Emerson Hough

The Purchase Price

Emerson Hough

The Purchase Price

1st Edition | ISBN: 978-3-75236-023-3

Place of Publication: Frankfurt am Main, Germany

Year of Publication: 2020

Outlook Verlag GmbH, Germany.

Reproduction of the original.

THE PURCHASE PRICE

OR, THE CAUSE OF COMPROMISE

By

EMERSON HOUGH

CHAPTER I

"Madam, you are charming! You have not slept, and yet you smile. No man could ask a better prisoner."

She turned to him, smiling faintly.

"I thank you. At least we have had breakfast, and for such mercy I am grateful to my jailer. I admit I was famished. What now?"

With just the turn of a shoulder she indicated the water front, where, at the end of the dock on which they stood, lay the good ship, *Mount Vernon*, river packet, the black smoke already pouring from her stacks. In turn he smiled and also shrugged a shoulder.

"Let us not ask! My dear lady, I could journey on for ever with one so young and pleasant as yourself. I will give you my promise in exchange for your parole."

Now her gesture was more positive, her glance flashed more keenly at him. "Do not be too rash," she answered. "My parole runs only while we travel together privately. As soon as we reach coach or boat, matters will change. I reserve the right of any prisoner to secure life, liberty and the pursuit of happiness. I shall endeavor, believe me—and in my own way."

He frowned as she presently went on to make herself yet more clear. "It was well enough when we traveled in our own private express, from Washington here to Pittsburgh for then there was no chance for escape. I gave my parole, because it pleased you and did not jeopardize myself. Here my jailer may perhaps have some trouble with me."

"You speak with the courage and fervor of the true leader of a cause. Madam," he rejoined, now smiling. "What evil days are these on which I have fallen—I, a mere soldier obeying orders! Not that I have found the orders unpleasant; but it is not fair of you to bring against mankind double weapons! Such is not the usage of civilized warfare. Dangerous enough you are as woman alone, without bringing to your aid those gifts of mind suited to problems which men have been accustomed to arrogate to themselves."

"Arrogate is quite the right word. It is especially fit for a jailer."

This time the shaft went home. The florid countenance of young Captain Carlisle flushed yet ruddier beneath its tan. His lips set still more tightly under the scant reddish mustache. With a gesture of impatience he lifted his military hat and passed a hand over the auburn hair which flamed above his white forehead. His slim figure stiffened even as his face became more stern. Clad in the full regimentals of his rank, he made a not unmanly figure as he stood there, though hardly taller than this splendid woman whom he addressed—a woman somewhat reserved, mocking, enigmatic; but, as he had said, charming. That last word of description had been easy for any man who had seen her, with her long-lashed dark eyes, her clear cheek just touched with color, her heavy dark hair impossible to conceal even under its engulfing bonnet, her wholly exquisite and adequate figure equally unbanished even by the trying costume of the day. She stood erect, easy, young, strong, fit to live; and that nature had given her confidence in herself was evidenced now in the carriage of head and body as she walked to and fro, pausing to turn now and then, impatient, uneasy, like some caged creature, as lithe, as beautiful, as dangerous and as puzzling in the matter of future conduct. Even as he removed his cap, Carlisle turned to her, a man's admiration in his eyes, a gentleman's trouble also there.

[Illustration: Carlisle turned, a man's admiration in his eyes]

"My dear Countess St. Auban," said he, more formally, "I wish that you might never use that word with me again,—jailer! I am only doing my duty as a soldier. The army has offered to it all sorts of unpleasant tasks. They selected me as agent for your disappearance because I am an army officer. I had no option, I must obey. In my profession there is not enough fighting, and too much civilian work, police work, constable work, detective work. There are fools often for officers, and over them politicians who are worse fools, sometimes. Well, then, why blame a simple fellow like me for doing what is given him to do? I have not liked the duty, no matter how much I have enjoyed the experience. Now, with puzzles ended and difficulties beginning, you threaten to make my unhappy lot still harder!"

"Why did you bring me here?"

"That I do not know. I could not answer you even did I know."

"And why did I come?" she mused, half to herself.

3

"Nor can I say that. Needs must when the devil drives; and His Majesty surely was on the box and using his whip-hand, two days ago, back in Washington. Your own sense of fairness will admit as much as that."

She threw back her head like a restless horse, blooded, mettlesome, and resumed her pacing up and down, her hands now clasped behind her back.

"When I left the carriage with my maid Jeanne, there," she resumed at length; "when I passed through that dark train shed at midnight, I felt that something was wrong. When the door of the railway coach was opened I felt that conviction grow. When you met me—the first time I ever saw you, sir,—I felt my heart turn cold."

"Madam!"

"And when the door of the coach closed on myself and my maid,—when we rolled on away from the city, in spite of all I could do or say—, why, then, sir, you were my jailer. Have matters changed since then?"

"Madam, from the first you were splendid! You showed pure courage. 'I am a prisoner!' you cried at first—not more than that. But you said it like a lady, a noblewoman. I admired you then because you faced me—whom you had never seen before—with no more fear than had I been a private and you my commanding officer."

"Fear wins nothing."

"Precisely. Then let us not fear what the future may have for us. I have no directions beyond this point,—Pittsburg. I was to take boat here, that was all. I was to convey you out into the West, somewhere, anywhere, no one was to know where. And someway, anyway, my instructions were, I was to lose you —to lose you. Madam, in plain point of fact. And now, at the very time I am indiscreet enough to tell you this much, you make my cheerful task the more difficult by saying that you must be regarded only as a prisoner of war!"

Serene, smiling, enigmatic, she faced him with no fear whatever showing in her dark eyes. The clear light of the bright autumn morning had no terrors for youth and health like hers. She put back a truant curl from her forehead where it had sought egress to the world, and looked him full in the face now, drawing a deep breath which caused the round of her bosom to lift the lace at her throat. Then, woman-like, she did the unlocked for, and laughed at him, a low, full ripple of wholesome laughter, which evoked again a wave of color to his sensitive face. Josephine St. Auban was a prisoner,—a prisoner of state, in fact, and such by orders not understood by herself, although, as she knew very well, a prisoner without due process of law. Save for this tearful maid who stood yonder, she was alone, friendless. Her escape, her safety even, lay in her own hands. Yet, even now, learning for the first time this much definitely regarding the mysterious journey into which she had been entrapped—even now, a prisoner held fast in some stern and mysterious grasp whose reason and whose nature she could not know—she laughed, when she should have wept!

"My instructions were to take you out beyond this point," went on Carlisle; "and then I was to lose you, as I have said. I have had no definite instructions as to how that should be done, my dear Countess." His eyes twinkled as he stiffened to his full height and almost met the level of her own glance.

"The agent who conveyed my orders to me—he comes from Kentucky, you see—said to me that while I could not bow-string you, it would be quite proper to put you in a sack and throw you overboard. 'Only,' said he to me, 'be careful that this sack be tightly tied; and be sure to drop her only where the water is deepest. And for God's sake, my dear young man,' he said to me, 'be sure that you do not drop her anywhere along the coast of my own state of Kentucky; for if you do, she will untie the sack and swim ashore into my constituency, where I have trouble enough without the Countess St. Auban, active abolitionist, to increase it. Trouble '—said he to me—'thy name is Josephine St. Auban!'

"My dear lady, to that last, I agree. But, there you have my orders. You are, as may be seen, close to the throne, so far as we have thrones in this country."

"Then I am safe until we get below the Kentucky shore?" she queried calmly.

"I beg you not to feel disturbed,—" he began.

"Will you set me down at Louisville?"

"Madam, I can not."

"You have not been hampered with extraordinary orders. You have just said, the carte blanche is in your hands."

"I have no stricter orders at any time than those I take from my own conscience, Madam. I must act for your own good as well as for that of others."

Her lip curled now. "Then not even this country is free! Even here there are secret tribunals. Even here there are hired bravos."

"Ah, Madam, please, not that! I beg of you—"

"Excellently kind of you all, to care so tenderly for me—and yourselves! I, only a woman, living openly, with ill will for none, paying ray own way, violating no law of the land—"

"Your words are very bitter, Madam."

"The more bitter because they are true. You will release me then at Cairo, below?"

"I can not promise, Madam. You would be back in Washington by the first boats and trains."

"So, the plot runs yet further? Perhaps you do not stop this side the outer ways of the Mississippi? Say, St. Louis, New Orleans?"

"Perhaps even beyond those points," he rejoined grimly. "I make no promises, since you yourself make none."

"What are your plans, out there, beyond?"

"You ask it frankly, and with equal frankness I say I do not know. Indeed, I am not fully advised in all this matter. It was imperative to get you out of Washington, and if so, it is equally imperative to keep you out of Washington. At least for a time I am obliged to construe my carte blanche in that way, my dear lady. And as I say, my conscience is my strictest officer."

"Yes," she said, studying his face calmly with her steady dark eyes.

It was a face sensitive, although bony and lined; stern, though its owner still was young. She noticed the reddish hair and beard, the florid skin, the blue eye set deep—a fighting eye, yet that of a visionary.

"You are a fanatic," she said.

"That is true. You, yourself, are of my own kind. You would kill me without tremor, if you had orders, and I—"

"You would do as much!"

"You are of my kind, Madam. Yes; we both take orders from our own souls. And that we think alike in many ways I am already sure."

"None the less—"

"None the less, I can not agree to set you down at Cairo, or at any intermediate point. I will only give my promise in return for your own parole. That, I would take as quickly as though it were the word of any officer; but you do not give it."

"No, I do not. I am my own mistress. I am going to escape as soon as I can."

He touched his cap in salute. "Very well, then. I flattered myself we had done well together thus far—you have made it easy. But now—no, no, I will not say it. I would rather see you defiant than to have you weaken. I love courage, and you have it. That will carry you through. It will keep you clean and safe as well."

Her face clouded for the first time.

"I have not dared to think of that," she said. "So long as we came in the special train, with none to molest or make me afraid—afraid with that fear which a woman must always have—we did well enough, as I have said; but now, here in the open, in public, before the eyes of all, who am I, and who are you to me? I am not your mother?"

"Scarcely, at twenty three or four." He pursed a judicial lip.

"Nor your sister?"

"No."

[Illustration: The *Mount Vernon*]

"Nor your wife?"

"No." He flushed here, although he answered simply.

"Nor your assistant in any way?"

His face lighted suddenly.

"Why not?" said he. "Can't you be my amanuensis,—that sort of thing, you see? Come, we must think of this. This is where my conscience hurts me—I can't bear to have *my* duty hurt *you*. That, my dear Countess, cuts me to the quick. You will believe that, won't you?"

"Yes, I believe that. Jeanne," she motioned to her maid who stood apart all this time, "my wrap, please. I find the air cool. When the body is weak or worn, my dear sir, the mind is not at its best; and I shall need all my wits."

"But you do not regard me as your enemy?"

"I am forced to do so. Personally, I thank you; professionally, I must fight you. Socially, I must be—what did you say,—your amanuensis? So! We are engaged in a great work, a treatise on our river fortifications, perhaps? But since when did army officers afford the luxury of amanuenses in this simple republic? Does your Vehmgericht pay such extraordinary expenses? Does your carte blanche run so far as that also?"

"You must not use such terms regarding the government of this country," he protested. "Our administration does not suit me, but it has pleased a majority of our people, else it would not be in power, and it is no Vehmgericht, The law of self preservation obtains in this country as with all nations, even in Europe. But we have planned no confiscation of your property, nor threatened any forfeiture of your life."

"No, you have only taken away that which is dearer than anything else, that which your government guarantees to every human being in this country—liberty!"

"And even that unconstitutional point shall remain such no longer than I can help, Madam. Do not make our journey longer by leaving it more difficult. God knows, I am beset enough even as it is now. But be sure our Vehmgerichte, as you are pleased to call it, shall never, at least while I am its agent, condemn you to any situation unsuited to a gentlewoman. A very high compliment has been paid you in holding you dangerous because of your personal charm. It is true, Madam, that is why you were put out of Washington—because you were dangerous. They thought you could get the ear of any man—make him divulge secrets which he ought to keep—if you just asked him to do it—for the sake of Josephine St. Auban!" He jerked out his sentences, as though habitual reticence and lack of acquaintance with women left it difficult for him to speak, even thus boldly.

"Oh, thank you, thank you!" She clapped her hands together, mockingly.

"Before now, women less beautiful than you have robbed men of their reason, have led them to do things fatal as open treason to their country. These men were older than you or I. Perhaps, as you will agree, they were better able to weigh the consequences. You are younger than they, younger than I, myself; but you are charming—and you are young. Call it cruel of me, if you like, to take you by the hand and lead you gently away from that sort of danger for just a few days. Call me jailer, if you like. None the less it is my duty, and I shall call it in part a kindness to you to take you away from scenes which might on both sides be dangerous. Some of the oldest and best minds of this country have felt—"

"At least those minds were shrewd in choosing their agent," she rejoined. "Yes; you are fanatic, that is plain. You will obey orders. And you have not been much used to women. That makes it harder for me. Or easier!" She smiled at him again, very blithe for a prisoner.

"It ought to have been held down to that," he began disconsolately, "I should have been all along professional only. It began well when you gave me your parole, so that I need not sit nodding and blinking, over against you also nodding and blinking all night long. Had you been silly, as many women would have been, you could not this morning be so fresh and brilliant—even though you tell me you have not slept, which seems to me incredible. I myself slept like a boy, confident in your word. Now, you have banished sleep! Nodding and blinking, I must henceforth watch you, nodding—and blinking, unhappy, uncomfortable; whereas, were it in my power, I would never have you know the first atom of discomfort."

"There, there! I am but an amanuensis, my dear Captain Carlisle."

He colored almost painfully, but showed his own courage. "I only admire the wisdom of the Vehmgerichte. They knew you were dangerous, and I know it. I have no hope, should I become too much oppressed by lack of sleep, except to follow instructions, and cast you overboard somewhere below Kentucky!"

"You ask me not to attempt any escape?"

"Yes."

"Why, I would agree to as much as that. It is, as you say, a matter of indifference to me whether I leave the boat at Cairo or at some point farther westward. Of course I would return to Washington as soon as I escaped from bondage."

"Excellent, Madam! Now, please add that you will not attempt to communicate with any person on the boat or on shore."

"No; that I will not agree to as a condition."

"Then still you leave it very hard for me."

She only smiled at him again, her slow, deliberate smile; yet there was in it no trace of hardness or sarcasm. Keen as her mind assuredly was, as she smiled she seemed even younger, perhaps four or five and twenty at most. With those little dimples now rippling frankly into view at the corners of her mouth, she was almost girlish in her expression, although the dark eyes above, long-lashed, eloquent, able to speak a thousand tongues into shame, showed better than the small curving lips the well-poised woman of the world.

Captain Edward Carlisle, soldier as he was, martinet as he was, felt a curious sensation of helplessness seize upon him as he met her, steady gaze, her alluring smile; he could not tell what this prisoner might do. He cursed the fate which had assigned such a duty, cursed especially that fate which forced a gallant soldier to meet so superb a woman as this under handicap so hard. For almost the first time since they had met they were upon the point of awkwardness. Light speech failed them for the moment, the gravity of the situation began to come home to both of them. Indeed, who were they? What were they to the public under whose notice they might fall—indeed, must fall? There was no concealing face and figure of a woman such as this; no, not in any corner of the world, though she were shrouded in oriental veil. Nay, were she indeed tied in a sack and flung into the sea, yet would she arise to make trouble for mankind until her allotted task should be complete! How could they two answer any question which might arise regarding their errand, or regarding their relations as they stood, here at the gateway of the remoter country into which they were departing? How far must their journey together continue? What would be said regarding them?

Carlisle found it impossible to answer such questions. She herself only made the situation the more difficult with her high-headed defiance of him.

Hesitating, the young officer turned his gaze over the wide dock, now covered with hurrying figures, with massed traffic, with the confusion preceding the departure of a river boat. Teams thundered, carts trundled here and there, shoutings of many minor captains arose. Those who were to take passage on the packet hurried forward, to the gangway, so occupied in their own affairs as to have small time to examine their neighbors. The very confusion for the time seemed to afford safety. Carlisle was upon the point of drawing a long breath of relief; but even as he turned to ask his companion to accompany him aboard the boat he caught sight of an approaching figure which he seemed to recognize. He would have turned away, but the keen-witted woman at his side followed his gaze and paused. There approached these two now, hat in hand, a gentleman who evidently intended to claim acquaintance.

This new-comer was a man who in any company would have seemed striking. In complexion fair, and with blue or gray eyes, he was tall as any Viking, as broad in the shoulder. He was smooth-faced, and his fresh skin and well-developed figure bespoke the man in good physical condition through active exercise, yet well content with the world's apportionment. His limbs were long, his hands bony and strong. His air, of self-confident assurance, seemed that of a man well used to having his own way. His forehead was high and somewhat rugged. Indeed, all his features were in large mold, like the man himself, as though he had come from a day when skin garments made the proper garb of men. As though to keep up this air of an older age, his long fair hair was cut almost square, low down on the neck, as though he were some Frank fresh from the ancient forests. Over the forehead also this square cut was affected, so that, as he stood, large and confident, not quite *outre*, scarce eccentric, certainly distinguished in appearance, he had a half-savage look, as though ignorant or scornful of the tenderer ways of civilization. A leader this man might be, a poor follower always.

Yet the first words he uttered showed the voice and diction of a gentleman. "My dear Captain," he began, extending his hand as he approached, "I am indeed charmed! What a delight to see you again in our part of the world! I must claim the pleasure of having met you once—two years ago, in St. Louis. Are you again on your way to the frontiers?"

The tone of inquiry in his voice was just short of curious, indeed might have been called expectant. His gaze, admiring yet polite, had not wholly lost opportunity to list the attractions of this lady, whose name had not yet been given him.

The gentleman accosted declined to be thus definite; adding only, after the usual felicitations, "Yes, we are going down the river a little way on the Vernon here."

"For some distance?"

"For quite a distance."

"At least, this is not your first journey down our river?"

"I wish it might be the last. The railway is opening up a new world to us. The stage-coach is a thing of the past."

"I wish it might be, for me!" rejoined the stranger.
"Unfortunately, I am obliged to go West from here over the National Road, to look at some lands I own out in Indiana. I very much regret—"

There was by this time yet more expectancy in his voice. He still bowed, with respectful glances bent upon the lady. No presentation came, although in the easy habit of the place and time, such courtesy might perhaps have been expected. Why this stiffness among fellow travelers on a little river packet?

[Illustration: He still bowed, with respectful glances.]

The tall man was not without a certain grave audacity. A look of amusement came to his face as he gazed at the features of the other, now obviously agitated, and not a little flushed.

"I had not known that your sister—" he began. His hand thus forced, the other was obliged to reply: "No, the daughter of an old friend of mine, you see—we are *en voyage* together for the western country. It has simply been my fortune to travel in company with the lady. I present you, my dear sir, to Miss Barren. My dear Miss Barren, this is State Senator Warville Dunwody, of Missouri. We are of opposite camps in politics."

The tall man bowed still more deeply. Meantime, Josephine St. Auban in her own way had taken inventory of the new-comer. Her companion hastily sought to hold matters as they were.

"My dear Senator Dunwody," he said, "we were just passing down to the boat to see that the luggage is aboard. With you, I regret very much that your journey takes you from us."

The sudden consternation which sat upon Dunwody's face was almost amusing. He was very willing to prolong this conversation. Into his soul there had flashed the swift conviction that never in his life had he seen a woman so beautiful as this. Yet all he could do was to smile and bow adieu.

"A fine man, that Dunwody, yonder," commented the young captain, as they parted, and as he turned to his prisoner. "We'll see him on in Washington some day. He is strengthening his forces now against Mr. Benton out there. A strong man—a strong one; and a heedless."

"Of what party is he?" she inquired, as though casually.

"What a man's party is in these days," was his answer, "is something hard to say. A man like Dunwody is pretty much his own party, although the Bentonites call him a 'soft Democrat.' Hardly soft he seems, when he gets in action at the state capital of Missouri yonder. Certainly Dunwody is for war and tumult. None of this late weak-kneed compromise for him! To have his own way—that is Dunwody's creed of life. I thank God he is not going with us now. He might want his own way with you, from the fashion of his glances. Did you see? My word!" Young Carlisle fumed a shade more than might have seemed necessary for military reasons.

Josephine St. Auban turned upon him with her slow smile, composedly looking at him from between her long, dark lashes.

"Why do you say that?" she inquired.

"Because it is the truth. I don't want him about."

"Then you will be disappointed."

"Why do you say that? Did you not hear him say that he was going West by coach from here?"

"You did not give him time. He is not going West by coach."

"What do you mean?"

"He will be with us on the boat!"

CHAPTER II

When Captain Edward Carlisle made casual reference to the "weak-kneed compromise," he simply voiced a personal opinion on a theme which was in the mind of every American, and one regarded with as many minds as there were men. That political measure of the day was hated by some, admired by others. This man condemned it, that cried aloud its righteousness and infallibility; one argued for it shrewdly, another declaimed against it loudly. It was alike blessed and condemned. The southern states argued over it, many of the northern states raged at it. It ruined many political fortunes and made yet other fortunes. That year was a threshold-time in our history, nor did any see what lay beyond the door.

If there existed then a day when great men and great measures were to be born, certainly there lay ready a stage fit for any mighty drama—indeed, commanding it. It was a young world withal, indeed a world not even yet explored, far less exploited, so far as were concerned those vast questions which, in its dumb and blind way, humanity both sides of the sea then was beginning to take up. America scarce more than a half century ago was for the most part a land of query, rather than of hope.

Not even in their query were the newer lands of our country then alike. We lay in a vast chance-medley, and never had any country greater need for care and caution in its councils. By the grace of the immortal gods we had had given into our hands an enormous area of the earth's richest inheritance, to have and to hold, if that might be; but as yet we were not one nation. We had no united thought, no common belief as to what was national wisdom. For three quarters of a century this country had grown; for half a century it had been divided, one section fighting against another in all but arms. We spoke of America even then as a land of the free, but it was not free; nor on the other hand was it wholly slave. Never in the history of the world has there been so great a land, nor one of so diverse systems of government.

Before these travelers, for instance, who paused here at the head of the Ohio River, there lay the ancient dividing line between the South and the North. To the northwest, between the Great Lakes and the Ohio, swept a vast land which, since the days of the old Northwest Ordinance of 1787, had by *national* enactment been decreed for ever free. Part of this had the second time been declared free, by *state* law also. To the eastward of this lay certain states where slavery had been forbidden by the laws of the several states,

13

though not by that of the nation. Again, far out to the West, beyond the great waterway on one of whose arms our travelers now stood, lay the vast provinces bought from Napoleon; and of these, all lying north of that compromise line of thirty-six degrees, thirty minutes, agreed upon in 1820, had been declared for ever free by *national* law. Yet beyond this, in the extreme northwest, lay Oregon, fought through as free soil by virtue of the old Northwest Ordinance, the sleeping dog of slavery being evaded and left to lie when the question of Oregon came up. Along the Pacific, and south of Oregon, lay the new empire of California, bitterly contended over by both sections, but by her own self-elected *state* law declared for ever free soil. Minnesota and the Dakotas were still unorganized, so there the sleeping dog might lie, of course.

To the south of that river on which our voyagers presently were to take ship, lay a section comprising the southern states, in extent far larger than all the northern states, and much stronger in legislative total power in the national halls of Congress. Here slavery was maintained by laws of the *states* themselves. The great realm of Texas, long coveted by the South, now was joined to the ranks of the slave-holding states, by virtue of a war of somewhat doubtful justice though of undoubted success. Above Texas, and below the line of thirty-six degrees, thirty minutes, lay a portion of what was known as the Indian country, where in 1820 there had been made no *prohibition* of slavery by the *national* government.

Above the line of thirty-six degrees, thirty minutes, there thrust up a portion of Texas which had no law at all, nor had it any until a very recent day, being known under the title of "No Man's Land." Yet on to the westward, toward free California, lay a vast but supposedly valueless region where cotton surely would not grow, that rich country now known as Utah, Nevada, Arizona and New Mexico. This region, late gained by war from Mexico, soon to be increased by purchase from Mexico on the South, was still of indeterminate status, slavery not being prohibited but permitted, by *federal* action, although most of this territory had been free soil under the old laws of Mexico. Moreover, as though sardonically to complicate all these much-mingled matters, there thrust up to the northward, out of the permitted slavery region of the South, the state of Missouri, quite above the fateful line of thirty-six degrees, thirty minutes, where slavery was permitted both by *federal* and *state* enactment.

Men spoke even then, openly or secretly, of disunion; but in full truth, there had as yet been no actual union. In such confusion, what man could call unwise a halting-time, a compromise? A country of tenures so mixed, of theories so diverse, could scarcely have been called a land of common government. It arrogated to itself, over all its dominion, the title of a free republic, yet by its own mutual covenant of national law, any owner of slaves in the southern states might pursue what he called his property across the dividing line, and invoke, in any northern state, the support of the state or national officers to assist him in taking back his slaves. As a republic we called ourselves even then old and stable. Yet was ever any country riper for misrule than ours? Forgetting now what is buried, the old arguments all forgot, that most bloody and most lamentable war all forgot, could any mind, any imagination, depict a situation more rife with tumult, more ripe for war than this? And was it not perforce an issue, of compromise or war; of compromise, or a union never to be consummated?

Yet into this heterogeneous region, from all Europe, itself convulsed with revolution, Europe just beginning to awaken to the doctrine of the rights of humanity, there pressed westward ever increasing thousands of new inhabitants—in that current year over a third of a million, the largest immigration thus far known. Most of these immigrants settled in the free country of the North, and as the railways were now so hurriedly crowding westward, it was to be seen that the ancient strife between North and South must grow and not lessen, for these new-comers were bitterly opposed to slavery. Swiftly the idea national was growing. The idea democratic, the idea of an actual self-government—what, now, was to be its history?

North of the fated compromise line, west of the admitted slave state of Missouri, lay other rich lands ripe for the plow, ready for Americans who had never paid more than a dollar an acre for land, or for aliens who had never been able to own any land at all. Kansas and Nebraska, names conceived but not yet born,—what would they be? Would the compromise of this last summer of 1850 hold the balances of power even? Could it save this republic, still young and needy, for yet a time in the cause of peace and growth? Many devoutly hoped it. Many devoutly espoused the cause of compromise merely for the sake of gaining time. As neither of the great political parties of the day filled its ranks from either section, so in both sections there were many who espoused, as many who denied, the right of men to own slaves. We speak of slavery as the one great question of that day. It was not and never has been the greatest. The question of democracy—that was even then, and it is now, the greatest question.

Here on the deck of the steamer at the little city of Pittsburg, then gateway of the West, there appeared men of purposes and beliefs as mixed as this mixed country from which they came. Some were pushing out into what now is known as Kansas, others going to take up lands in Missouri. Some were to pass south to the slave country, others north to the free lands; men of all sorts and conditions, many men, of many minds, that was true, and all hurrying into new lands, new problems, new dangers, new remedies. It was a great and splendid day, a great and vital time, that threshold-time, when our western traffic increased so rapidly and assuredly that steamers scarcely could be built rapidly enough to accommodate it, and the young rails leaped westward at a speed before then unknown in the world.

Carried somehow, somewhither, for some reason, on these surging floods, were these travelers, of errand not wholly obvious to their fellows, yet of such sort as to call into query alike the nature of their errand and their own relations. It is easily earned repetition to state that Josephine St. Auban's was a presence not to be concealed. Even such a boat as the Mount Vernon offered a total deck space so cramped as to leave secrecy or privacy well out of the question, even had the motley and democratic assemblage of passengers been disposed to accord either. Yet there was something in the appearance of this young woman and her companion which caused all the heterogeneous groups of humanity to make way for them, as presently they approached the gang-plank.

Apparently they were not unexpected. The ship's clerks readily led the way to apartments which had been secured in advance. Having seen to the luggage of his charges, whom he disposed in a good double state-room, the leader of the party repaired to his own quarters. Tarrying no longer than to see his own luggage safe aboard, he commanded one of the men to fetch him to the office of the captain.

The latter gentleman, busy and important, dropped much of his official way when he found whom he was accosting. "This is quite unexpected, sir," he began, removing his cap and bowing.

"Captain Rogers," began the other, "you have been advised to some extent of my plans by telegram from Washington."

The captain hesitated. "Is this with the lady's consent? I must consider the question of damages."

"There will be no damages. Your owners will be quite safe, and so will you."

"Are there any charges of any kind against——?"

"That is not for you to ask. She is under my care, and must not disembark until I say the word. You will kindly give her a place at my table. There must be no idle curiosity to annoy her. But tell me, when shall we reach the mouth of the river? Is it not possible to save some time by avoiding some of the smaller stops?"

"But our freight, our passengers——" The captain passed a hand across his brow, much perplexed. The other showed a sudden firmness.

"My errand demands secrecy and speed alike. There must be no communication between this boat and the shore, so far as this young lady is concerned. Meantime, if all is ready, it would please me mightily if we could start."

The captain pulled a bell rope. "Tell the mate to cast off," he said, to the man who answered. An instant later the hoarse boom of the boat's whistles roared out their warning. There came a crush of late-comers at the gangway. Shouts arose; deck hands scrambled with the last packages of freight; but presently the staging was shipped and all the lines cast free. Churning the stained waters into foam with her great paddles, the *Mount Vernon* swung slowly out into the narrow stream.

[Illustration: The Captain pulled a bell rope.]

"Now, Captain Rogers," went on Captain Carlisle, tersely, "tell, me who's aboard;" and presently he began to ponder the names which, in loose fashion, the clerk assembled from his memory and his personal acquaintance.

"Hm, Hm!" commented the listener, "very few whom I know. Judge Clayton from the other side, below Cairo. State Senator Jones, from Belmont—"

"You know Mr. Jones? Old 'Decline and Fall' Jones? He never reads any book excepting Gibbon's *Decline and Fall of the Roman Empire*. Always declines a drink when offered, but he's sure to fall a moment later!" Thus the smiling clerk.

"Well, I may see Mr. Jones, possibly Judge Clayton. There's no one else." He seemed not dissatisfied.

Alas! for human calculations and for human hopes! Even as he left the captain's room to ascend the stair, he met face to face the very man whose presence he least desired.

"Dunwody!" he exclaimed.

The gentleman thus addressed extended a hand. "I see you are safe aboard. Myself, too, I am very glad."

"I thought you said you were going—"

"I was, but I changed my mind at the last moment. It is far more comfortable going down by boat than it is by stage. Then, the thought of the pleasure of your society on the journey—" He was smiling, rather maliciously.

"Yes, yes, of course!" somewhat dismally.

"But now, to be frank with you, you don't seem altogether happy.

Why do you want to be rid of me? What harm have I done?" smiled Dunwody.

"Oh, my dear sir!"

"May not one change his mind if he likes?"

"My dear sir, there is no argument about that."

"Certainly not! The only argument is on the previous question—When are you going to introduce me as you should, to that extremely beautiful young lady who is with you?"

"Good God, my very dear sir!"

"You are not 'my dear sir' at all, so long as you try to hoodwink me," persisted Dunwody, still smiling. "Come, now, what are you doing here, west bound with a young and charming person who is not your wife, widow, mother, daughter, *fiancee* or sister—who is not—"

"That will do, if you please!" Carlisle's hot temper named into his freckled face.

"Why so touchy?"

"It is within a man's rights to choose his own company and his own ways. I am not accountable, except as I choose."

The other man was studying him closely, noting his flush, his irritation, his uneasiness. "But what I am saying now is that it is cruel, unusual, inhuman and unconstitutional to be so selfish about it. Come, I shall only relent when you have shown yourself more kind. For instance, in the matter of her table in the dining-room—"

"The lady has expressed a desire to remain quite alone, my dear sir. I must bow to her will. It is her privilege to come and go as she likes."

"She may come and go as she likes?" queried Dunwody, still smiling. There was a look on his face which caused Carlisle suddenly to turn and examine him sharply.

"Naturally."

"Without your consent, even?"

"Absolutely so."

"Then why should she have sent me this little message?" demanded Dunwody suddenly. He presented a folded bit of paper, snapping it on the back with a finger.

A still deeper flush spread over the young officer's telltale face. He opened and read: "If you care to aid a woman who is in trouble, come to me at room 19 when you can."

"When did you receive this?" he demanded. "By God!" he added, to himself, "she did it, too!"

"Within the moment. Her maid brought it."

"You didn't have this before you came on board—but of course, that wasn't possible."

Dunwody looked at him keenly. "You have just heard me," he said. "No, I don't deny there are some things here which I can't understand. You are covering up something, my dear Captain, of course, but just what I do not know. Your station in life, your presence in this country, so far from home! —" He smiled now in a way which his antagonist considered sinister. Yet what defense could be made without exposing secrets which were not his to uncover?

"Come," went on Dunwody, "let's be frank about it. You may trust me, of course. But—neither sister, wife, nor servant—could you blame any man, especially any man who had a direct message like this, for wanting, or, say, even demanding a meeting? Haven't I the right? Come, now!"

Carlisle made no immediate answer, and was about to turn on his heel, finding it hard to restrain himself. He paused, however.

"Very good, then. To show how little you know me, and how much you wrong both this lady and myself, you shall meet her, as you say. Not that you have earned the right."

CHAPTER III

The *Mount Vernon*, favored by a good stage of water, soon cleared the narrow Monongahela channel, passed the confluence, and headed down under full steam, all things promising well for a speedy and pleasant run. The sky was blue and cloudless, and the air fresh with the tang of coming autumn. Especially beautiful were the shores which they now were skirting. The hues of autumn had been shaken down over mile after mile of wide forest which appeared in a panorama of russet and gold and red, to grow the more resplendent when they should arrive opposite the high bluffs which line the stream almost to the town of Wheeling.

Below these upper reaches, then the least settled and wildest portion of the country along the Ohio, the river flattened and widened, the current becoming more gentle, and the shores, though not yet wholly cleared of their forests, presenting here and there scenes of rural rather than of savage beauty. Civilization had not as yet taken full hold along this rich valley. The old town of Marietta, the cities of Louisville and Cincinnati, the villages huddled at mouths of such rivers as came down from the Virginia hills, or the larger settlements marking points near the debouchments of slower streams like the Muskingum and Wabash, which crossed the flatter lands beyond, made the chief points of traffic and of interest in those days of west bound travel.

On the upper deck or along the rails of the lower deck, many passengers were gazing out at the varying pictures of the passing shores. Not so the young officer, erstwhile accosted as jailer of a woman, later hinted to be something else than jailer. With eyes cast down, he spent most of his time pacing up and down alone. Yet it was not an irresolute soul which reposed beneath the half-frigid exterior. He presently arrived upon a plan of action.

The public, too, had its rights, he concluded, and the woman as a woman had her rights also to her good fame. He must not harm her name. Best then, to disarm suspicion by playing the game wholly in the open. The midday meal now being announced by loud proclamation of the boat's gong, he turned, and soon rapped at the door of room nineteen.

Jeanne, the tearful but faithful maid who shared her mistress' fortunes, by this time had done what she could to mend her lady's appearance. The traces of travel had been quite removed, by virtue of the contents of such valises as they had with them. Good health and youth, as well as good courage, fought for Josephine St. Auban, as well as good sense and a philosophy of travel learned by experiences in other lands. If indeed she had not slept, at least her face did not betray that fact. Her color was good, her eye was clear. Her dark hair, brushed low over the temples in the fashion of the day, was fresh and glossy. Moreover, her habiliments were such as to cause most of the feminine occupants of the boat to make careful note, when she had accepted Carlisle's escort and entered the dining-room. She walked with calmness to the table reserved for her, and with inclination of the head thanked him as he arranged her chair for her. Thus in a way the gauntlet was by both thrown down to all present.

Most of those present without hesitation showed their interest. The hum of the dingy tables slackened and ceased. A score of women frowned at a score of men whose glances wandered undutifully. Who was she, and what? That question certainly passed in the minds of most in the crowded little room. Meantime, Josephine St. Auban's own eyes were not unregardful.

"I see that my guess was quite correct," she said at length, smiling full at her guardian.

At once he caught her thought. "Oh, about Mr. Dunwody," he assented, assuming a carelessness which she read through at once. "Yes, I met him—a while ago. He told me he had suddenly decided to change his plans and take the Vernon down the river, instead of going by stage. Very natural of him, too, I should say. I would be much distressed to think of myself traveling by coach, even in weather pleasant as this. He has keen eyes, though, has he not?" he added resentfully.

"That is to say—"

"So hard hit that he threatens a duel or worse if I do not at once further his desire to pursue his acquaintance. It's not myself he's so eager to meet. He has no love for me, that's sure, long ago."

"Indeed?" She kept her eyes fixed on her plate. If a slight flush tinged her cheek it scarce was visible. "Is that all?" she asked at length.

"Madam, you yourself could best answer your own question." He looked at her keenly, not showing his case; not telling her that Dunwody had shown him her hasty note. Not the flicker of an eyelash betrayed her own thought. Surely, she had courage. Surely, she meant trouble.

"How delightful!" she resumed at length calmly. "Not that I weary of your company, sir; but I told you my parole was ended when we reached the boat. Suppose, now, I should stand up here and cry out that I am being restrained of my liberty. What would be the result?"

"I should be hung at the yard-arm instantly! I should be lynched. Dunwody would come in the lead, crashing over the tables. I fear Dunwody, even bearing a rope, as we used to say—in Virgil, was it?"

"Admirable! Now, since that is true, suppose you and I make some sort of terms! I'm tired of being jailed, even in a traveling jail. I told you fairly I should try to escape; and so I shall."

He needed no second look to catch the resolution in her glance. "Our game is somewhat desperate, Madam, I admit," said he, "I scarcely know whether you are in my hands or I in yours. As I have already given you consideration, let us hope you will do as much for me, remembering at least the delicacy of my position. I'm under orders; and I'm responsible for you."

"Yes?" she rejoined. "Now, as to what I suggest, it is this: You shall leave the boat at Louisville or Cincinnati. Your errand is already sufficiently well done. You have got me out of Washington. Suppose we set Cincinnati as the last point of our common journey?"

"But what then for you. Madam?"

"As to that, I can not tell. Why should you care? Do not be concerned over details. You have brought me into this situation. I must escape from it in my own way."

"You sting me deeply. I've had to do this, just as an executioner may have to cut off a head; but a thousand times I ask your pardon. A thousand times you, yourself, have made me ashamed. Come, when we part, shall it not be as friends? You have won my respect, my admiration. I wish I were entitled to your own. You've been perfect. You've been splendid."

"Look," she said, without raising her eyelids.

He turned. Dunwody was making his way toward them among the tables.

"My dear Senator," said Carlisle, choking down his wrath as the Missourian reached them and bowed his salutations, "I have the greatest pleasure in the world in keeping my promise to you. I am delighted to have you join our little party at this time. You remember the Countess—I would say, Miss Barren?"

"I have not so soon forgotten," answered Dunwody. His commanding eyes still sought her face. Beyond a slight bow and one upward glance, she did not display interest; yet in truth a sudden shiver of apprehension came into her heart. This was a different sort of man she now must endeavor to handle. What was it that his straight glance meant?

It was a singular situation in which these three found themselves. That she had asked the aid of this new-comer was a fact known to all three of them. Yet of the three, none knew precisely the extent of the others' knowledge. Dunwody at least was polite, if insistent, in his wish to learn more of this mysterious young woman who had appealed to him for aid, yet who now made no further sign. Who was she? What *sort* was she? he demanded of himself. God! if she was one sort. And why should she *not* be that sort? Did not the River carry many sorts? Was not the army ever gallant? What officer ever hesitated in case of a fair damsel? And what fair damsel was not fair game in the open contest among men—that old, old, oldest and keenest of all contests since this hoary world began?

"I am sure the fatigue of the journey across the mountains must have left you quite weary," he ventured, addressing her. "There's only the choice of sleeping, or of hanging over the deck rail and looking at these hills." He waved a hand toward a window, whence might be seen the near-by shores.

Josephine St. Auban showed no sign of perturbation as she answered: "Not so weary as busy. The duties of an amanuensis leave one small time for recreation." Her face was demureness itself.

[Illustration: Josephine showed no sign of perturbation.]

The situation assumed swift complications. Carlisle caught his cue, with alertness fairly to be called brilliant. "Yes," said he, "the young lady is of foreign education and family, and is most skilful in these respects. I should find it difficult to carry forward my literary work without her able assistance. It is a boon which even few public men have shared with myself. You know, I am in the West in view of certain writings." He virtuously sat erect, with a fine air, presently pushing back his chair.

Dunwody looked from one to the other in perplexity. He had expected to find a woman claiming his aid, or rather his acquaintance under excuse of a plea for aid. He found both these apparently in league against him, and one of these apparently after all not what he had thought! His face flushed. Meantime Josephine St. Auban arose, bowed, and left them.

When the two men found themselves alone, Dunwody, for a time lost in moody silence, at length broke out into a peal of laughter. "Well, human nature is human nature, I suppose. I make no comment, further than to say that I consider all the lady's fears were groundless. She has been well treated. There was no need to call for *my* aid. The army is hard to defeat, Captain, and always was!"

"I had not myself regarded any officer in the light of an oppressor of the distressed amanuensis," he went on. "But come now, who is she? You started to call her 'Countess.' Since when have countesses gone into secretarying? Tut! Tut! and again, my dear man, Tut!"

"Sir," replied Carlisle, "I recall that when I was a youth, some of us, members of the Sabbath-school class, occasionally would ask our teacher a question on the Scriptures which he could not answer. In that case he always said, 'My dear young friends, there are some things which are not for man to know.'"

"I accept my temporary defeat," said Dunwody slowly. "We'll see. But come, now, Captain, time is passing and the tables are yearning for trouble. The army is distinguished not alone in love. Draw-poker hath its victories, not less than war. I told Jones and Judge Clayton and one or two others that I was pining for a little game of draw. What do you say? Should not all lesser questions be placed in abeyance?"

"That," said the other, "comes to me at the present moment in the nature of an excellent compromise measure. I am agreed!"

Fencing thus, neither sure of his adversary, they now made their way to one of the larger saloons, which ordinarily was devoted to those who preferred to smoke, mayhap to chew, perhaps even to do worse; for the door leading to the bar-room of the boat was near at hand. A darky boy stood grinning, arranging a table, offering cards and tobacco in a tempting tray. The two drew up leisurely to the table, and presently were joined by the gentlemen whom Dunwody had mentioned. For the time, then, as two of the four reflected, there was a truce, a compromise.

CHAPTER IV

THE GAME

They made a group not uninteresting as they gathered about the table in the deck saloon. The youngest of the four received the deference generally accorded the uniform he wore, and returned the regard due age and station in the civilian world. For the moment rid of one annoying question, he was quite his better self, and added his quota in the preliminary badinage of the game. Across the table from him sat Judge Henry Clayton of New Madrid, a tall and slender gentleman with silky white mustaches and imperial, gentle of speech, kindly of countenance, and with soft, white hands, whose long fingers now idly raised and let fall some of the parti-colored tokens of the game.

[Illustration: They made a group not uninteresting.]

At Clayton's side, Dunwody, younger, larger and more powerful, made something of a contrast. Both these gentlemen had removed their coats and hung them across the backs of chairs, evidently intending a serious session. In this procedure the last of the party now followed suit,—the Honorable William Jones, state senator from Belmont, Missouri. Seating himself, the latter now in turn began shuffling a pack between fingers short, puffy, freckled and experienced. His stooped shoulders thrust forward a beardless round face, whose permanently arched eyebrows seemed to ask a continuous question, his short, dark hair receded from a high forehead, and a thick mid-body betokened alike middle age and easy living. A planter of the back country, and a politician, his capital was a certain native shrewdness and little else. Of course, in company such as this, and at such a day, the conversation must drift toward the ever fruitful topic of slavery.

"No, sir," began the Honorable William Jones, indulging himself in the luxury of tobacco as he addressed his companions, "there ain't no doubt about it. Us Southerners orto take all that new country west of the Missoury, clean acrost to the Pacific."

The older gentleman smiled at him. "You forget California," said he. "She is already in, and free by her own vote."

"An' a crime aginst the natural rights of the South! Sir, the institution of slavery is as old as history. It is as old as the first settlement of agricultural man upon one piece of ground. It's as old as the idea of sovereignty itself."

Dunwody gave a sly wink at his neighbor, Judge Clayton. The latter sank back in his chair resigned. Indeed, he proceeded to precipitate what he knew was to come.

"Sir, England herself," he assented gravely, "is the oldest of slavers. The Saxons, of whom we speak as the fathers of freedom, were the worst slave masters in the world—they sold their very kin into slavery at times."

The Honorable William Jones was impatient of interruption. "Comin' to our own side of the sea, gentlemen, what do we find? New England foremost in the slave trade! New York, ownin' onct more slaves than Virginny ever did! Georgia was fo'ced to take on slave labor, although she had tried to do without it. *Every* race, *every* nation, sirs, has accepted the theory of slave labor. What says Mr. Gibbon in his great work—in his remarkable work, his treasure house of learnin'—*The Decline and Fall of the Roman Empire*—if I had my copy here I could put my finger on to the very place where he says it, sirs. Why, sirs, in the *Decline and Fall*—I could show you the very line and chapter if I had my copy here—but it's up in my room—I could show you the very chapter on slavery, by the Lord Harry! sir, where Mr. Foote, of the state of Mississippi, in his last speech down in that country, sirs,—"

"Now, now, Jones," Dunwody raised a restraining hand at length, "just sit down. Don't go get your copy of the *Decline and Fall*. We're willing to take some of that for granted. Let's get at the pleasant task of taking away all the money of this Free Soil gentleman from the North. *Non* politics, *non* religion, *sed* poker! That's why we're here."

The Honorable William Jones, his eloquence thus dammed up, seemed to experience a sudden restriction of the throat, and coughed once or twice. "I will go against the said poker just onct," said he; "but, ahem!"

"I would suggest," said Dunwody, "that before we tempt the gods of fortune we should first pour a libation for their favor. What do you say, sir?" He turned to Jones and winked at Clayton.

"No, no, no, sir! No, I thank you just as much, but I never drink more than onct in a day. At home it varies. On some days I like my liquor in the mornin', some days just before bedtime, especially if there is any malary about, as there is in most of my country—indeed, I think there is some malary in these Ohio bottoms up here."

"That fact is beyond dispute," ventured Judge Clayton gravely. "In short, I myself feel in danger as we pass through these heavy forests."

"Quite so," assented the Honorable William Jones. "Sometimes I take a drink in the mornin' before breakfast, especially if there is malary around, as I said; sometimes before dinner, but only one; or, sometimes right after dinner, like now. Difference among men, ain't there? Some say it's wrong to drink before breakfast. Others say one drink then goes farther'n six later in the day. For me, now, only one drink a day. Unless—that is, of course—unless there is some very special occasion, such as—"

"Such as that offered by this most malarious country," ventured the judge gravely.

"Well, yes, since you mention it, on such an occasion as this. But Tom—" turning to the colored boy, "Make it very light; ver-r-ry light. Hold on thah, you rascal, not too light!"

The Honorable William Jones set an example in which he was joined temperately by the judge, the others contenting themselves in completing their arrangements for the game. The tokens were distributed, and in accordance with the custom of the time, the table soon was fairly well covered with money of divers sorts, gold coin, a lesser amount of silver, bills issued by many and divers banks in this or that portion of the country.

Silence fell when the game really began. The Honorable William Jones at first ever and anon threatened to erupt into Roman facts and figures, but chilly glances made his answer. Half an hour, and the passing of time was forgot.

At first the cards ran rather severely against the judge, and rather in favor of the historian, who played "the said poker" with such thoroughness that presently there appeared before him a ragged pile of currency and coin. Dunwody and Carlisle were losers, but finally Dunwody began to edge in upon the accumulated winnings of his neighbor on the right. An hour passed, two hours, more. The boat plowed on down-stream. Presently the colored boy began to light lamps. There came to the faces of all the tense look, the drawn and lined visage which is concomitant to play for considerable stakes. A frown came on the florid countenance of the young officer. The pile of tokens and currency before him lessened steadily. At last, in fact, he began to show uneasiness. He thrust a hand into a pocket where supplies seemed to have grown scarce. There is small mercy in a game of poker hard played, but at least one of his opponents caught some such signal of distress. Dunwody looked up from his own last hand.

"Don't leave us just yet, friend," he said. "You may draw on me for all you like, if you care to continue. We shall see that you get a ticket back home. No man can ask more than that!"

"I have a thousand acres of cotton land 'n a hunnerd niggers waitin' for me to git home," said the Honorable William Jones, "an' by hockey, I raise the ante to twenty dollars right hyer! Are you all comin' in?"

"I have at least that much left in my locker," answered Judge

Clayton. "What do you say to doubling that?"

"Suit me," said Dunwody briefly; they nodded assent all around, but the younger man ventured:

"Suppose I sit with you for one jack-pot, gentlemen. The hour is growing late for me, and I must plead other duties. When a man is both busy and broke, it is time for him to consider."

"No, no," expostulated the Honorable William Jones, who long since had forgotten his rule regarding one drink a day. "No, no, not broke, and not busy! Not at all!"

"I don't know," said Dunwody. "Suppose we make it one more jack-pot all around?" They agreed to this. It was Judge Clayton's deal.

"Gimme at least three," began the senator from Belmont, puckering out his lips in discontent.

"Three good ones," consented the judge. "How many for the rest of you?"

Dunwody shook his head. "I'll stand as it is, please."

The judge quietly discarded two cards, Carlisle having done the same. The betting now went about with more than one increase from the Honorable William Jones, whose eyes apparently were seeing large. At last the "call" came from Carlisle, who smilingly moved the bulk of his remaining fortune toward the center of the table. Thereupon, with a bland and sane smile, the Honorable William Jones shook his head and folded his cards together. The judge displayed queens and tens, the gentleman opposite queens and deuces. Dunwody laid down his own hand, which showed aces and fours. They all sighed.

"Gentlemen, you all deserve to win," said Dunwody. "I feel like a thief."

"I have a thousand acres of niggers 'n four hunnerd cotton lands," remarked the Honorable William Jones, amiably, "says you can't do it again. I can prove it from Mr. Gibbon's *Cline 'n Fall.*"

Judge Clayton rose, laughing, slapping Dunwody on the shoulder and giving an arm to Mr. Jones, whom he assisted to his room.

CHAPTER V

SPOLIA OPIMA

Dunwody remained seated at the table, carelessly shuffling the cards between his fingers. Once in a while he cast an amused glance toward Carlisle, and at last remarked, as though continuing an arrested thought:

"Amanuensis, is she?" He chuckled. The other ventured no reply.

"My dear sir, at your age, I congratulate you! The choice of an amanuensis is one very important for a public man, not less so, I imagine, for a military man. Consider the need—"

"I think that will do, my dear Dunwody," rejoined Carlisle at length, the hot blood in his face. "Frankly, this conversation is unwelcome to me."

"I'll tell you what I'll do with you," exclaimed the Missourian suddenly. "I'll bet you every cent in this pile of my winnings here that that young lady isn't your amanuensis, and never has been. I'll bet its like that she is no relative of yours. I'll bet it all over again that she is the most beautiful woman that ever set foot on a boat on this river, or ever set foot on any land. Moreover, I'll bet again—"

"You might win a certain share of these wagers," smiled the young officer, willing to pass by a possible argument. "Moreover, I am quite willing to discuss arrangements for changing the term of servitude of this young lady. I've been doing a little thinking about one or two matters since this morning."

"What!"

"Quite right. I wouldn't care to restrain her in any way, if she cared to travel in other company. Our work is well advanced toward completion, as it is."

"Yet you came here with her? Then what—?"

"Never mind what the relation may have been, my dear fellow. It irks me now. Especially does this sort of conversation irk me, because it is not fair to the young lady herself."

Dunwody drew in his breath with a strong sigh. He sat up straight in his chair, then rested an arm on the table, as he leaned forward toward the other. "A young lady has had a poor protector who would not protect her name. Of course!"

"In any case," smiled Carlisle, forcing the frown away from his face, "my fortunes need mending now. Do you think I could continue a journey down the river in company so strong at cards as yours? At a later time, if you like, I will endeavor to get my revenge."

"Suppose you have it now," said Dunwody calmly. "Haven't you just heard me say I haven't the means?"

"You have as much as I have."

"Tut! tut! I don't borrow to play cards."

"You do not need to borrow. I say, your stake equals mine, and we will play at evens, too. Come, deal one hand, poker between two, and to the hilt."

The other man looked at him and gazed at the heaped pile of coins and notes which lay before him. He himself was no pale-blooded opponent, nor usually disposed to slight the opportunities of the game. "I don't understand," said he finally. "Certainly I am not willing to pledge my land and 'niggers,' like our friend from Belmont here. Perhaps my fall has been hard enough not to tempt me to go on with my sort of luck. Suppose I decline!"

"You don't understand me," said Dunwody, looking him fair in the face. "I said that your stake can easily be equal with this on the table. I'll play you just two out of three jack-pots between the two of us. You see my stake."

"But mine?"

"You can make it even by writing one name—and correctly—here on a piece of paper. Full value—yes, ten times as much as mine! You are giving odds, man!"

"I don't understand you."

"You don't want to understand me. Come, now. You, as an army man, ought to know something of the history of poker in these United States. Listen, my friend. Do you recall a certain game played by a man higher in authority— younger than he is to-day—a game played upon a snowbound train in the North country? Do you remember what the stakes were—then? Do you recall that that man later became a president of the United States? Come. There is fine precedent for our little enterprise."

The swift flush on the face of the other man made his answer.
Dunwody went on mercilessly:

"He played then much as you do now. There was against him then, as there is now against you, a man who admired not so much just one woman in all the world as, let us say, one particular woman then and there present. Perhaps you remember his name—Mr. Parish—later ennobled by the German government and long known as a land baron in New York. Come! Think of it! Picture that snowbound train, that great citizen, and Parish, playing and playing, until at last it came to the question of a woman—not so beautiful as this one here, but in her own way shrewd, *the same sort of woman*, I might say—mysterious, beautiful, and—no, don't protest, and I'll not describe. You remember very well her name. It was pleasant property not so long ago for everybody. They played for the *love*, not for the hand, of that woman. Parish won her. Do you remember now?"

The younger man sat looking at him silently, his face now grown quite pale. "I am unwilling, sir, to allow any man to mention such details regarding the past life of my commander-in-chief, a president of the United States. It is not seemly. My profession should free me, by its very nature, from conversation such as this. My errand should free me. My place as a gentleman should free me, and her, from such discussion. It must, it shall, sir!"

"Forgive me," said Dunwody, coloring. "Your rebuke is just. I ask your pardon freely; but remember, what I say here is between us two, and no one else. Why deny yourself the luxury of remembering such a game as that? It was a man's game, and well worth the playing. Your former head of the army, at least, lost; and he paid. The other won. All Ogdensburg can tell you about that to-day. They lived there—together—Parish and the woman, till he went abroad. Yes, and she was a prisoner there not simply for a short time; she lived and died there. Whatever Parish did, whoever he was, he never loved any other woman as he did that one. And by the Lord! when it comes to that, no other woman in that town ever was loved more than she by everybody. Odd creatures, women, eh? Who can find them out? Who can weigh them, who can plumb their souls? But, my God! who can do without them?"

Carlisle made no answer, and Dunwody went on. "She had political intrigues back of her, just as this woman here has, for all I know. But one lost in that game, and the other, won. I've often wondered about that particular game of cards, my friend,—whether after all she loved the man who won her, right or wrong,—what became of her,—who she was? But now, tell me, was not our drunken friend right? Has human nature changed since Rome? And has not the conqueror always ruled? Have not the *spolia opima*, the rarest prizes, always been his?"

Carlisle only sat silent, looking at him, pale now, and rigid. He still made no comment.

"So now I say," went on Dunwody, "here is that same situation, twice in one lifetime! It's ominous, for somebody. There is trouble in the air, for some or all of us. But I say I offer you fair play, even, man to man. I ask no questions. I will not take any answers, any more than those two would have allowed any, that day on the train there, when they played, ten years or more ago. That was

31

a foreign woman. So is this, I think. She is the most beautiful woman I have ever seen. I have looked her in the face. I shall never see such another face again. Man, I'm mad over her. And you've just said you'd loose your hold on her, whatever it is—for her sake. By God! once my hold was on her, she never should get away—again."

"What do you propose?" asked the other hoarsely.

"I propose only to offer you that same game over again!" replied Dunwody. "Man, what an uncanny thing this is! But, remember one thing,—no matter what comes, I shall never mention our meeting here. I am not your keeper."

"Sir," broke out the other, "you embarrass me unspeakably. You do not know the circumstances. I can not tell—"

"Pardon me, I make no taunts, and I have said I tell no tales. But my word of honor, man,—I will play you,—two out of three, to see—who takes her." His voice was low, tense, savage.

The younger man sat back in his chair. One knowing his tempestuous nature might have expected anger, consternation, resentment, to remain on his face. On the contrary, a sudden light seemed to come into his countenance. Suddenly he stifled a smile! He passed a hand across his brow, as though to assure himself. It was not so much confidence or resolution as half deliberation which shone in his eye as he cast a glance upon the heap of money on the opposite side of the table. Yet no sordid thought, no avarice was in his gaze. It was the look of the fanatic, the knight errant, resolved upon deed of risk or sacrifice for sake of a woman's wish; but with it was the amusement of a man who foresaw that difficulties lay ahead of him who essayed the role of jailer to Josephine, Countess St. Auban. What now passed across his countenance, little by little, therefore, was relief, relaxation from a strain, a solution of some doubtful problem. In brief, there seemed offered to him now the opportunity to terminate an errand which suddenly had grown distasteful to him and dangerous both to him and to his charge. At one stroke he might secure for himself riddance of the company of an embarrassing companion who already had served notice of her intention to desert him; and might also keep silent this man, whom she had asked for aid. As for him, she would take his measure quickly enough if he presumed in any way. Would not the purpose of his journey have been accomplished, might not he himself return to his work, would not each of these three have been served to his or her own liking, should now the suggestion of this eager man be accepted? If he won at the cards, why then—if he lost—but that he resolved not to do! The greatest misfortune possible, to his perplexed soul, was that the cards should not be against him. As he reflected upon these things, he hesitated. It was but to gain time.

"Senator Dunwody," said he, at length, "you and I are from different parts of the country—from two different worlds, you might say. You believe in slavery and the extension of it—I believe in just the reverse. I would sacrifice my professional future, if need were, in that belief." The other nodded, but his eyes did not waver.

"Very good! Now, I want to say to you this much. The young lady who has been with me is dangerous. She is an abolitionist of the strictest sect. She is very likely an European revolutionist, among other things. She is dangerous as such. I think I can say this much, and break no pledge of confidence."

"That isn't how she is dangerous to me. But is that the crime for which you transport her for life?" smiled the other. His shot came so close that his companion raised a hand.

"I don't deny, don't explain, don't argue," he retorted curtly. "I only say that I shall be willing to part with her services and turn her over to your own care, if you *both* so like. We know she has appealed to you for aid. My own errand, if you please, is near to its close. It has been—"

"Cut the cards, man!" cried the Missourian. It was lucky that he interrupted. He was just in time to prevent the other from making the mistake of saying what was the truth—that he was in any case about to leave the young lady to her own devices, and by her own request. The game which he most valued now was not on the table before him. He was playing it in his own mind. In short, duty or no duty, he was resolved to end the role of jailer and prisoner, for sake of the prisoner herself. Let others attempt the unpleasant task if they liked. Let others condemn if they liked. He, Carlisle, could be jailer no longer. Yet he deliberated well the risk he ran.

"It would be ruin to me if this were known, Senator Dunwody, and of that you are perfectly aware."'

"I know that as well as you, but there can be honor even in politics, war, or—love. I have given you my word. Deal!"

"You are impatient. You rejoice as a strong man to run a race, my dear sir."

"I *do* run a race. I *am* strong. Play! It is in the cards that I must win."

"But if you should lose?"

"I shall not lose!"

His insistence, his confidence, almost caused the older man to laugh. "No, my friend," said he to himself, "you shall not lose!" But what he said aloud was, "You must not be excited, Dunwody. You may need all your nerve. I thought you cooler in times of stress."

"You don't know me. I don't know myself. Perhaps it is ice in your blood—I don't know,—it's fire in mine."

"Very well,—I hope you like the cards I have given you." But there was no ice in the red flush on Carlisle's sanguine face,

"Give me four more," cried the Missourian, flinging down his own cards with hands that trembled.

"Quite right, sir, you shall have them. But how you tremble! I wouldn't have so poor a nerve as yours for all the money in the world, my dear Senator. You act as though there were four hundred acres of niggers at stake, as Mr. Jones would say!"

"Go on! You don't know what there is at stake."

"So, now. You have your four cards. For myself—though you are so excited you wouldn't notice it if I did not call your attention to it—I take but three. You are an infant, man. See that you be not delivered into the hands of the enemy."

They looked now each into his renewed hand of five cards. Dunwody swept a stack of money toward the center of the table. "A thousand dollars against one look from her eye!"

"My dear sir," rejoined the other calmly, "you are raised to the extent of two glances—one from each eye."

"Another thousand for the touch of her glove."

"I come back. You shall have a pair."

"A thousand more to hear the sound of her step—another thousand for one smile!"

Carlisle's voice trembled, but he forced himself under control. "My dear sir, you shall have all you wish! I am sure if she could see you now she herself would be disposed to smile. You do not yet understand that woman. But now, suppose that the betting has gone far enough? What cards have you? For myself, I discover that I have drawn four kings. I trust that you have four aces of your own."

There was sincerity in this wish, but Dunwody answered gloomily: "You gave me three tens and a pair of fives, with what I held. You have won the first round."

He dashed a hand, and cleared the square of matted hair from his forehead, which now was beaded. Red, florid, full-blooded, balked in his eagerness, he looked as savage as some denizen of the ancient forest, in pursuit as reckless, as ill-suited with ill-fortune.

"My deal," said he, at length, in a voice half a growl. And later, "How many?"

"I shall, if you please, require but one card," was the quiet answer. Dunwody himself required two. They sat narrowly eying each other, although there was in this close duel small advantage for either except in the run of the cards themselves.

"It is perhaps needless for us to waste time, since I can not divide my stakes," smiled the younger gentleman.

Again with a half growl, Dunwody threw down his cards, face upward. His teeth were clenched, all his muscles set, all his attitude strained, tense.

"You have won, my dear Senator! I failed to improve my four cards, which, it is true, were of one color, but which I regret to say still remain of the one color and of no better company!"

"It is even!" exclaimed Dunwody. "Come!"

The cards went around once more, and once more the officer asked for a single card. Once again he lost.

Dunwody drew back with a deep sigh. "Look!" he said, "of my three cards, two were what I wanted—aces, aces, man!—four of them! By every token, I have won. It's fate!"

The face of his opponent was a study. His eyebrows went up in pleasant expostulation at the other's eagerness. "So, then," said he, "I suppose I must pay my stake, much to my regret. Ah! how fortune has run against me to-day. And so, here it is,—I write her name for you once more—this time her real name, so far as any in America know it—thus,—Josephine, Countess St. Auban, of France, of Hungary, of America, abolitionist, visionary, firebrand. There, then,—though I think you will find the matter of taking possession somewhat difficult to compass—so far as I am concerned, she is, with all my heart, yours to have and to hold, *if you can*! My duty to her is over. Yours begins, I hope!"

Dunwody found no speech. He was pale, and breathing fast.

Gravity increased in the other's demeanor. His face now looked drawn, weary. "I beg, my dear sir," he said, "nay, I entreat and command you, to make all gentle and kind use of this which the gods have given you. I confess nothing whatever, except that I am hungry and tired to extinction. I congratulate the winner, and consider myself fortunate to be allowed to go in peace to my own place—penniless, it is true, but at least with a conscience quite clear." The frown on his face, the troubled gaze of his eyes, belied his last words. "It's no part of my conscience to coerce a woman," he added defiantly. "I can't do it —not any longer."

"It is well to be a cheerful loser," returned Dunwody, at last. "I couldn't blame any man for being coerced by—her! I admit that I am. But after this, what will be your plans?"

"I purpose leaving the boat at the first suitable stop, not farther down than Louisville, at least. Perhaps Cincinnati would be yet better. By the fortunes of war you will, therefore, stand in my stead. I've changed my mind, suddenly. I told the young lady that we would continue on together, even beyond Cairo. But now—well, to the victor, as Mr. Marcy has said, belong the spoils. Only, there are some titles which may not be negotiated. A quitclaim is by no means a warranty. You'll discover that." He smiled grimly.

The other made no answer. He only stood to his full height and stretched out his great arms. He seemed a figure come down unchanged from some savage day.

CHAPTER VI

THE NEW MASTER

Alone in her state-room all these hours, Josephine St. Auban had abundant time to reflect upon the singular nature of her situation. At first, and very naturally, she was disposed to seek the protection of the boat's officers, but a second thought convinced her of the unwisdom of that course. As to this stranger, this stalwart man of the West, she had appealed to him and he had made no sign. She had no friend, no counselor. A feeling of inefficiency, of smallness and helplessness, swept over her. For the first time in her life she found herself hard and fast in the grasp of events over which she had absolutely no control. She was prisoner to her own good fame. She dared not declare herself. She dared not cry out for help. None would believe her story. She herself did not fully understand all the circumstances connected with her unlawful banishment from the capital of the proudest and freest republic of the world.

[Illustration: Josephine St. Auban had abundant time to reflect]

It was while still in this frame of mind that, on the day following, there came to her a messenger bearing the card of Warville Dunwody. She gazed at it for some moments undecided, debating. She tried to reason. Had she trusted rather to woman's vaticination, matters had been better for her. What she actually did was to summon Jeanne to complete some hurried toilet preparations. Then she set out to meet the sender of the card.

There was no occupant of the saloon excepting one, who rose as she entered, hesitating. On the instant a sudden change swept over Dunwody's face. Was it at first assuredness it had borne? "I am glad that you have thus honored me," he said simply.

"It is much pleasanter to move about as one may," she answered. "But where is our friend, Captain Carlisle, this morning? Is he ill, or simply unmindful of one so unimportant as myself? I have not heard from him."

"He left the boat last night," answered Dunwody gravely, his eyes fixed on her face.

"Left the boat—he is gone? Why, he sent me no word, and I thought—at least, he said—"

"He has, Madam, like Cataline, evaded, broken forth, absconded. But as to leaving word for you, he was not quite so heartless as all that. I have a message for you."

With a word craving permission she opened the message. It was brief.

"MY DEAR COUNTESS:"
"You will be glad to know that so far as your late
jailer is concerned, your captivity is at an end. I am
leaving the boat at the next stop, and since that falls in
the night-time, I will not disturb you. Senator
Dunwody has kindly consented to act as your guardian in
my stead, and from your message to him, I judge that
in any case you would prefer his care to mine."

"My dear Countess, they are not merely idle words
when I say to you that you have won my respect and
admiration. Be on your guard, and allow me to
advise you in the interest of yourself and others to
remain—silent."
"YOUR OBLIGED AND DUTIFUL SERV'T—"

No reasons were urged, no apologies offered. Obviously, the signature was in such circumstances better omitted.

The effect of this note, strange to say, was to fill its recipient not with satisfaction, not even with surprise, but with sudden horror. She felt abandoned, forsaken, not pausing to reflect that now she had only what she had demanded of her late companion,—guardian, she now hastily called him, and not jailer. Unconsciously she half-arose, would have left the room. Her soul was filled with an instinctive, unformulated dread.

As to Dunwody himself, ruthless and arrogant as was his nature, he bore no trace of imperiousness now. The silent lips and high color of the face before him he did not interpret to mean terror, but contempt. In the fortunes of chance he had won her. In the game of war she was his prisoner. Yet no ancient warrior of old, rude, armored, beweaponed, unrelenting, ever stood more abashed before some high-headed woman captive. He had won—what? Nothing, as he knew very well, beyond the opportunity to fight further for her, and under a far harder handicap, a handicap which he had foolishly imposed on himself. This woman, seen face to face, yes, she was beautiful, desirable, covetable. But she was not the sort of woman he had supposed her. It was Carlisle, after all, who had won in the game!

For two moments he debated many things in his mind. Did not women of old sometimes relent? He asked himself over and over again the same questions, pleaded to himself the same arguments. After all, he reasoned, this was only a woman. Eventually she must yield to one sort of treatment or the other. He had not reflected that, though the ages in some ways have stood still, in others they have gone forward. In bodily presence woman has not much changed, this age with that. The canons of art remain the same, the ideals of art are the same. These and those lines, gracious, compelling,—this and that color, enchanting, alluring, so much white flesh, thus much crown of tresses—they have for ages served to rob men of reason. They have not changed. What this man could not realize was that there may be changes not of color and of curve.

Not so long as all this they gazed at each other, measured, took ground, gaging each the adversary opposite.

"Do not go!" he almost commanded. She was half way to the door.

"Why not, sir?" She wheeled on him fiercely.

"Because,—at least, you would not be so cruel—"

"I thank you, but I am leaving the boat at the first opportunity. It is impossible for us to continue an acquaintance formed thus irregularly."

"On the contrary, my dear!" The ring in his voice terrified her, but his terms angered her yet more.

"I do not in the least understand you, sir! I am accustomed to do quite as I like. And you may address me as the Countess St. Auban."

"Why should we talk of this?" he retorted. "Why talk to me of countesses? To me you are something better as you stand,—the most beautiful girl, the most splendid human being, I ever saw in all my life. If you are doing quite as you like, why should you ask me to come to your aid? And why will you not now accept my aid when it is offered? The relations under which you have been traveling with this other gentleman were not quite clear to me, but such as they were—"

"Do you lack courage, sir, to say that he has quit-claimed me to you? Am I still a prisoner? Are you to be my new jailer? By what right, then?"

Dunwody had not gathered all the story of this woman and her earlier guardian; more than she herself could guess what had been Carlisle's motive or plan in leaving her to her own devices. That she was the victim simply of a daring kidnapping could, not have occurred to him. What then did she mean by talking of prisoners?

"After all, you were not that amanuensis which you yourself claimed to be?"

"I was not. Of course I was not. I am the Countess St. Auban. It is not necessary for me to serve any man, in my capacity."

"Why, then, did you say you were?"

"Because I thought I was still to be in that gentleman's charge. I did not know he was about to desert me. I preferred his company to worse."

"He has only given you your own wish—I hope it is still your wish. I hope it is not 'worse.'"

"I beg you to forget that little note from me. I was only frightened at the thought of a long journey which I did not know then might end so soon. I only fancied I was in need of help."

"Tell me one thing," he began irrelevantly. "You are countess, as you say. Who is your husband, and where is he?"

"You have no right to ask. I must leave you now. Ah! If indeed I had a protector here—some man of that country where men fight—"

"I have said that you shall not leave."

"But this passes belief. It is insult, it is simple outrage! I am alone—I come to you asking protection in the name of a man's chivalry,—an American's. This is what I receive! You declare yourself to be my new jailer. What is being done with me? I never saw Captain Carlisle until three days ago. And you have met me once, before this moment! And you are a Southerner; and, they tell me—"

"That once was enough."

"Your pardon, sir! Which way does the conversation tend?"

"To one end only," he resumed sullenly, desperately. "You shall not leave. If you did, I should only follow you."

"How excellent, to be taken by one brigand, handed over to another brigand, and threatened with perpetual attendance of the latter! Oh, excellent indeed! Admirable country!"

"You despise the offer of one who would be a respectful servitor."

She mocked at him. "How strange a thing is man! That is the first argument he makes to a woman, the first promise he makes. Yet at once he forgets the argument and forgets the promise. What you desire is to be not my servant, but my master, I should say. You fancy you are my master? Well, then, the situation seems to me not without its amusing features. I am a prisoner, I am set free. I am sought to be again put in durance, under duress, by a man who claims to be my humble servitor—who also claims to be a gentleman! It is most noble of you! I do not, however, comprehend."

The dull flush on his face showed at least no weakening on his own part.

"Come now!" he exclaimed impatiently, "let us arrive at the issue."

"And what honorable enterprise is it which you propose?"

"To make it short, Madam, I propose to take you home with me. Now you have heard it." He spoke in a desperate, icy calm.

[Illustration: I propose to take you home with me.]

"You flatter me! But how, if I may ask, do you intend to accomplish all that?"

"I have not thought so far along. In peace, if you please: it would be much better."

"But, my God!" she exclaimed, pausing in her walk up and down. "You speak as though you meant these things! Could it be there, out there—beyond the great river—yes, my other jailer told me that we were not to stop this side! I suppose you are my new keeper, then, and not my friend? Duty again, and not chivalry! Is that what you mean?"

"I hardly know what I mean," he answered miserably. "I like all this no better than yourself. But let us begin with what is certain. Each hour, each day I may be able to hold you here is that much gained. I can't let you go."

"Most excellent! You begin well. But I shall not submit to such insults longer. Such treatment is new to me. It shall not go unrevenged. Nor shall it continue now."

"It is too late!" he broke in. "I know how much I have taken leave of my own self-respect, but there are times when one takes leave of everything—cares for nothing that lies between him and one purpose. It would do no good for you to claim the protection of others—even if I had to fight all the boat's officers, I might win. But in that case you could only lose. You would have to explain who you are, why you are here. You would not be believed."

"What I wish to know is only one thing," she rejoined. "Not offering terms, I want to know what is the alternative you have proposed. Let us see if we can not reason calmly over this matter." She also was suddenly cold and pale. The hand of a swift terror was upon her now.

"You ask me to reason, and I answer I have no reason left. You ask me what I propose, ask what we should do, and I answer I do not know. But also I know that if you left me, I should never see you again."

"But what difference, then? You are, I presume, only my new constable."

"There could be no social chance for me—I've ruined that. You would exact defeat of me as surely as you met me, there."

"Social chance?—Social—! Well, the *bon Dieu*! And here you exact defeat for yourself. But what defeat? Come, your speech sounds more personal than professional. What can you possibly think yourself to be, but my new jailer?"

"I'm not so sure. Look, each turn of the wheels takes us farther away from the places where society goes on in its own grooves. Out here we manage the world in our own ways."

Unconsciously the eyes of both of them turned down the river, along which the boat now steadily continued its course. He went on somberly.

"Out there," he said, pointing toward the west, "out beyond the big river, there's a place where the wilderness sweeps. Out there the law is that of the old times. It is far away."

"How dare you speak in such way to me?" she half whispered, low and tense. "And you claim manhood!"

"No," he said, sighing. "I—claim nothing. I deny nothing. I assert nothing— except that I'm going to be not your Jailer, but your keeper. Yes, I'm going to hold you, keep you! You shall not get away. Why," he added, pacing apart for a moment. "I have no shame left. I've planned very little. I thought I might even ask you to be a guest at my own plantation. My place is out on the edge of the world, thirty miles back from the river. An amanuensis is as reasonable there as on this boat, in the company of a frontier army man."

"That, then, is your robber castle, I suppose."

"I rule there, Madam," he said simply.

"Over thrall and guest?"

"Over all who come there, Madam."

"I've heard of the time," she went on icily, "when this country was younger, how the *seigneurs* who held right under the old French kings claimed the law of the high, low and middle justice. Life, death, honor, all lay in their hands— in the hands of individuals. But I thought those times past. I thought that this river was different from the St. Lawrence. I thought that this was a republic, and inhabited by men. I thought the South had gentlemen—"

"You taunt me, my dear lady, my dear girl. But be not so sure that times have changed. Out beyond, there, where we are going, I could put you a mile back from the river, and you would find yourself in a wilderness the most pathless in the world to-day, worse than the St. Lawrence ever knew at any time, more lawless, more beyond the reach of any law. These lands out here are wild; yes, and they breed wild men. They have been the home of others besides myself, lawless, restless under any restraint. If you come to wildernesses, and if you come to the law of the individual, I say we're only just approaching that sort of thing right now, and here."

She looked at him, some inarticulate sort of sound in her throat, fully frightened now, seeing how mistaken she had been. He went on:

"Out there in the big valleys beyond the river, you would indeed disappear. No man could guess what had become of you. You would never be found again. And without any doubt or question, Madam, if you force me to it, you shall have your answer in that way. I'm not a boy to be fooled with, to be denied. I rule out there, over free and thrall. There's where you're going. Your other jailer told you the truth!"

She looked at him slowly and fully now, the color fading from her face. Her soul had touched the steel in his own soul. She knew that, once aroused, this man would hesitate at nothing. Crowded beyond his limit, there was no measure he would not employ. Other means must be employed with such a nature as his. She temporized.

"Listen. You are a man of family and traditions,—my late guardian told me. You have been chosen to a position of trust, you are one of the lawmakers of your own state. Do you ever stop to reflect what you are doing, how you are abandoning yourself, your own traditions, your own duties, when you speak as you have been speaking to me? I had committed no crime. I am held by no process of law. You take risks."

"I know. I have thrown it all away in the balance. If these things were known, I would be ruined." He spoke dully and evenly, indifferently.

"I lack many things, Madam," he resumed at length. "I do not lack honesty even with myself, and I do not lie even to a woman. That's the trouble. I have not lied to you. Come now, let us understand. I suppose it's because I've been alone so much. Civilization does not trouble us much back there. These are my people—they love me—I hold them in my hand so long as I live up to their standards. Maybe I've thrown them away, right now,—my people."

"You are not living up to your standards."

"No, but I can not make you understand me. I can not make you understand that the great thing of life isn't the foolish ambition of a man to get into a state legislature, to make laws, to see them enforced. It isn't the original purpose of man to get on in politics or business, or social regard. Man is made to love some woman. Woman is made to be loved by some man. That's life. It's all of it. I know there's nothing else."

"I have heard my share of such talk, perhaps, in this or that corner of the world," she answered, with scorn. "Excellent, for you to force it upon a woman who is helpless!"

"Talk doesn't help, but deeds will. You're going along with me. I would swear you belonged to me, if need be. As, by the Almighty God! I intend you some day shall. All the officers of the law are sworn to help a man claim what is his own, this side or that of the slave line. All the stars in the sky are sworn to help a man who feels what I feel. Don't tempt me, don't try to drive me—it will never do. I'll be harder to handle than the man who lost you to me last evening in a game of cards,—and who went away last night and left you—to me."

As she gazed at him she saw his hands clenched, his mouth twitching. "You would do that, even—" she began. "I have never known men grew thus unscrupulous. A game—a game at cards! And I—was lost—I!—I! And also won? What can you mean? Am I then indeed a slave, a chattel? Ah, indeed, now am I lost! My God, and I have no country, no kin, no God, to avenge me!"

A sort of sob caught in his throat. "I was wrong!" he cried suddenly. "I always say the wrong word, do the wrong thing, take the wrong way. But—don't you remember about Martin Luther? He said he couldn't help himself. 'Here stand I, I can not otherwise, God help me!' That's just the way with me—you blame me, but I tell you I can not otherwise. And I've told the truth. I've made wreck of everything right now. You ask me to make plans; and I tell you I can not. I would take you off the boat by force rather than see you go away from me. This thing is not yet worked out to the end. I'm not yet done. That's all I know. You'll have to go along with me."

A sudden revulsion swept over him. He trembled as he stood, and reached out a hand.

"Give me a chance!" he broke out, sobered now. "It was a new thing, this feeling. Come, you sent for me—you asked me—that other man placed me in his stead as your guardian. He didn't know I would act in this way, that's true. I own I've been brutal. I know I've forgotten everything, but it came over me all at once, something new. Why, look at us two together—what could stop us? Always I've lacked something: I did not know what. Now I know. Give me my chance. Let me try again!"

In this strange, strained position, she caught, in spite of herself, some sort of genuine note underneath the frankness of his ungovernable passion. For once, she was in a situation where she could neither fathom motives nor arrange remedies. She stood in sheer terror, half fascinated in spite of all.

They both were silent for a while, but at length she resumed, not so ungently: "Then let there be this contract between us, sir. Neither of us shall make any further scene. We'll temporize, since we can do no better. I gave parole once.

I'll not give it again, but I'll go a little farther on westward, until I decide what to do."

Impulsively he held out his hand to her, his mouth twitching with emotion, some sort of strange impulse shining in his eyes,

"Be my enemy, even," he said, "only, do not leave me. I'll not let you go."

CHAPTER VII

A CONFUSION IN CHATTELS

Their conversation was brought to an end by sounds of hurrying feet upon the decks above them. The hoarse boom of the steamer's whistle indicated an intended landing. A swift thought of possible escape came to the mind of Josephine St. Auban. When Dunwody turned in his troubled pacing up and down the narrow floor of the cabin, he found himself alone.

"Jeanne!" cried she, running from the stair to the door of her state-room. "Hurry! Quick, get your valises! We'll leave the boat here, at once!" Escape, in some fashion, to some place, at once, that was her sole thought in the panic which assailed her.

But when presently, as the boat drew in along the dock, she made ready to go ashore and hurriedly sought a servant to take care of the luggage, it was the captain of the *Mount Vernon* himself who came to meet her.

"I am sorry, Madam," he began, his cap in hand, "but your passage was booked farther down the river than this point. You are mistaken. This is not Cairo."

"What of that, sir? Is it not the privilege of a passenger to stop at any intermediate point?"

"Not in this case, Madam."

"What do you mean?" she blazed out at him in anger on first impulse. But even as she did so there came over her heart once more the sick feeling of helplessness. Though innocent, she was indeed a prisoner! As much as though this were the Middle Ages, as though these were implacable armed enemies who stood about her, and not commonplace, every-day individuals in a commonplace land, she was a prisoner.

"You shall suffer for this!" she exclaimed. "There must be a law somewhere in this country."

"That is true, Madam," said the captain, "and that is the trouble. I'm told that my orders come from the *highest* laws. Certainly I have no option in the matter. I was told distinctly not to let you off without his orders—not even to allow you to send any word ashore."

"But the gentleman who accompanied me is no longer on the boat. He left me word that our journey in common was ended. See, here is his note."

"All I can say, Madam, is that this is not signed, and that he did not tell me he was going to leave. I can not allow you to go ashore at this point. In fact, I should consider you safer here on the boat than anywhere else."

"Are there then no gentlemen in all the world? Are you not a man yourself? Have you no pity for a woman in such plight as mine?"

"Your words cut me deeply, my dear lady. I want to give you such protection as I can. Any man would do that. I am a man, but also I am an officer. You are a woman, but apparently also some sort of fugitive, I don't know just what. We learn not to meddle in these matters. But I think no harm will come to you —I'm sure not, from the care the gentlemen used regarding you. Please don't make it hard for me."

The boat was now alongside the dock at the river settlement, and there was some stir at the gangway as room was made for the reception of additional passengers. As they looked over the rail they discovered these to be made up of a somewhat singular group. Two or three roughly dressed men were guarding as many prisoners. Of the latter, two were coal black negroes. The third was a young woman apparently of white blood, of comely features and of composed bearing in spite of her situation. A second glance showed that all these three were in irons. Obviously then the law, which at that time under the newly formed Compromise Acts allowed an owner to follow his fugitive slaves into any state, was here finding an example, one offering indeed all the extremes of cruelty both to body and to soul.

"For instance, young lady, look at that," went on the boat captain, turning to Josephine, who was carried back by the incoming rush of the new passengers. "It is something we see now and again on this river. Sometimes my heart aches, but what can I do? That's the law, too. I have learned not to meddle."

[Illustration: "That's the law, too"]

"My God! My God!" exclaimed Josephine St. Auban, her eyes dilating with horror, forgetting her own plight as she looked at the spectacle before her. "Can these things really be in America! You submit to this, and you are men? Law? Is there *any* law?"

She did not hear the step behind them, but presently a voice broke in.

"If you please, Captain Rogers," said Warville Dunwody, "I think it will not be necessary to restrain this lady in any way. By this time she knows it will be better not to make any attempt to escape."

Jeanne, the maid, was first to see the distress in the face of her mistress.

"*Infame! Infame!*" she cried, flying at them, her hands clenched, her foot stamping. "Dogs of pigs, you are not men, you are not gentlemen! See now! See now!"

Tears stood in the eyes of Jeanne herself. "Come," said she, and put an arm about her mistress, leading her back toward the door of the cabin.

"This is bad business, sir," said the older man, turning to Dunwody. "I don't understand all this case, but I'm almost ready to take that girl's part. Who is she? I can't endure much longer seeing a woman like that handled in this way. You'll some of you have to show me your papers before long."

"You ask me who she is," replied Dunwody slowly, "and on my honor I can hardly tell you. She is temporary ward of the government, that much is sure. You know very well the arm of the national government is long. You know, too, that I'm a state senator and also a United States marshal in Missouri."

"But where do you come into this case, Senator?"

"I came into it last night at a little after nine o'clock," rejoined Dunwody. "Her former guardian has turned her over to me. She does not leave the boat till I do, at Cairo, where I change for up-river; and when I go, she goes. Don't pay any attention to any outcry she may make. She's my—property."

Captain Rogers pondered for a time, but at length his face broke out into a sort of smile. "There may be trouble ahead for you," he began. "It is like my old friend Bill Jones in there. He buys him a young filly last spring. Goes over to bring the filly home, and finds she isn't broke, and wild as a hawk. So he puts a halter on her and starts off to lead her home. The filly rears up, falls over and breaks her neck; so he's out his money and his pains. Some sorts of women won't lead."

"They all do in time," rejoined Dunwody grimly. "This one must."
The old boat captain shook his head.

"Some of them break their necks first," said he. "This one's got blood in her too, I tell you that."

Dunwody made no answer except to turn and walk down the deck. The captain, pondering on matters entirely beyond his comprehension, but forced to accept the assurances of men such as these who had appeared as guardians of this mysterious young woman, now returned to his own quarters. "I reckon it's none of my business," he muttered. "Some high-class forger or confidence worker that's beat the government somehow, maybe. But she don't look it— I'll be damned if she looks it. I wonder—?"

Dunwody, left to himself, began moodily to walk up and down the narrow deck, his hands behind his back. On his face was the red fighting flush, but it was backed by no expression of definite purpose, and his walk showed his mental uncertainty. All at once he turned and with decision passed down the stairs to the lower deck. He had heard voices which he recognized.

Judge Clayton had joined the party in charge of the fugitives, and was now in conversation with the overseer, a short man clad in a coarse blue jacket, with high boots and greasy leather trousers. The latter was expatiating exultantly upon his own bravery and shrewdness in effecting the recapture of his prisoners.

"Why, Jedge," said he, "fust off it di'n't look like we'd ever git track of 'em at all. I cotched the trail at Portsmouth at last, and follered 'em back into Ohio. They was shore on the 'underground' and bound for Canada, or leastways Chicago. I found 'em in a house 'way out in the country—midnight it was when we got thar. I'd summonsed the sher'f and two constables to go 'long. Farm-house was a underground railway station all right, and the farmer showed fight. We was too much fer him, and we taken 'em out at last, but one of the constables got shot—some one fired right through the winder at us. This Lily gal was the wust of the lot, and I don't put it a-past her to 'a' done some of the shootin' herself. But we brung 'em all along.

"Now, Jedge," he continued, "of co'se, I think I can do something for these two bucks Bill and Jim—this gal only persuaded 'em to run away with her. But if I was you, I shore would sell that Lily gal South, right away. She's bound fer to make trouble, and nothin' but trouble, fer you as long as you keep her round the place."

The speaker, coarse and ignorant, presented a contrast to the tall, dignified and quiet gentleman whom he accosted, and who now stood, with hands in pockets, looking on with genuine concern on his face.

"Lily," said he at length, "what makes you act this way? Haven't you always been treated well down there at home?"

"Yas, sir, I reckon so," replied the girl sullenly; "well as anybody's niggahs is!"

"Then why do you want to run off? This is the third time in the last year. I've been kind to you—I say, Dunwody," he went on, turning suddenly as he saw the latter approach—"haven't I always treated my people right? Haven't I always given them everything in the world they ought to have?"

"Yes, Judge, that's the truth, and any neighbor of yours will say it," assented Dunwody as he joined the group. "What's wrong then? This Lily girl run off again? Seems to me you told me about her."

"Yes," said Judge Clayton, rubbing a finger across his chin in perturbation, "the poor thing doesn't know when she's well off. But what am I to do with her, that's the question? I don't believe in whipping; but in this case, Wilson, I'm going to turn over those two boys to you. I won't have the girl whipped even yet. I'll see you when we get down to Cairo," he added, turning away. "We'll have to change there to the Sally Lee, for the Vernon doesn't stop at our landing. She's going straight through to Memphis."

As Judge Clayton walked away, Dunwody turned to the overseer, whom he had seen before on the Clayton plantations.

"So you had trouble this time?" he ventured.

"Heap of it, sir," replied the overseer, taking off his cap. "It was that fine yaller lady there that made most of it. She's the one that's a-fo_mint_in' trouble right along. She's a quiet lookin' gal, but she ain't. It's all right what the jedge says to me, but I'm goin' to have a little settle_ment_ with this fine lady myself, this time."

The girl heard him plainly enough, but only turned moodily back toward the coil of rope where sat the two blacks who had been her companions. From these she kept her skirt as remote as though they were not of her station. Dunwody approached the overseer, and put a gold double-eagle in his hand.

"Listen here, Wilson," said he, "you seem to be able to handle such people discreetly. Now I've got a prisoner along, up-stairs, myself—never mind who she is or how she comes here. As you know, I'm a United States marshal for this district, and this prisoner has been turned over to me. I'm going on up home, beyond St. Genevieve, and I've got to change down there at Cairo myself, to take the up-river boat."

"Mulattress?" listlessly inquired Wilson, after grinning at the coin. "They're the wust. I'd rather handle straight niggers my own self."

"Well," said Dunwody, "now that you mention it, I don't know but they would be easier to handle. This prisoner is about as tall as that girl yonder, and she's a whole lot lighter, do you understand? Of a dark night—say about the time we'd get down to Cairo, midnight—well wrapped up, and the face of neither showing, it might be hard to tell one of them from the other."

"How'll you trade?" grinned Wilson. "Anybody kin git a mighty good trade for this yaller lady of ours here. If she was mine I'd trade her for a sack of last year potatoes. I reckon Jedge Clayton'll be sick enough of her, time he gets expenses of this last trip paid, gittin' her back."

"I'm not trading," said Dunwody, frowning and flushing. "But now I'll tell you what I want you to do, when we get into Cairo. I may have trouble with my prisoner, and I don't know any better man than yourself to have around in a case like that. Do you think, if I left it all to you, you could handle it?"

"Shore I could—what's the use of your troublin' yourself about it, Colonel Dunwody? This here's more in my line."

Dunwody turned away with a sudden feeling of revulsion, almost of nausea at the thought now in his mind. It was a few moments later that he again approached Wilson.

"There's a French girl along with this prisoner of mine," said he. "Just take them both along together. I reckon the French girl won't make any disturbance—it's the other—the lady—her mistress. She's apt to—to 'fomint' trouble. Handle her gently as you can. You'll have to have help. The captain will not interfere. You just substitute my prisoner for yours yonder at Cairo— I'll show you where she is when the time comes. Once you have her aboard my boat for St. Genevieve, you can come back and take care of your own prisoners here. There may be another eagle or so in it. I am not asking questions and want none asked. Do your work, that's all."

"You don't need to be a-skeered but what I'll do the work, Colonel," smiled Wilson grimly. "I've had a heap o' trouble the last week, and I'm about tired. I'll not stand no foolishness."

Had any friend seen Warville Dunwody that night, he must have pronounced him ten years older than when the Mount Vernon had begun her voyage.

CHAPTER VIII

"All very well, gentlemen! All very well!" repeated the man who sat at the head of the table. "I do not deny anything you say. None the less, the question remains, what were we to do with this woman, since she was here? I confess my own relief at this message from our agent, Captain Carlisle, telling of her temporary disappearance."

As he spoke, he half pushed back his chair, as though in impatience or agitation over the problem which evidently occupied his mind. A man above medium height, somewhat spare in habit of body, of handsome features and distinguished presence, although with hair now slightly thinned by advancing years, he seemed, if not by natural right, at least by accorded authority, the leader in this company with whose members he was not unwilling to take counsel.

Those who sat before him were his counselors, chosen by himself, in manner ratified by law and custom. They made, as with propriety may be stated, a remarkable body of men. It were less seemly openly to determine their names and their station, since they were public men, and since, as presently appeared, they now were engaged on business of such nature as might not be placed in full upon public records.

At least it may be stated that this meeting was held in the autumn of the year 1850, and in one of the great public buildings of the city of Washington. Apparently it was more private than official in its nature, and apparently it now had lasted for some time. The hour was late. Darkness presently must enshroud the room. Even now the shadows fell heavy upon the lofty portraits, the rich furnishings, the mixed assemblage of somewhat hodgepodge decorations. Twice an ancient colored man had appeared at the door with lighted taper, as though to offer better illumination, but each time the master of the place had waved him away, as though unwilling to have present a witness even so humble as he. Through the door, thus half opened, there might have been seen in the hall two silent and motionless figures, standing guard.

Obviously the persons here present were of importance. It was equally obvious that they sought no intrusion. Why, then, in a meeting so private and so serious, should there come a remark upon a topic certainly not a matter of state in the usual acceptance of the term? Why should the leader have been concerned over the slight matter of a woman's late presence here in Washington?

As though to question his associates, the speaker turned his glance down the long table, where sat figures, indistinct in the gathering gloom. At his right hand, half in shadow, there showed the bold outlines of a leonine head set upon broad shoulders. Under cavernous brows, dark eyes looked out with seriousness. Half revealed as it was, here was a countenance fairly fit to be called godlike. That this presence was animated with a brain whose decision had value, might have been learned from the flitting gaze of the leader which, cast now on this or the other, returned always to this man at the right. There were seven gentlemen of them in all, and of these all were clad in the costume of the day, save this one, who retained the fashion of an earlier time. His coat might have come from the Revolution, its color possibly the blue of an earlier day. The trousers fitted close to massive and shapely limbs, and the long waistcoat, not of a modish silk, was buff in color, such as might one time have been worn by Washington himself. This man, these men, distinguished in every line, might have been statesmen of an earlier day than that of Calhoun, Clay and Benton. Yet the year of 1850, that time when forced and formal peace began to mask the attitude of sections already arrayed for a later war, might have been called as important as any in our history.

The ranks of these men at the table, too, might have been called arranged as though by some shrewd compromise. Even a careless eye or ear might have declared both sections, North and South, to have been represented here. Grave men they were, and accustomed to think, and they reflected, thus early in Millard Fillmore's administration, the evenly balanced political powers of the time.

The headlong haste of both sections was in the year 1850 halted for a time by the sage counsels of such leaders as Clay, in the South, even Webster, in the North. The South claimed, after the close of the Mexican War and the accession of the enormous Spanish territories to the southwest, that the accepted line of compromise established in 1820, by which slavery might not pass north of the parallel of latitude thirty-six degrees, thirty minutes, should be extended westward quite to the Pacific Ocean. She grumbled that, although she had helped fight for and pay for this territory, she could not control it, and could not move into it legally the slaves which then made the most valued part of a southern man's property. As against this feeling, the united politicians had thrown to the hot-headed Southerners a sop in the form of the Fugitive Slave Act. The right for a southern owner to follow and claim his slave in any northern state was granted under the Constitution of the United States. Under the compromise of 1850, it was extended and confirmed.

The abolitionists of the North rose in arms against this part of the great compromise measure; a law which, though constitutional, seemed to them nefarious and infamous. The leaders in Congress, both Whig and Democrat, feared now, therefore, nothing in the world so much as the outbreak of a new political party, which might disorganize this nicely adjusted compromise, put an end to what all politicians were fond of calling the "finality" of the arrangement, and so bring on, if not an encounter of armed forces, if not a rupture of the Union, at least what to them seemed almost as bad, the disintegration of the two great parties of the day, the Whigs and Democrats.

If compromise showed in this meeting of men from different sections, it was, therefore, but a matter in tune with the time. Party was at that day not a matter of geography. There existed then, however, as there exists to-day, the great dividing line between those who are in and those who are out. Obviously now, although they represented different sections of the country, these men likewise represented the party which, under the adjusted vote of the day, could be called fortunate enough to dwell within the gates of Washington and not in the outer darkness of political defeat.

The dark-browed man at the leader's right presently began to speak. His voice, deep and clear as that of a great bronze bell, was slow and deliberate, as fittingly voicing an accurate mind.

"Sir," he said, "this matter is one deserving our most careful study, trivial though at first blush it would seem. As to the danger of this woman's machinations here, there is no question. A match may produce convulsion, explosion, disaster, when applied to a powder magazine. As you know, this country dwells continually above an awful magazine. At any time there may be an explosion which will mean ruin not only for our party but our country. The Free Soil party, twice defeated, does not down. There is a nationalist movement now going forward which ignores the Constitution itself. With you, I dread any talk, any act, of our own or another nation, which shall even indirectly inflame the northern resentment against the fugitive law."

"On that, we are perfectly agreed, sir," began the original speaker, "and then —"

"But then, sir, we come to the question of the removal of this unwelcome person. She herself is a fugitive from no law. She has broken no law of this land or of this District. She has a right to dwell here under our laws, so long as she shall obey them, and there is no law of this District, nor this republic, nor of any state, any monarchy, not even any law of nations, which could be invoked to dismiss her from a capital where, though unwelcome, she has a right to remain. I may be unwelcome to you, you to me, either of us to any man; yet, having done no treason, so long as we pay our debts and observe the

54

law, no man may raise hand or voice against us."

"Quite right!" broke in the leader again. "But let us look simply at the gravity of it. They say it is treason not only against our own country but against a foreign power which this woman is fomenting. The Austrian attache, Mr. Hulsemann, is altogether rabid over the matter. He said to me privately——"

"Then most improperly!" broke in the tall dark man.

"Improperly, but none the less, insistently, he said that his government will not tolerate her reception here. He charges her with machinations in Europe, under cover of President Taylor's embassy of investigation into Hungarian affairs. He declares that Russia and Austria are one in their plans. That, I fear, means also England, as matters now stand in Europe."

"But, sir," broke in the vibrant voice of a gentleman who sat at the left of the speaker, concealed in the shadow cast by the heavy window drapings, "what is our concern over that? It is our boast that this is a free country. As for England, we have taken her measure, once in full, a second time at least in part; and as for Austria or Russia, what have we to do with their territorial designs? Did they force us to fight, why, then, we might fight, and with proper reason."

"True again, sir!" said the leader, recognizing the force of the murmur which greeted this outburst. "It is not any of these powers that I fear. They might bluster, and still not fight; and indeed they lack any rational cause for war. But what I fear, what all of us fear, gentlemen, is the danger here, inside our own walls, inside our own country."

Silence again fell on all. They looked about them, as though even in this dimly lighted room they felt the presence of that ominous shadow which lay over all the land—the menace of a divided country.

"That is the dread of all of us," went on the leader. "The war with Mexico showed us where England stands. She proved herself once more our ancient enemy, showed that her chief desire is to break this republic. Before that war, and after it, she has cultivated a friendship with the South. Why? Now let the abolitionist bring on this outbreak which he covets, let the North and South fly at each other's throats, let the contending powers of Europe cross the seas to quarrel over the spoils of our own destruction—and what then will be left of this republic? And yet, if this compromise between North and South be broken as all Europe desires, and as all the North threatens, precisely those matters will come hurrying upon us. And they will find us divided, incapable of resistance. That is the volcano, the magazine, over which we dwell continually. It passes politics, and puts us as patriots upon the question of the endurance of our republic.

"And I tell you now, gentlemen," he concluded, "as you know very well yourselves, that this woman, here in Washington, would hold the match ready to apply to that magazine. Which of you does not see its glimmering? Which of you doubts her readiness? There was not twenty-four hours to argue the matter of her—her temporary absence. We'd have had Austria all about our ears, otherwise. Gentlemen, I am mild as any, and most of any I am sworn to obey the laws, and to guarantee the safeguards of the Constitution; but I say to you—" and here his hand came down with an emphasis unusual in his nature —"law or no law, Constitution or no Constitution, an exigency existed under which she had to leave Washington, and that upon that very night."

"But where is she now?" ventured another voice. "This young army captain simply says in his report that he left her on the *Mount Vernon* packet, en route down the Ohio. Where is she now; and how long before she will be back here, match in hand?"

"It is the old, old case of Eve!" sighed one, who leaned a bony arm upon the walnut, and who spoke in the soft accents which proclaimed him of the South. "Woman! It is only the old Garden over again. Trouble, thy name is Woman!"

"And specifically, its name is Josephine, Countess St. Auban!" drawled another, opposite. A smile went around among these grave and dignified men; indeed, a light laugh sounded somewhere in the shadow. The face of the leader relaxed, though not sufficiently to allow light comment. The dark man at the right spoke.

"The great Napoleon was right," said he. "He never ceased to prove how much he dreaded woman at any juncture of public affairs. Indeed, he said that all the public places of the government should be closed to them, that they should be set apart and distinguished from the managers of affairs."

"And so do we say it!" broke in the leader. "With all my heart, I say it."

The tall man bowed, "It was the idea of Napoleon that woman should be distinguished always by a veil and gown, a uniform of unworthiness and of danger. True, Napoleon based his ideas on his studies in the Orient. Us he accused of treating woman much too well. He declared woman, by virtue of her birth, to be made as man's inferior and his slave, and would tolerate no other construction of the relation of the sexes. According to Napoleon, women tyrannize over us Americans, whereas we should tyrannize over them. It was plain, in his conception, that the main province of woman is in making fools of men."

"In some ways, Napoleon was a thoughtful man," remarked, a voice to the left; and once more a half subdued smile went around.

"I yield to no man in my admiration for the fair sex—" began the tall, dark man. The smile broke into open laughter. The leader rapped sharply on the table edge, frowning. The tall man bowed once more, as he resumed.

"—but, viewed from the standpoint, of our diplomacy, the matter here is simple. Last week, at the reception where the representatives of Austria were present this woman appeared, properly introduced, properly invited, it is true, but wholly unwelcome socially, in certain quarters. The attache and his wife left the roof, and made plain to their host their reasons for doing so."

"Yes, and it was public shame that they should take such action. The woman had the right of her host's protection, for she was there by invitation!" Thus the bony man in the shadows.

Again the leader rapped on the table. "Gentlemen, gentlemen!" he began, not wholly humorously. "Let us have a care. Let us at least not divide into factions here. We all of us, I trust, can remember the case of Peggy O'Neil, who split Washington asunder not so long ago. She was the wife of one of President Jackson's cabinet members, yet when she appeared upon a ball-room floor, all the ladies left it. It was Jackson and Eaton against the world. That same situation to-day, granted certain conditions, might mean a war which would disrupt this Union. In fact, I consider Josephine St. Auban to-day more dangerous than Mrs. Eaton at her worst."

"But we have just heard what rights we have before the law, sir," ventured a hesitating, drawling voice, which had earlier been heard. "How can we take cognizance of private insult given by a foreign power in only quasi-public capacity? I conceive it to be somewhat difficult, no matter what the reception in the society of Washington, to eject this woman from the city of Washington itself; or at least, very likely difficult to keep her ejected, as you say, sir."

"Where should she go?" demanded yet another voice. "And why should she not come back?"

Impatiently, the leader replied: "Where? I do not know. I do not *want* to know. I *must* not know! Good God, must we not bear ourselves in mind?"

"Then, sir, in case of her sudden return, you ask an agent?" said a keen, clear, and incisive voice, which had not yet been heard. "Gentlemen, shall we cast lots for the honor of watching the Countess St. Auban in case of her undesired return?"

The grim demand brought out a hasty protest from a timid soul: "To that, I would not agree." A sort of shuffle, a stir, a shifting in seats seemed to take place all about the table.

"Very well, then," went on the clear voice, "let us employ euphemism in terms and softness in methods. If we may not again kidnap the lady, why may we not bribe her?"

"It could not be done," broke in the dark man toward the head of the table. "If I know the facts, this woman could not be bought for any ransom. She has both station and wealth accorded her, so the story goes, for some service of her family in the affairs of France. But she will none of monarchies. She turned democrat, revolutionist, in France, and on the hotter stage of Hungary —and so finally sought this new world to conquer. She is no artless miss, but a woman of the world, brilliant and daring, with ideas of her own about a world-democracy. She is perhaps devout, or penitent!"

"Nay, let us go softly," came the rejoinder from the shadows. "Woman is man's monarch only part of the time. We need some man who is a nice judge of psychological moments and nicely suited methods. We stand, all of us, for the compromise of 1850. That compromise is not yet complete. The question of this unwelcome lady still remains to be adjusted. Were Mr. Clay not quite so old, I might suggest his name for this last and most crucial endeavor of a long and troublous life!"

"By the Eternal Jove!" broke in the dark man at the right, shaking off the half-moodiness which had seemed to possess him. "When it comes to wheedling, age is no such bar. I call to mind one man who could side with Old Hickory in the case of Mrs. Peggy Eaton. I mean him whom we call the Old Fox of the North."

"He was a widower, even then, and hence immune," smiled the man across the table. "Now he is many years older."

"Yet, none the less a widower, and all the more an adjuster of nice matters. He has proven himself a politician. It was his accident and not his fault not to remain with us in our party! Yet I happen to know that though once defeated for the presidency and twice for the nomination, he remains true to his Free Soil beliefs. It has just occurred to me, since our friend from Kentucky mentions it, that could we by some fair means, some legal means—some means of adjustment and compromise, if you please, gentlemen,—place this young lady under the personal care of this able exponent of the *suaviter in modo*, and induce him to conduct her, preferably to some unknown point beyond the Atlantic Ocean, there to lose her permanently, we should perhaps be doing our country a service, and would also be relieving this administration of one of its gravest concerns. Best of all, we should be using a fox for a cat's-paw, something which has not often been done."

The matter-of-fact man who presided straightened his shoulders as though with relief at some sign of action; yet he did not relax his insistent gravity sufficiently to join the smile that followed this sally.

"Let us be sure, gentlemen, of one thing at a time," he resumed. "As we come to this final measure suggested by our friend from Kentucky, I am at a loss how further to proceed. What we do can not be made public. We can not sign a joint note asking this distinguished gentleman to act as our intermediary."

"At the time of the ratification of the Constitution by the convention of 1787," began the dark man who had earlier spoken, "there arose a difficulty as to the unanimity of those signing. At the suggestion of Doctor Franklin and Mr. Gouverneur Morris, there was a clause added which stated that the Constitution was signed '*as by the states actually present*,' this leaving the individual signers not personally responsible! I suggest therefore, sir, that we should evade the personal responsibility of this did you put it to the vote of the *states* represented here."

"I rely upon the loyalty and the unanimity of my family," replied the leader, with more firmness than was wont. "Gentlemen, are we then agreed? Does Massachusetts consent? Is Virginia with us? Is New York agreeable? Does Kentucky also agree?"

There was no murmur of dissent, and the leader, half rising, concluded;

"Gentlemen, we agreed four days ago that the Countess St. Auban should leave Washington not later than that night. We are now agreed that, in case of her return, she shall if possible be placed under the charge, not of any responsible figure of *our* party, but of a gentleman distinguished in the councils of an *opposing* party, whose abolitionist beliefs coincide somewhat with her own. Let us hope they will both get them to Missouri, the debating ground, the center of the political battle-field to-day. But, Missouri or Hungary, Kentucky or France, let us hope that one or both of them shall pass from our horizon.

"There remains but one question, as earlier suggested by Kentucky: if we agree upon New York as our agent, who shall be our emissary to New York, and how shall he accomplish our purpose with that gentleman? Shall we decide it by the usual procedure of parliamentary custom? Do you allow the —the Chair—" he smiled as he bowed before them—"to appoint this committee of one? I suppose you agree that the smaller the committee and the more secret the committee's action, the better for us all?"

There was silence to this. A moment's hesitation, and the speaker announced his decision. "The gentleman from Kentucky is appointed to execute this task for the people of the United States. Let us hope he never will have need to serve."

It cost the self-control of some to remain silent at this, and the courage of the remaining member also to preserve the silence which meant his acceptance of a task so difficult and distasteful.

"Sir," hastily went on the original speaker, "our thanks are due to you. We shall limit you with no instructions. All the money required by you as agent, or required by your agent, shall of course be forthcoming, and you shall quietly have also the assistance of all the secret service, if so desired. None of us must know what has become of the Countess St. Auban, now or later. You have heard me. Gentlemen, we adjourn."

He stepped now to the door, and admitted the ancient colored man, with his lights. The curtains were drawn, shutting out even the twilight gloom. And now the lights blazed up, illuminating an historic stage.

The chief of the deliberations now became the host, and motioned his guests to the corner of the apartments where stood a long sideboard of dark mahogany, bearing different crystal decanters. Himself refraining, as did one or two others, he passed glasses, motioned to the ancient colored man, and, raising his own hand, proposed them a toast.

"Gentlemen,—the Union!"

They bowed to him ceremoniously, each in his way, with reverence, touching lips to his glass. As they parted, one for a moment stood alone, the dark man who had sat at the speaker's right. For a moment he paused, as though absorbed, as finally he set down his glass, gazing steadily forward as though striving to read what lay in the future.

"The Union!" he whispered, almost to himself.

It might have been the voice, as it was the thought of all those who, now passing, brought to a close this extraordinary meeting.

The Union!

CHAPTER IX

Meantime, events which might have held interest in certain circles in Washington had they been known, passed on their course, and toward that very region which had half in jest been named as the storm center of the day —the state of Missouri, anomalous, inchoate, discordant, half North, half South, itself the birth of compromise and sired by political jealousy; whither, against her will, voyaged a woman, herself engine of turbulence, doubt and strife, and in company now of a savage captor who contemplated nothing but establishing her for his own use in his own home.

Tallwoods, the home plantation of the Dunwody family in the West, now the personal property of the surviving son, state senator Warville Dunwody of Missouri, presented one of the contrasts which now and again might have been seen in our early western civilization. It lay somewhat remote from the nearest city of consequence, in a region where the wide acres of the owner blended, unused and uncultivated, with those still more wild, as yet unclaimed under any private title. Yet in pretentiousness, indeed in assuredness, it might have rivaled many of the old estates of Kentucky, the Carolinas, or Virginia; so much did the customs and ambitions of these older states follow their better bred sons out into the newer regions.

These men of better rank, with more than competency at their disposal, not infrequently had few neighbors other than the humble but independent frontiersman who left for new fields when a dog barked within fifty miles of his cabin. There were neighbors within half that distance of Tallwoods, settlers nestled here or there in these enfolding hills and forests; but of neighbors in importance equal to that of the owner of Tallwoods there were few or none in that portion of the state. The time was almost feudal, but wilder and richer than any feudal day, in that fief tribute was unknown. The original landlord of these acres had availed himself of the easy laws and easy ways of the time and place, and taken over to himself from the loose public domain a small realm all his own. Here, almost in seclusion, certainly in privacy, a generation had been spent in a life as baronial as any ever known in old Virginia in earlier days. A day's ride to a court house, two days to a steamer, five hours to get a letter to or from the occasional post—these things seem slight in a lifelong accustomedness; and here few had had closer touch than this with civilization.

[Illustration: Tallwoods]

The plantation itself was a little kingdom, and largely supplied its own wants. Mills, looms, shops,—all these were part of the careless system, easy and opulent, which found support and gained arrogance from a rich and generous environment. The old house itself, if it might be called old, built as it had been scarce thirty years before, lay in the center of a singular valley, at the edge of the Ozark Hills. The lands here were not so rich as the wide acres thirty miles or more below, where on the fat bottom soil, black and deep, the negroes raised in abundance the wealth-making crop of the country. On the contrary, this, although it was the capital of the vast Dunwody holdings thereabout, was chosen not for its agricultural richness so much as for its healthfulness and natural beauty.

In regard to these matters, the site could not better have been selected. The valley, some three or four miles across, lay like a deep saucer pressed down into the crest of the last rise of the Ozarks. The sides of the depression were as regular as though created by the hands of man. Into its upper extremity there ran a little stream of clear and unfailing water, which made its entrance at an angle, so that the rim of the hills seemed scarcely nicked by its ingress. This stream crossed the floor of the valley, serving to water the farms, and, making its way out of the lower end by a similar curious angle, broke off sharply and hid itself among the rocks on its way out and down from the mountains—last trace of a giant geology which once dealt in continental terms, rivers once seas, valleys a thousand miles in length. Thus, at first sight, one set down in the valley might have felt that it had neither inlet nor outlet, but had been created, panoplied and peopled by some Titanic power, and owned by those who neither knew nor desired any other world. As a matter of fact, the road up through the lower Ozarks from the great Mississippi, which entered along the bed of the little stream, ended at Tallwoods farm. Beyond it, along the little river which led back into the remote hills, it was no more than a horse path, and used rarely except by negroes or whites in hunting expeditions back into the mountains, where the deer, the wild turkey, the bear and the panther still roamed in considerable numbers at no great distance from the home plantation.

Tallwoods itself needed no other fence than the vast wall of hills, and had none save where here and there the native stone had been heaped up roughly into walls, along some orchard side. The fruits of the apple, the pear and the peach grew here handsomely, and the original owner had planted such trees in abundance. The soil, though at first it might have been, called inhospitable, showed itself productive. The corn stood tall and strong, and here and there the brown stalks of the cotton plant itself might have been seen; proof of the wish of the average Southerner to cultivate that plant, even in an environment not wholly suitable. All about, upon the mountain sides, stood a heavy growth of deciduous trees, at this time of the year lining the slopes in flaming reds and golds. Beyond the valley's rim, tier on tier, stately and slow, the mountains rose back for yet a way—mountains rich in their means of frontier independence, later to be discovered rich also in minerals, in woods, in all the things required by an advancing civilization.

Corn, swine and cotton,—these made the wealth of the owner of Tallwoods' plantation and of the richer lands in the river bottoms below. These products brought the owner all the wealth he needed. Here, like a feudal lord, master of all about him, he had lived all his life and had, as do all created beings, taken on the color and the savor of the environment about him. Rich, he was generous; strong, he was merciful; independent, he was arrogant; used to his own way, he was fierce and cruel when crossed in that way. Not much difference, then, lay between this master of Tallwoods and the owner of yonder castle along the embattled Rhine, or the towered stronghold of some old lord located along an easy, wandering, English stream; with this to be said in favor of this solitary lord of the wilderness, that his was a place removed and little known. It had been passed by in some manner through its lack of appeal to those seeking cotton lands or hunting grounds, so that it lay wholly out of the ken and the understanding of most folk of the older states.

If in Tallwoods the owner might do as he liked, certainly he had elected first of all to live somewhat as a gentleman. The mansion house was modeled after the somewhat stereotyped pattern of the great country places of the South. Originally planned to consist of the one large central edifice of brick, with a wing on each side of somewhat lesser height, it had never been entirely completed, one wing only having been fully erected. The main portion of the house was of two stories, its immediate front occupied by the inevitable facade with its four white pillars, which rose from the level of the ground to the edge of the roof, shading the front entrance to the middle rooms. Under this tall gallery roof, whose front showed high, white and striking all across the valley, lay four windows, and at each side of the great double doors lay yet other two windows. On either side of the pillars and in each story, yet other two admitted light to the great rooms; and in the completed wing which lay at one side of the main building, deep embrasures came down almost to the level of the ground, well hidden by the grouped shrubbery which grew close to the walls. The visitor approaching up the straight gravel walk might not have noticed the heavy iron bars which covered these, giving the place something the look of a jail or a fortress. The shrubs, carelessly, and for that reason more attractively planted, also stood here and there over the wide and smooth bluegrass lawn.

The house was built in the edge of a growth of great oaks and elms, which threw their arms out over even the lofty gables as though in protection. Tradition had it that the reason the building had never been completed was that the old master would have been obliged to cut down a favorite elm in order to make room for it; and he had declared that since his wife had died and all his children but one had followed her, the house was large enough as it was. So it stood as he had left it, with its two tall chimneys, one at each end of the mid-body of the house, marking the two great fireplaces, yet another chimney at the other end of the lesser wing.

Straight through the mid-body of the house ran a wide hall, usually left open to all the airs of heaven; and through this one could see far out over the approach, entirely through the house itself, and note the framed picture beyond of woods glowing with foliage, and masses of shrubbery, and lesser trees among which lay the white huts of the negroes. Still to the left, beyond the existing wing, lay the fenced vegetable gardens where grew rankly all manner of provender intended for the bounteous table, whose boast it was that, save for sugar and coffee, nothing was used at Tallwoods which was not grown upon its grounds.

So lived one, and thus indeed lived more than one, baron on American soil not so long ago, when this country was more American than it is to-day— more like the old world in many ways, more like a young world in many others. Here, for thirty years of his life, had lived the present owner of Tallwoods, sole male of the family surviving in these parts.

It might have been called matter of course that Warville Dunwody should be chosen to the state legislature. So chosen, he had, through sheer force of his commanding nature, easily become a leader among men not without strength and individuality. Far up in the northern comer, where the capital of the state lay, men spoke of this place hid somewhere down among the hills of the lower country. Those who in the easier acres of the northwestern prairie lands reared their own corn and swine and cotton, often wondered at the half-wild man from St. Francois, who came riding into the capital on a blooded horse, who was followed by negroes also on blooded horses, a self-contained man who never lacked money, who never lacked wit, whose hand was heavy, whose tongue was keen, whose mind was strong and whose purse was ever open.

The state which had produced a Benton was now building up a rival to Benton. That giant, then rounding out a history of thirty years' continuous service in the Senate of the United States, unlike the men of this weaker day, reserved the right to his own honest and personal political belief. He steadily refused to countenance the extending of slavery, although himself a holder of slaves; and, although he admitted the legality and constitutionality of the

Fugitive Slave Act, he deplored that act as much as any. To the eventual day of his defeat he stood, careless of his fate, firm in his own principles, going down in defeat at last because he would not permit his own state legislature—headed then by men such as Warville Dunwody and his friends—to dictate to him the workings of his own conscience. Stronger than Daniel Webster, he was one of those who would not obey the dictates of that leader, and he *did* set up his "conscience above the law." These two men, Benton and Dunwody, therefore, were at the time of which we write two gladiators upon the scenes of a wild western region, as yet little known in the eastern states, though then swiftly coming forward into more specific notice.

Perhaps thirty or forty slaves were employed about Tallwoods home farm, as it was called. They did their work much as they liked, in a way not grudging for the main part. Idle and shiftless, relying on the frequent absence of the master and the ease of gaining a living, they worked no more than was necessary to keep up a semblance of routine. In some way the acres got plowed and reaped, in some way the meats were cured, in some way the animals were fed and the table was served and the rooms kept in a semi-tidiness, none too scrupulous. Always in Tallwoods there was something at hand ready to eat, and there was fuel whereby fires might be made. Such as it was, the hospitality of the place was ready. It was a rich, loose way of life, and went on lazily and loosely, like the fashion of some roomy old vehicle, not quite run down, but advancing now and then with a groan or a creak at tasks imposed.

But now, another and most important matter for our note—there was no woman's hand at Tallwoods. The care was that of servants, of slaves. When things grew insupportable in their shiftlessness the master lashed out an order and got what he demanded; then soon matters sank back again to their old state. None might tell when the master would ride away, and when gone none could say when he would return. Since the death of his mother no woman's control had ruled here, nor, in spite of the busy tongues at the larger cities above, did there seem likelihood that any would soon share or alter the fortunes of Tallwoods. Rumors floated here and there, tongues wagged; but Tallwoods lay apart; and Tallwoods, as commonly was conceded, had ways of its own.

It was to these remote and somewhat singular surroundings that there approached, on the evening of a bland autumn day, along the winding road which followed the little stream, the great coach of the master of Tallwoods, drawn by four blooded carriage horses, weary, mud-stained and flecked with foam. At the end of the valley, where the road emerged from its, hidden course among the cliffs, the carriage now halted. Dunwody himself sprang down from the driver's seat where he had been riding in order to give the occupants of the coach the more room. He approached the window, hat in hand.

"My dear lady," said he, "this is the end of our journey. Yonder is my home. Will you not look at it?"

It was a pale and languid face which greeted him, the face of a woman weary and even now in tears. Hastily she sought to conceal these evidences of her distress. It was the first time he had seen her weeping. Hitherto her courage had kept her cold and defiant, else hot and full of reproofs. This spectacle gave him concern. His face took on a troubled frown.

"Come now, do not weep, my dear girl,—anything but that."

"What, then, is it you would say?" she demanded. "It makes little difference to me where you are taking me."

He threw open the coach door and extended a hand to aid her in alighting. "Suppose we walk up from here," he said. "I know you are tired by the ride. Besides," he added, with pride, "I want to show you Tallwoods."

Scarce touching his hand, she stepped down. Dunwody motioned to the driver to advance, and in spite of the protests of the maid Jeanne, thus left alone within, the coach rolled on up the driveway ahead of them.

It was in fact a beautiful prospect which lay before the travelers thus arrived. The sun was low in the west, approaching the rim of the hills, and its level rays lighted the autumn foliage, crossed the great trees, brightened the tall white pillars. It even illuminated the grounds beyond, so that quite through the body of the house itself its golden light could be seen on the farther slopes, framing the quaint and singular picture thus set apart. All around rose the wide cup of the valley, its sides as yet covered by unbroken decoration of vivid or parti-colored foliage. Here and there the vivid reds of the wild sumac broke out in riot; framed lower in the scale were patches of berry vines touched by the frost; while now and again a maple lifted aloft a fan of clean scarlet against the sky,—all backed by the more somber colors of the oaks and elms, or the now almost naked branches of the lindens.

These enfolding forests gave a look of protectedness to this secret place. They left a feeling not of discomfort but of shelter. Moreover, the grass underfoot was soft and still green. Some sort of comeliness, picturesque though rude, showed in the scant attempts to modify nature in the arrangement of the grounds. And there, noble and strong, upon a little eminence swelling at the bottom of the valley's cup, lay the great house, rude, unfinished, yet dignified. If it seemed just this side of elegance, yet the look of it savored of comfort. To a woman distracted and wearied it should have offered some sort of rest. To her who now gazed upon it the sight afforded only horror. This then was the place. Here was to be her trial. This was the battle-ground.

Dunwody lingered, hoping to hear some word of satisfaction.

"The hills are beautiful, the trees are beautiful, and the sky," she said, at length. "What God has done here is beautiful. But God Himself is gone."

Rage filled him suddenly. "At any rate, this is what I have and all I have," he said. "Like it, woman, or by that God! hate it! Here you are, and here you stay, until—until I die or until God returns. You are the only woman in it for me when you step into that house there. You are its mistress. I rule here. But what you want shall be yours at any time you want it. You can think of nothing in the world that shall not be brought to you when you ask for it. My servants are yours. Choose from them as many as you like."

"Slaves for your slave? You are full of kindness indeed! But I shall never be what you delicately call the mistress of Tallwoods."

"By the Lord! girl, if I thought that would be true—if I thought for one moment that it were true—" in a half-frenzy he threw out his arm, rigid. An instant later he had lapsed into one of the moods new to him. "There is no punishment I don't deserve," he said. "All the time I have hurt you, when I'd rather cut my tongue out than hurt you. I've seen you, these few days. God knows, at the hardest—me at the worst—you at the worst. But your worst is better than the best of any other woman I ever saw. I'm going to have you. It's you or nothing for me, and I'm going to have you. Choose your own title here, then, Madam. This is your home or your prison, as you like."

For a moment Josephine paused, looking around her at the surrounding hills. He seemed to catch her thought, and smiled at her.

"Twenty miles to the nearest house that way, Madam. None at all that other way. Every path known and guarded by my people. No paths at all in these hills out yonder. Wild animals in them, little food in them for man or woman not used to living wild. You would be helpless in one day, if you tried to get put. We'd find you before you'd gone five miles. Don't attempt any foolishness about trying to escape from here. You're mine, I say. I shall not let you go."

Yet in spite of his savagery, his face softened in the next moment. "If it could only be in the right way! Look at me, look at you. You're so very beautiful, I'm so strong. There is only one right way about it. Oh, woman!

"But come," he resumed with a half sigh, seeking in a rough way to brush back a wisp of hair from his forehead, to join the tangled mane upon his crest; "I hate myself as much as you hate me, but it's your fault—your fault that you are as you are—that you set me mad. Let's try to forget it for to-night, at least. You're tired, worn out. I'm almost tired myself, with all this war between us."

She was silent as they slowly advanced, silent as a prisoner facing prison doors; but he still went on, arguing.

"Think of what you could do here, how happy we could be here. Think of what we could do, together. There isn't anything I wouldn't try to do. Why, I could do *anything*; and I'd bring everything I got, everything, back to you,— and set it down at your feet and say, 'I brought you this.' What would I care for it, alone? What does it mean to me? What glory or success do I want? Without you, what does all this world, all my life, all I can do, mean to me after this? I knew long ago I couldn't be happy, but I didn't know why, I know now what I wanted, all along. I can do something in the world, I can succeed, I can be somebody now—and now I want to, want to! Oh, I've lacked so much, I've longed so much. Some way the world didn't seem made right. I wondered, I puzzled, I didn't know, I couldn't understand—I thought all the world was made to be unhappy—but it isn't, it's made for happiness, for joy, for exultation. Why, I can see it plainly enough now—all straight out, ahead of me,—all straight ahead of us two!"

"How like a man you are!" she said slowly. "You seek your own success, although your path lies over a woman's disgrace and ruin."

"Haven't you ever thought of the other side of this at all? Can't a woman ever think of mercy to a man? Can't she ever blame herself just for being Eve, for being the incarnate temptation that she is to any real man? Can't she see what she is to him? You talk about ruin—I tell you it's ruin here, sure as we are born, for one or both of us. I reckon maybe it's for both."

"Yes, it is for both."

"No. I'll not admit it!" he blazed out. "If I've been strong enough to pull you down, I'm strong enough to carry you up again. Only, don't force the worst part of me to the front all the time."

"A gentle wooer, indeed! And yet you blame me that I can not see a man's side in a case like this."

"But in God's name, why should a man see any but a man's side of it? Things don't go by reason, after all. The world goes, I reckon, because there is a man's side to it. Anyhow, I am as I am. Whatever you do here, whatever you are, don't try to wheedle me, nor ask me to see your side, when there is only one side to this. If any man ever lifted hand or eye to you, I'd kill him. I'll not give up one jot of the right I've got in you, little as it is—I've taken the right to hold you here and talk to you. But when you say you'll not listen to me, then you do run against my side of it, my man's side of it; and I tell you once more, I'm the owner of this place. I live here. It's mine. I rule here, over free and thrall."

With rude strength and pride he swept an arm widely around him, covering half the circle of the valley. "It's mine!" he said slowly. "Fit for a king, isn't it? Yes, fit for a queen. It is almost fit for you."

His hat was in his hand. The breeze of the evening, drawing down the valley, now somewhat chilled, lifted the loose hair on his forehead. He stood, big, bulky and strong, like some war lord of older days. The argument on his lips was that of the day of skins and stone.

She who stood at his side, this prisoner of his prowess, taken by his ruthless disregard of wish or rights of others, stood even with his shoulder, tall, deep-bosomed, comely, as fair and fit and womanly a woman as man's need has asked in any age of the world. In the evening light the tears which had wet her eyes were less visible. She might indeed have been fit queen for a spot like this, mate for a man like this.

And now the chill of autumn lay in the twilight. Night was coming—the time when all creatures, save ravening night feeders, feel apprehension, crave shelter, search out a haven for repose. This woman was alone and weary, much in need of some place to rest her head. Every fiber in her heart craved shelter, comfort, security, protection.

Dunwody turned, offered her a hand, and led her to the wide double doors.

CHAPTER X

"Sally, come here," called Dunwody to one of the row of grinning negro servants who were loosely lined up in the hall, as much in curiosity as deference, to give their master his only welcome home. "Take this lady up to the room in the east part. See that she has everything she wants. She is not to be disturbed there until morning, do you hear, Sally? When you come down I want to see you again. You others there, make your duty to this lady. Call her Miss Josephine. When she wants anything, you jump and get it. Go on, now."

They scattered grinning, all but the bent and grizzled old woman Sally, who now came forward. She looked with blank brown eyes at the new-comer, herself inscrutable as the Sphinx. If she commented mentally on the droop of the young woman's mouth and eyes, at least she said nothing. It was not her place to ask what white folk did, or why. She took up the traveling-bags and led the way up the narrow stairway which made out of the central hall.

"Sally," said Josephine, turning, when they reached the stairway, "where's my own maid—the other—Jeanne?"

"I dunno, Ma'am," said Sally. "I reckon she's all right, though. Dis heah's yuah room, Ma'am, if you please." She shuffled ahead, into a tall and wide room, which overlooked the lawn and the approaching road.

Once alone, Josephine flung herself face downward upon the bed and burst into a storm of tears, her fine courage for once outworn. She wept until utterly spent. Sally, after leaving the room, had returned unnoticed, and when at last Josephine turned about she saw the old woman standing there. A hard hand gently edged under her heaving shoulder. "Thah now, honey, doan' cry! God A'mighty, girl, doan' cry dat-a-way. What is wrong, tell me." Sympathy even of this sort was balm to a woman wholly unnerved. Josephine found her head on the old negro woman's shoulder.

[Illustration: Her fine courage for once outworn.]

"Now you jus' lay right quiet, Ma'am," went on Sally. "I'se gwine to git you a little something warm to drink and something to eat right soon, and den I'se gwine put you-all to bed nice and clean, and in de mawnin' you'll feel like you was anotheh lady, you suttinly will, Ma'am."

"Who are you?" demanded Josephine, turning to look into the old and wrinkled face.

"I'se jus' Sally."

"I suppose you are keeper of the prison," commented Josephine bitterly.

"Dis ain't no prisum, Ma'am, I'se bin heah a long time 'mong dese triflin' niggahs. Dis ain't no prisum—but God knows, Ma'am, we needs a lady heah to run things. Is you come foh dat?"

"No, no," said Josephine. "I'm just—I'm just—I'm going away as soon as I can."

"Sho, now! Huc'cum you heah, Ma'am?"

"It was a mistake."

"I didn't know white folks evah done nothin' they didn't want to do," commented Sally. "But doan' you mind. Ef you wants me, jes' call for Sally."

"Tell me, Sally, isn't there any Mrs. Dunwody here?" demanded Josephine suddenly.

The face of the old woman remained inscrutable, and Josephine could see no sign except that a sort of film crossed her eyes, as though veiling some inmost thought.

"Ef dey was, I doan' reckon you-all would have come heah, would you? Now you lay down and git comf'table. Doan' you worry none, Ma'am. You gwine be fine, by mawnin'. You suttinly is a right handsome lady, Ma'am!"

The old woman shuffled from the room, to join her master at the foot of the stairs.

"Where is she, Sally?" demanded Dunwody, "and how is she?"

"She's right tired, suh," said Sally non-committally. And then, "Mighty fine lookin' lady, suh. An' she is a lady! Huc'cum her here, Marse Warv'l? Whut you-all—"

"What did she say to you?"

"Nothin' 'cept she's gwine git away right soon. White folkes' business ain't none o' my business."

"Well, never you mind about all that, Sally. Now listen. It's your business to keep her there, in that room. When she wants anything, get it. But don't you talk to her, you understand. I reckon you do understand, don't you?"

"I reckon I does, suh."

"Well, all right then. If she goes to walk, keep her in sight. She doesn't send out letters to any one, and doesn't talk to strangers, do you understand?"

71

"I reckon I does, suh."

Old Sally stood looking at him for a time with her small brown eyes half-covered under her gray brows. At last, with something of the liberty of the old servant she said, "Marster, is you married to that dere lady? Ef you isn't, is you gwine marry her?"

"If I told you you'd know too much, Sally. It's enough for you to know that you're responsible for her. If she turns up missing any time, you'll be missing yourself not long after."

"I reckon I will," said Sally chuckling; and then shuffled off about her own duties.

CHAPTER XI

Left alone, Josephine St. Auban at last attempted to pull herself together. With the instinct of a newly caged animal, she made a little tour of the room. First she noted the depth of the windows, their height above the ground. No escape there, that was sure—unless one, cat-like, could climb down this light ladder up which the ivy ran between the cornice and the ground. No, it was a prison.

In the room itself were good yet simple furnishings. The wall paper was of a small and ancient figuring. In places it hung torn. The furniture was old mahogany, apparently made in an earlier generation. An engraving or so hung askew upon the wall, a broken bust stood on a bracket. The tall tester bed, decorated with a patchwork silken covering, showed signs of comfort, but was neither modern nor over neat. The room was not furnished in poverty, but its spirit, its atmosphere, its feeling, lacked something, a woman could have told what.

She pushed back the heavy dresser, but the wall was without opening behind it. She looked for the key to the door, and was glad to find the lock in order. For the first time now she laid off her bonnet, unfastened her wrap. With a hand which trembled she made some sort of attempt at toilet, staring into the mirror at a face scarcely recognized as her own. The corners of its mouth were drooping plaintively. A faint blue lay beneath the eyes.

She faced the fact that she must pass the night alone. If it is at night that the shadows fall upon the soul, then most of all does woman, weak and timorous animal, long for some safe and accustomed refuge place, for a home; and most of all does she shrink from unfamiliar surroundings. Yet she slept, wearied to exhaustion. The night was cool, the air fresh from the mountains coming in through the opened window, and bringing with it calm.

Dawn came. A chirping cedar bird, busy in the near-by shrubbery, wakened her with a care-free note. She started up and gazed out with that sudden wonder and terror which at times seize upon us when we awake in strange environment. Youth and vitality resumed sway. She was alive, then. The night had passed, then. She was as she had been, herself, her own, still. The surge of young blood came back in her veins. The morning was there, the hills were there, the world was there. Hope began once more with the throb of her perfect pulse. She stretched a round white arm and looked down it to her hand. She held up her fingers against the light, and the blood in them, the soul in them, showed pink and clean between. Slowly she pushed down the patchwork silk. There lay her splendid limbs and body. Yes, it was she, it was herself, her own. Yes, she would live, she would succeed, she would win! All of which, of course, meant to her but one thing—escape.

A knock came at the door, really for the third time, although for the first time heard. Old Sally entered, bearing her tray, with coffee.

"Now you lay right still whah you is, Ma'am," she began. "You-all wants a li'l bit o' coffee. Then I'll bring you up some real breakfus'—how you like yuah aigs? Ma'am, you suttinly is lookin' fine dis mawnin'. I'll fetch you yuah tub o' watah right soon now."

In spite of herself Josephine found herself unable to resist interest in these proceedings. After all, her prison was not to be without its comforts. She hoped the eggs would be more than two.

The old serving woman slowly moved about here and there in the apartment, intent upon duties of her own. While thus engaged, Josephine, standing femininely engaged before her glass, chanced to catch sight of her in the mirror. She had swiftly slipped over and opened the door of a wardrobe. Over her arm now was some feminine garment.

"What have you there?" demanded Josephine, turning as swiftly.

"Jus' some things I'se gwine take away to make room for you, tha'ss all, Ma'am."

Josephine approached and took up in her own hands these evidences of an earlier occupancy of the room. They were garments of a day gone by. The silks were faded, dingy, worn in the creases from sheer disuse. Apparently they had hung untouched for some time.

[Illustration: They were garments of a day gone by.]

"Whose were these, Sally?" demanded Josephine.

"I dunno, Ma'am. I'se been mos'ly in the kitchen, Ma'am."

Josephine regarded her closely. No sign of emotion showed on that brown mask. The gray brows above the small eyes did not flicker. "I suppose these may have belonged to Mr. Dunwody's mother," said Josephine carelessly.

"Yassam!"

"His sister?"

"Yassam!"

"Or his wife, perhaps?"

"Yassam, ef they really wuz one."

"Was there ever?" demanded Josephine sharply.

"Might a-been none, er might a-been a dozen, fur's I know. Us folks don' study much 'bout whut white folks does."

"You must have known if there was any such person about—you've been here for years. Don't talk nonsense!"

Temptation showed on Sally's face. The next instant the film came again over the small brown eyes, the mask shut down again, as the ancient negro racial secretiveness resumed sway. Josephine did not ask for what she knew would be a lie.

"Where is my own maid, Jeanne?" she demanded. "I am anxious about her."

"I dunno, Ma'am."

"Is she safe—has she been cared for?"

"I reckon she's all right."

"Can you bring her to me?"

"I'll try, Ma'am."

But breakfast passed and no Jeanne appeared. From the great house came no sounds of human occupancy. Better struggle, conflict, than this ominous waiting, this silence, here in this place of infamy, this home of horror, this house of some other woman. It was with a sense of relief that at length she heard a human voice.

Outside, beneath the window, quavering sounds rose. The words were French, Canadian French, scarce distinguishable to an ear trained only in the Old World. It was an old man singing, the air perhaps that of some old chanson of his own country, sung by villagers long before:

"Souvenirs du jeune age
Sont gravis dans mon coeur,
Quand je pense au village,
Revenant du bonheur—"

The old voice halted, at length resuming, idly: "*Quand je pense—quand je pense.*" Then after humming the air for a little time it broke out as though in the chorus, bold and strong:

"Rendes-moi ma patrie, ou laisses-moi mourir!"

The words came to her with a sudden thrill. What did they not mean to the alien, to the prisoner, to the outcast, anywhere in all the world! "Give me back my country, or let me die!"

She stepped to the window and looked down. An old man, brown, bent and wrinkled, was digging about the shrubbery, perhaps preparing some of the plants for their winter sleep. He was clad in leather and linsey, and seemed ancient as the hills. He resumed his song. Josephine leaned out from the casement and softly joined in the refrain:

"Rendez-moi ma patrie, ou laissez-moi mourir!"

[Illustration: An old man, brown, bent and wrinkled]

The old man dropped his spade. "*Mon Dieu!*" he exclaimed, and looked all about, around, then at last up.

"Ah! *Bon jour*, Mademoiselle!" he said, smiling and taking off his old fur cap. "You spik also my language, Mademoiselle?"

"*Mais oui*, Monsieur," rejoined Josephine; and addressed him further in a few sentences on trivial topics. Then, suddenly resolved, she stepped out of her own room, passed softly down the stair, out through the wide central hall, and so, having encountered no one, joined the ancient man on the lawn. It chanced he had been at labor directly in front of one of the barred lower windows. He now left his spade and stepped apart, essaying now a little broken English.

"You seeing my song al_so_, Mademoiselle? You like the old song from Canadian village, aye? I seeing heem many tam, me."

"Who are you?" demanded Josephine.

"Me, I am Eleazar, the ol' trap' man. Summers, I work here for Monsieur Dunwodee. Verr' reech man, Monsieur Dunwodee. He say, 'Eleazar, you live here, all right.' When winter come I go back in the heel, trap ze fur-r, Madame, ze cat, ze h'ottaire, ze meenk, sometime ze coon, also ze skonk. Pret' soon I'll go h'out for trap now, Mademoiselle."

"How long have you been here, Eleazar?" she asked.

"Many year, Mademoiselle. In these co'ntree perhaps twent'—thirt' year, I'll don' know."

"Were you here when the lady lived here?" she demanded of him directly.

He frowned at this suddenly. "I'll not know what you mean, Mademoiselle."

"I mean the other lady, the wife of Mr. Dunwody."

"My faith! Monsieur Dunwody he'll live h'alone here, h'all tam."

She affected not to understand him. "How long since she was here, Eleazar?" she demanded.

"What for you'll talk like those to me? I'll not know nossing, Mademoiselle. I'll not even know who is Mademoiselle, or why she'll been here, me. I'll not know for say, whether 'Madame,' whether 'Mademoiselle.' *Mais* 'Mademoiselle'—*que je pense.*"

She looked about her hastily. "I'm here against my wish, Eleazar. I want to get away from here as soon as I can."

He drew away in sudden fright. "I'll not know nossing at all, me," he reiterated.

"Eleazar, you like money perhaps?"

"Of course, yes. *Tout le monde il aime l'argent.*"

"Then listen, Eleazar. Some day we will walk, perhaps. How far is it to Cape Girardeau, where the French people live?"

"My son Hector he'll live there wance, on Cap' Girardeau. He'll make the tub, make the cask, make the bar_rel_. Cap' Girardeau, oh, perhaps two— t'ree day. Me, I walk heem once, maybe so feefty mile, maybe so seexty mile, in wan day, two-t'ree a little more tam, me. I was more younger then. But now my son he'll live on St. Genevieve, French place there, perhaps thirtee mile. Cap' Girardeau, seventy-five mile. You'll want for go there?" he added cunningly.

"Sometime," she remarked calmly. Eleazar was shrewd in his own way. He strolled off to find his spade.

Before she could resume the conversation Josephine heard behind her in the hall a step, which already she recognized. Dunwody greeted her at the door, frowning as he saw her sudden shrinking back at sight of him.

"Good morning," he said. "You have, I hope, slept well. Have you and Eleazar here planned any way to escape as yet?" He smiled at her grimly. Eleazar had shuffled away.

"Not yet."

"You had not come along so far as details then;" smilingly.

"You intruded too soon."

"At least you are frank, then! You will never get away from here excepting on one condition."

She made no answer, but looked about her slowly. Her eyes rested upon a little inclosed place where some gray stones stood upright in the grass; the family burial place, not unusual in such proximity to the abode of the living, in that part of the country at the time.

"One might escape by going there!" she pointed.

"They are my own, who sleep there," he said simply but grimly. "I wish it might be your choice; but not now; not yet. We've a lot of living to do yet, both of us."

She caught no note of relenting in his voice. He looked large and strong, standing there at the entrance to his own home. At length he turned to her, sweeping out his arm once more in a gesture including the prospect which lay before them.

"If you could only find it in your heart," he exclaimed, "how much I could do for you, how much you could do for me. Look at all this. It's a home, but it's just a desert—a desert—the way it is now."

"Has it always been so?"

"As long as I can remember."

"So you desire to make all life a desert for me! It is very noble of you!"

Absorbed, he seemed not to hear her. "Suppose you had met me the way people usually meet—and you some time had allowed me to come and address you—could you have done that, do you reckon?" He turned to her, an intent frown on his face, unsmiling.

"That's a question which here at least is absurd," she replied.

"You spoke once of that other country, abroad,—" he broke off, shaking his head. "Who are you? I don't feel sure that I even know your name as yet."

"I am, as you have been told, Josephine, Countess St. Auban. I am French, Hungarian, American, what you like, but nothing to you. I came to this country in the interest of Louis Kossuth. For that reason I have been misunderstood. They think me more dangerous than I am, but it seems I am honored by the suspicions of Austria and America as well. I was a revolutionist yonder. I am already called an abolitionist here. Very well. The name makes little difference. The work itself—"

"Is that how you happened to be there on the boat?"

"I suppose so. I was a prisoner there. I was less than a chattel. I was a piece of property, to be staked, to be won or lost at cards, to be kidnapped, hand-cuffed, handled like a slave, it seems. And you've the hardihood to stand here and ask me who I am!"

"I've only that sort of hardihood, Madam, which makes me ride straight. If I had observed the laws, I wouldn't have you here now, this morning."

"You'll not have me long. If I despise you as a man without chivalry, I still more do so because you've neither ambition nor any sense of morals."

"You go on to improve me. I thank you, Mademoiselle—Eleazar was right. I heard him. I like you as 'Mademoiselle.'"

"What difference?" she flared out. "We are opposed at all angles of the human compass. There is no common meeting ground between us. Let me go."

He looked at her full in the face, his own features softened, relenting for a time, as though her appeal had touched either his mental or his moral nature. Then slowly, as he saw the excellence of her, standing there, his face dropped back into its iron mold. "You are a wonderful woman," he said, "wonderful. You set me on fire—and it's only eight o'clock in the morning. I could crush you—I could tear you to pieces. I never saw your like, nor ever shall. Let you go? Yes! When I'm willing to let my blood and soul go. Not till then. If I were out in that graveyard, with my bones apart, and your foot crossed my grave, I'd get up and come, and live again with you—live—again. I say, I could live again, do you hear me?"

She broke out into a torrent of hot speech. He did not seem to hear her. "The wrong of it," said he, "is that we should fight apart and not together. Do as you like for to-day. Be happy as you can. Let's live in the present, as we were, at least for to-day. But to-night—"

He turned swiftly, and left her, so that she found left unsaid certain questions as well as certain accusations she had stored for this first meeting.

CHAPTER XII

That night, Josephine St. Auban did not sleep. For hours she tossed about, listening. Infrequently, sounds came to her ears. Through the window came now and again faint notes of night-faring birds, south bound on their autumnal migration. Once in a while a distant step resounded in the great building, or again there came the distant voices of the negroes singing in their quarters beyond. The house had ceased its daily activities. The servants had left it. Who occupied it now? Was she alone? Was there one other?

In apprehension which comes to the senses in the dark watches of the night— impressions, conclusions, based upon no actual or recognized action of the physical senses—Josephine rose, passed to the window and looked out. The moonlight lay upon the lawn like a broad silver blanket. Faint stars were twinkling in the clear sky overhead. The night brooded her planets, hovering the world, so that life might be.

The dark outlines of the shrubbery below showed black and strong. Upon the side of a near-by clump of leafless lilacs shone a faint light, as though from one of the barred windows below. The house was not quite asleep. She stilled her breath as she might, stilled her heart as she might, lest its beating should be heard. What was about to happen? Where could she fly, and how?

Escape by the central stairway would be out of the question, because by that way only could danger approach. She leaned out of the window. Catching at the coarse ivy vine which climbed up the old wall of the house, she saw that it ascended past her window to the very cornice where the white pillars joined the roof. The pillars themselves, vast and smooth, would have been useless even could she have reached them. Below, a slender lattice or ladder had been erected to the height of one story, to give the ivy its support. A strong and active person might by mere possibility reach this frail support if the ivy itself proved strong enough to hold under the strain. She clutched at it desperately. It seemed to her that although the smaller tendrils loosened, the greater arms held firm.

She stepped back into the room, listened, straining all her soul in a demand for certitude. As yet she had only dreaded to hear a sound, had not indeed done so. Now at last there came a footfall—was it true? It seemed not heavy enough for a man's step, but a man on secret errand might tread light. She flung herself upon the bed, her hands clasped, her lips moving in supplication.

But now it came again, that was it—it was a footfall. It approached along the hall, paused at the barricaded door. It was there outside, stopping. She heard a breath drawn. The knob was tried, silently at first, then with greater force. "Who is there?" she quavered. "Who is there?" she repeated. No answer came.

"Jeanne!" she cried aloud. "Oh, Jeanne! Jeanne! Sally!"

There was once a sound of a distant door opening. No voice came. Outside her own door now was silence.

She could endure no more. Though it were into flames, she must escape from this place, where came one to claim a property, not a woman; where a woman faced use, not wooing. God! And there was no weapon, to assure God's vengeance now, here, at once.

Half-clad as she was, she ran to the window, and unhesitatingly let herself out over the sill, clutching at the ivy as she did so. She feared not at all what now was before her. It is doubtful whether those who spring from a burning building dread the fall—they dread only that which is behind them.

As she now half-slid from the window, she grasped wildly at the screen of ivy, and as fate would have it caught one of its greater branches. It held fast, and she swung free from the sill, which now she could never again regain. She clung desperately, blindly, swung out; then felt the roots of the ivy above her rip free, one after another, far up, almost to the cornice. Its whole thin ladder broke free from the wall. She was flung into space. Almost at that instant, her foot touched the light lattice of the lower story. The ivy had crawled up the wall face and followed the cornice up and over somewhere, over the edge of the eaves, finding some sort of holding ground. It served to support her weight at least until she felt the ladder underfoot. At this in turn she clutched as she dropped lower, but frail and rotten as it was, it supported her but slightly. The next instant she felt, herself falling.

[Illustration: She grasped wildly at the screen of ivy.]

She dropped out and down, struck heavily, and had but consciousness enough left to half-rise. Before her eyes shone scores of little pointed lights. Then her senses passed away, and all went sweetly, smoothly and soothingly black about her....After ages, there came faint sounds of running feet. There was a sort of struggle of some sort, it seemed, in her first returning consciousness. Her first distinct feeling was one of wonder that Dunwody himself should be the first to bend over her, and that on his face there should seem surprise, regret, grief. How could he feign such things? She pushed at his face, panting, silent.

Jeanne now was there—Jeanne, tearful, excited, wringing her hands, offering aid; but in spite of Jeanne, Dunwody raised Josephine in his arms. As he did so he felt her wince. Her arm dropped loosely. "Good God! It is broken!" he cried. "Oh, why did you do this? Why did you? You poor girl, you poor girl! And it was all my fault—my fault!" Then suddenly, "Sally!—Eleazar!" he cried.

They came running now from all sides. Between them they carried Josephine back to her room and placed her once more upon her couch.

"Saddle up, Eleazar," commanded Dunwody. "Get a doctor—Jamieson—from St. Genevieve as fast as you can. The lady's arm is broken."

"Pardon, Monsieur," he began, "but it is far for St. Genevieve. Me, I have set h'arm before now. Suppose I set heem now, then go for the doc'?"

"Could you do that?" demanded Dunwody.

"Somehow, yes, me," answered Eleazar. Dunwody nodded. Without further speech the old man rolled up his sleeves and addressed himself to his task. Not without skill, he approached the broken ends of the ulna, which was fractured above the wrist. Having done this without much difficulty he called out for splints, and when some pieces of thin wood were brought him he had them shaped to his needs, adjusted about them his bandage and made all fast. His patient made no sound of suffering. She only panted, like a frightened bird held in the hand, although the sobbing of Jeanne filled the room. The forehead of Dunwody was beaded. He said nothing, not even when they had finished all they now could do to make her comfortable.

"*Au revoir*, Mademoiselle," said Eleazar, at length. "I go now for those doc'."

A moment later the room was cleared, none but Dunwody remaining. At last, then, they were alone together.

"Go away! Bring me Jeanne!" she cried at him. His lips only tightened.

"May I not have Jeanne?" she wailed again.

"Yes, you shall have Jeanne—you shall have anything you want," he answered at length, quietly. "Only get well. Forgive me all this if you can."

Josephine's lips trembled. "May I go?" she demanded of him.

There was a strange gentleness in his voice. "You're hurt. It would be impossible for you to go now. Don't be afraid. Don't! Don't!"

She looked at him keenly, in spite of her suffering. There seemed some change about him. At length, heavily, his head sunk, he left the room.

Jeanne herself, sobbing, tearful, withal overjoyed, rejoined her mistress. The two embraced as was best possible. As her senses cleared, a sort of relief came over Josephine. Now, she began to reason, for the time she was shielded by this infirmity; comforted also by the presence of one as weak and helpless as herself.

"It's an ill wind, Jeanne, which blows no one good," she smiled bravely. "See, now we are together again."

"Madame!" gulped Jeanne. "Madame!"

"Fie, fie, Jeanne! In time we shall be away from here."

"Madame, I like it not—this house. Something here is wrong. We must fly!"

"But, Jeanne, I am helpless. We must wait, now."

All that night and till morning of the next day they waited, alone, Dunwody not appearing, though continually old Sally brought up proofs of his solicitousness. At last there came the sound of hoofs on the gravel road, and there alighted at the door, dust-covered and weary, old Eleazar and Jamieson, the doctor of St. Genevieve. These were met by the master of Tallwoods himself.

"Listen now, Jamieson," said Dunwody, "You're here by my call. You understand me, and understand the rules of your own profession. Ask no questions here. Your patient has broken an arm—there has been an accident. That's all you need to know, I think. Your job is to get her well, as soon as you can. You're a doctor, not a lawyer; that's all."

He led the way to the door of Josephine's room, and the doctor, stained with travel as he was, entered. He was an old man, gray and lean, consumed in his time by fevers and chills, in the treatment of which he was perhaps more skilful than in surgery. He approached the couch not unkindly and stood in preliminary professional scrutiny of his patient. The face turned toward him, framed in its dark roll of hair, caused him to start with surprise. Even thus flushed in the fever of pain, it seemed to him no face ever was more beautiful. Who was she? How came she here? In spite of Dunwody's command many questions sprang to his own mind, almost to his lips. Yet now he only gently took up the bandaged arm.

"Pardon, my dear," he said quietly. "I must unwrap these bandages, to see how well Eleazar has done his work—you know, these doctors are jealous of each other! So now, easy, easy!"

He unrolled the rude bandages which, if not professionally applied, at least had held their own. He examined the splints, hummed to himself meantime.

"Fine!" he exclaimed. "Excellent! Now indeed I shall be jealous.

The old man has done a job as good as I could have done myself!
There was no need of my coming at all. But I'm glad I came, my
dear."

"But you aren't going away. Doctor—you will not go back!"

He pursed a lip as he gazed down over his steel bowed glasses. "I ought to get
back, my dear, because I have other patients, don't you see, and it's a long
ride. Why can't you let me go? You're young and healthy as a wild deer.
You're a perfectly splendid girl. Why, you'll be out of this in a couple of
weeks. How did you happen to fall that way?"

[Illustration: Why can't you let me go?]

She nodded toward the window. "I fell out—there—I was frightened."

"Yes, yes, of course—sleep walking, eh?"

Jamieson took snuff very vigorously. "Don't do it again. But pshaw! If I were
as young and strong as you are, I'd have my arm broken twice a week, just for
fun."

"Doctor, you're going!" she exclaimed. "But you must do something for me
—you must be my friend."

"Certainly, my dear, why not? But how can I help you? Dunwody's pledged
me to professional secrecy, you know." He grinned, "Not that even Warv'
Dunwody can run me very much."

He looked down at her, frowning, but at that moment turned to the door as he
heard Dunwody's step.

"How do you find the patient, Doctor?" asked Dunwody. Jamieson moved a
hand in cheerful gesture to his patient.

"Good-by, my dear. Just get well, now. I'm coming back, and then we'll have
a talk. Be good, now, and don't walk in your sleep any more." He took
Dunwody by the shoulder and led him out.

"I don't like this, Dunwody," he said, when they were out of earshot of the
room. "What's going on here? I'm your doctor, as we both know; but I'm
your friend, too. And we both know that I'm a gentleman, and you ought to
be. That's a lady there. She's in trouble—she's scared e'en a'most to death.
Why? Now listen. I don't help in that sort of work, my boy. What's up here?
I've helped you before, and I've held your secrets; but I don't go into the
business of making any more secrets, d'ye see?"

"There aren't going to be any more, Jamieson," rejoined Dunwody slowly.
"I've got to keep hers. You needn't keep mine if you don't feel like it. Get her

well, that's all. This is no place for her. As for me, as you know very well, there isn't any place anywhere for me."

The old doctor sighed. "Brace up to it, my son. But play the game fair. If it comes to a case of being kind to yourself or kind to a woman, why, take a gamble, and try being kind to the woman. They need it. I'm coming back: but now I must be getting on. First, I'm going to get something to eat. Where's the whisky?"

Dunwody for the time left him, and began moodily to pace apart, up and down the gallery. Here presently he was approached by Jeanne, the maid.

"Madame will speak to you!" announced that person loftily, and turned away scornfully before he had time to reply. Eager, surprised, he hastened up the stair and once more was at her bedside. "Yes?" he said. "Did you wish me for anything?"

Josephine pushed herself back against the head board of the bed, half supported by pillows. With her free hand she attempted to put back a fallen lock of dark hair. It was not care for her personal appearance which animated her, however, although her costume, arranged by her maid, now was that of the sick chamber. "Jeanne," she said, "go to the armoire, yonder. Bring me what you find there. Wait," she added to Dunwody. "I've something to show you, something to ask you, yes."

Jeanne turned, over her arm now the old and worn garments which Sally earlier had attempted to remove.

"What are these?" exclaimed Josephine of the man who stood by.

He made no reply, but took the faded silks in his own hands, looking at them curiously, as though he himself saw something unexpected, inexplicable.

"What are they, sir? Whose were they? You told me once you were alone here."

"I am," he answered. "Look. These are years old, years, years old."

"What are they? Whose were they?" she reiterated.

"They are grave clothes," he said simply, and looked her in the face. "Do you wish to know more?"

"Is she—was she—is she out there?" He knew she meant to ask, in the graveyard of the family.

"Why do you wish to know?" he inquired quietly. "Is it because you are a woman?"

"I am here because I am a woman. Well, then."

He looked at her, still silently, for a time. "She is dead," he said slowly. "Can't you let her lie dead?"

"No. Is she out there? Tell me."

"No."

"Is she dead? Who was she?"

"I have told you, I am alone here. I have told you, I've been alone, all my life, until you came. Isn't that enough?"

"Yes, you've said that; but that was not the truth."

"It depends upon what you mean by the truth."

"The man who could do what you have done with me would not stop at anything. How could I believe a word you said?" Then, on the instant, much as she had cause to hate him, she half regretted her speech. She saw a swift flush spring to his cheek under the thin florid skin. He moved his lips, but did not speak. It was quite a while before he made reply.

"That isn't just," he said quietly. "I wouldn't lie to you, not even to get you. If that's the way you feel about me, I reckon there couldn't, after all, be much between us. I've got all the sins and faults of the world, but not just that one. I don't lie."

"Then tell me."

"No. You've not earned it. What would be the use, if you didn't believe what I said?"

He held up the faded things before his eyes, turning them over calmly, looking at them directly, unshrinkingly. She could not read what was in his mind. Either he had courage or long accustomedness, she thought.

"I asked Sally," she half smiled.

"Yes?"

"And I'll ask her again. I don't want—I can't have, a—a room which belongs to another woman, which has belonged to another. I've not, all my life, been used to—that sort of place, myself, you see."

"You are entitled to first place. Madam, wherever you are. I don't know what you have been." He pointed to her own garments, which lay across a chair. "You don't know what she has been;" he indicated these that he held in his hand. "Very well. What could a mere liar, a coward, do to arrange an understanding between two women so mysterious? You sprang from the earth, from the sea, somewhere, I do not know how. You are the first woman for me. Is it not enough?"

"I told Sally, it might have been a sister, your mother—"

"Dead long ago. Out there." He nodded to the window.

"Which?" she demanded.

He turned to her full now, and put out a hand, touching the coverlid timidly almost. "You are ill," he said. "Your eyes shine. I know. It's the fever. It isn't any time now for you to talk. Besides, until you believe me, I can not talk with you any more. I've been a little rough, maybe, I don't know; but as God made this world, those trees, that sun yonder, I never said a word to you yet that wasn't true. I've never wanted of you what wasn't right, in my own creed. Sometimes we have to frame up a creed all for ourselves, don't you know that? The world isn't always run on the same lines everywhere. It's different, in places."

"Will you tell me all about it—about her, sometime?"

"If you are going away, why should you ask that? If you are going to be nothing to me, in all the world, what right have you to ask that of me? You would not have the right I've had in speaking to you as I have. That was right. It was the right of love. I love you! I don't care if all the world knows it. Let that girl there hear if she likes. I've said, we belong together, and it seems truth to me, the very truth; yes, and the very right itself. But some way, we hurt each other, don't we? Look at you, there, suffering. My fault. And I'd rather it had cost me a limb than to see you hurt that way. It cuts my heart. I can't rest over it. And you hurt me, too, I reckon, about as bad as anything can. Maybe you hurt me more than you know. But as to our rights to anything back of the curtain that's before us, before your life and mine, why, I can't begin until something else has begun. It's not right, unless that other is right, that I've told you. We belong together in the one big way, first. That's the premise. That's the one great thing. What difference about the rest, future or past?"

"You've not been much among women," she said.

"Very little."

"You don't understand them."

"I don't reckon anybody does."

"Jeanne told me that she heard, last night, a child crying, here in this house."

"Could it not have been a negro child?" He smiled at her, even as he stood under inquisition.

She noticed that his face now seemed pale. The bones of the cheeks stood out more now. He showed more gravity. Freed of his red fighting flush, the, flame of passion gone out of his eyes, he seemed more dignified, more of a man than had hitherto been apparent to her.

"*Non! Non!*" cried out Jeanne, who had benefited unnoticed to an extent undreamed hitherto in her experience in matter delicate between man and maid. Her mistress raised a hand. She herself had almost forgotten that Jeanne was in the room. "*Non! Non!*" reiterated that young person. "Eet was no neegaire child, *pas de tout, jamais de la vie*! I know those neegaire voice. It was a voice white, Madame, Monsieur! Apparently it wept. Perhaps it had hunger."

A sort of grim uncovering of his teeth was Dunwody's smile. He made no comment. His face was whiter than before.

"Whose child was it?" demanded Josephine, motioning to the garments he still held in his hands. "Hers?" He shook his head slowly.

"No."

"Yours?"

"No."

"Oh, well, I suppose it was some servant's—though the overseer, Jeanne says, lives across the fields, there. And there would not be any negroes living here in the house, in any case?"

"No."

"Was it—was it—yours?"

"I have no child. There will never be any for me in the world—except—under —" But now the flush came back into his face. Confused, he turned, and gently laid down the faded silks across a chair back, pulling it even with the one where lay Josephine's richer and more modern robes. He looked at the two grimly, sadly, shook his head and walked out of the room.

"Madame!" exclaimed Jeanne, "it was divine! But, *quelle mystere*!"

CHAPTER XIII

Dunwody joined Jamieson below, and the latter now called for his horse, the two walking together toward the door. They hardly had reached the gallery when there became audible the sound of hoof-beats rapidly approaching up the road across the lawn. A party of four horsemen appeared, all riding hard.

[Illustration: A party of four horsemen appeared.]

"Who're they?" inquired the doctor. "Didn't see any of them on the road as I came in."

"They look familiar," commented Dunwody. "That's Jones, and that's Judge Clayton, down below—why, I just left both of them on the boat the other day! It's Desha and Yates with them, from the other side of the county. There must be something up."

He advanced to meet the visitors. "Good morning, gentlemen. Light down, and come in."

All four got down, shook hands with Dunwody, gave their reins to servants, and joined him on his invitation to enter. Jamieson was known to all of them.

"Well, Colonel Dunwody," began the Honorable William Jones, "you didn't expect to see us so soon, did you? Reckon you'd ought to be all the gladder.

"You live here, my dear Colonel," he continued, looking about him, "in much the same state and seclusion remarked by Mr. Gibbon in his immortal work on the *Decline and Fall of Rome*—where he described the castles of them ancient days, located back in the mountainous regions. But it ain't no Roman road you've got, out thar."

"I was going to remark," interrupted Judge Clayton, "that Colonel Dunwody has anticipated all the modern requirements of hospitality as well as embodied all those of ancient sort. Thank you, I shall taste your bourbon, Colonel, with gladness. It is a long ride in from the river; but, following out our friend's thought, why do you live away back in here, when all your best plantations are down below? We don't see you twice a year, any more."

"Well," said the owner of Tallwoods, "my father might be better able to answer that question if he were alive. He built this for a summer place, and I use it all the year. I found the place here, and it always seemed too big to move away. We set three meals a day, even back here in the hills, and there's

89

quite a bunch of leaves we can put on the table. The only drawback is, we don't see much company. I'm mighty glad to see you, and I'm going to keep you here now, until—"

"Until something pops open," remarked the Honorable William, over the rim of his glass. Dunwody's neighbors nodded also.

Their host looked at them for a moment. "Are you here on any special errand —but of course there must be something of the sort, to bring you two gentlemen so close on my trail."

"We met up with these gentlemen down at the river," began Yates, "and from what they done told us, we thought we'd all better ride in along together, and have a little talk with you. Looks like there might be trouble in these parts before long."

"What sort of trouble?"

"It's this-a-way," broke in the Honorable William Jones. "The jedge an' I laid off at Cairo when you-all went on through. Next day, along comes a steamer from up-river, an' she's full of northern men, headed west; a damned sight more like a fightin' army than so many settlers. They're goin' out into the purairie country beyant, an' I think it's just on the early-bird principle, to hold it ag'inst settlers from this state. They're a lot of those damned black abolitionists, that's what they are! What's more, that Lily gal of the jedge's here, she's got away agin—she turned up missin' at Cairo, too—an' she taken up with this bunch of Yankees, an' is mighty apt to git clar off."

Judge Clayton nodded gravely. "The whole North is stirred up and bound to make trouble. These men seem to have taken the girl in without hesitation. They don't intend to stand by any compromise, at least. The question is, what are we going to do about it? We can't stand here and see our property taken away by armed invaders, in this way. And yet—"

"It looks," he added slowly, a moment later, "just as Thomas Jefferson said long ago, as though this country had the wolf by the ear, and could neither hold it nor let it go. For myself—and setting aside this personal matter, which is at worst only the loss of a worthless girl—I admit I fear that this slavery wolf is going to mean trouble—big trouble—both for the South and the North, before long."

"Douglas, over there in Illinois, hasn't brought up anything in Congress yet that's stuck," broke in the ever-ready Jones. "Old Caroliny and Mississip'— them's the ones! Their conventions show where we're goin' to stand at. We'll let the wolf go, and take holt in a brand new place, that's exactly what we'll do!"

Dunwody remained silent for a time. Doctor Jamieson took snuff, and looked quietly from one to the other. "You can count me in, gentlemen," said he.

Silence fell as he went on. "If they mean fight, let them have fight. If we let in one army of abolitionists out here, to run off our property, another will follow. As soon as the railroad gets as far west as the Missouri River, they'll come out in swarms; and they will take that new country away from us. That's what they want.

"The South has been swindled all along the line," he exclaimed, rising and smiting a fist into a palm. "We got Texas, yes, but it had to be by war. We've been juggled out of California, which ought to have been a southern state. We don't want these deserts of Utah and New Mexico, for they won't raise cotton. When we try to get into Cuba, the North and all the rest of the world protests. We are cut off from growth to the south by Mexico. On the west we have these Indians located. The whole upper West is air-tight abolitionist by national law. Now, where shall we go? These abolitionists are even wedging in west of us. This damned compromise line ought to be cut off the map. We ought to have a chance to grow!"

Strange enough such speech sounds to-day,—speech demanding growth for a part of a country, denying it for the whole, speech ignoring the nationalist tendency so soon to overwhelm all bounds, all creeds in the making of a mighty America that should be a home for all the nations. But as the gray-headed old doctor went on he only voiced what was the earnest conviction of many of the ablest men of his time, both of the South and the North.

"The South has been robbed. We paid our share of the cost of this last war, in blood and in money! We paid for our share in the new territory won for the Union! And now they deny us any share of it! A little band of ranters, of fanatics, undertake to tell a great country what it shall do, what it shall think, —no matter even if that is against our own interests and against our traditions! Gentlemen, it's invasion, that's what it is, and that's my answer, so far as my honest conscience and all my wisdom go. It's war! What's the next thing to do? Judge, we can take back your girl—the legal right to do that is clean. But we all know that that may be only a beginning."

"To me, sir," ventured Judge Clayton, "the legal side of this is very clear, leaving aside our right to recover my property. They are trying to shove their fanatical beliefs down our throats with rifle barrels. We never used to stand that sort of thing down here. I don't think we will begin it now!"

The Honorable William Jones helped himself to whisky, altogether forgetting his principle of taking but one drink a day. "If them damned abolitionists would only stay at home, we could afford to sit quiet an' let 'em howl; but when they come into our dooryard an' begin to howl, it's time somethin' ought to be did. I 'low we'll have to fight."

"We will fight," said Dunwody slowly and gravely. A faint picture of the possible future was passing before his mind.

"What boat are these men using?" asked Doctor Jamieson, turning to young Desha.

"Little old scow named the *Helen Bell*. She can't steam up-stream a hundred miles a week. She ties up every night. We can easy catch her, up above St. Genevieve, if we ride fast."

"That looks feasible to me," remarked Judge Clayton, and the others nodded their approval.

Judge Clayton dropped into a seat, as he replaced his glass on the nearest table. "By the way, Colonel Dunwody," said he, "there was something right strange happened on the Vernon, coming down the Ohio, and I thought maybe you could help us figure it out. There was another disappearance—that extraordinarily beautiful young lady who was there—you remember her? No one knew what became of her. When I heard about that Lily girl's escape, I sent my men with the two bucks on down home, with instructions for a little training, so they would not try the underground again right soon. But now—"

"Now about that Lily girl," interrupted the Honorable William Jones, who had once more forgotten his temperance resolutions,—"But hello, Colonel, what's this, wha-a-at's this?"

He picked up and exposed to view a small object which he saw lying on the hall floor. It was a small pin of shell and silver, such as ladies sometimes used for fastening the hair.

"Somehow, I got the idea you was a bachelor man," went on the Honorable William cheerfully. "Thought you lived here all alone in solitary splenjure; never looked at a woman in your whole life in the whole memory of man. But, looky-here, now, what's this?"

Dunwody, suddenly confused, could only wonder whether his face showed what he really felt. His guest continued his investigation.

"An' looky-there on the table!" pointing, where some servant apparently had placed, yet another article of ladies' apparel, dropped by accident, a dainty glove of make such as no servant of that country ever saw, much less used. "Come now," blithely went on the gentleman from Belmont. "Things is lookin' mighty suspicious, mighty suspicious. Why didn't you tell us when you-all was married?"

A sudden start might have drawn attention to Judge Clayton, but he controlled himself. And if a slight smile assailed his lips, at least he was able to suppress it. Nothing, however, could suppress the curiosity of the able student of Roman history. "I'll just take a little prowl around," said he.

He was rewarded in his search. A little hair-pin lay at the first step of the stair. He fell upon it with uproarious glee.

"Trail's gittin' hot," said he. "I reckon I'll go on up."

"No!" cried Dunwody suddenly, and sprang to the foot of the stair. "Please!— that is,—" he hesitated. "If you will kindly wait a moment, I will have the servants put your room in order for you before you go up."

"Oho!" cried the Honorable William. "Don't want us to find out a single thing! House o' mystery, ah, ha! Doctor here, too! Tell us, anybody died here to-day?"

Doctor Jamieson answered by quietly stepping to the side of Dunwody. Judge Clayton, without comment, joined them, and the three edged in between the exhilarated gentleman and the stairway which he sought to ascend.

"I was just saying, gentlemen," remarked Judge Clayton quietly, "that I was sure it would give us all much pleasure to take a stroll around these beautiful grounds with Colonel Dunwody."

He looked Dunwody calmly in the eye, and the latter knew he had a friend. He knew perfectly well that Judge Clayton did not for an instant suppose that these articles ever had belonged to any servant. On the contrary; it was possible he remembered where and in whose possession he had seen them before. But nothing more was said about the beautiful young lady of the *Mount Vernon*.

"You have a beautiful place here, Colonel Dunwody, beautiful!" said Clayton carelessly, casting an arm over the other's shoulders and leading the way to the front door. "It reminds me of our old family home back in Virginia. Come, gentlemen; let us have a more careful look at so well-chosen a locality. It is improved—improved, gentlemen, as well as it originally was chosen. But look at those hills!"

CHAPTER XIV

To the heated imagination of the Honorable William Jones something still remained to be explained, and he remained anxious to continue the conversation on the topic foremost in his mind.

"Look around here, gentlemen," said he, extending an eloquent arm. "Behold them mountings. Look at them trees surrounding this valley of secrets. The spoils of war belongs to him that has fit—the captives of the bow and spear are his'n. How said Brennus the Gaul, when he done vanquished Rome? 'Woe to the conquered!' said he. 'Woe to them that has fell to our arms!' Now it's the same right here. Look at—"

"I was just going to remark," suavely broke in Judge Clayton, "that of the many mountain views of our southern country, this seems to me one of the most satisfactory. I have never seen a more restful scene than this, nor a morning more beautiful. But, Missouri!" he added almost with mournfulness. "What a record of strife and turmoil!"

Dunwody nodded. "As when Missouri was admitted, for instance," he said smilingly.

"Precisely!" rejoined Clayton, biting meditatively at a plucked grass stem. "The South gets a state, the North demands one! When Missouri came in, Illinois also was admitted—one free against one slave state. Politics,— nothing more. Missouri would break the balance of power if she came alone and unpaired as a slave state, so the North paired her with Maine, and let her in, with a string tied to her! Slavery already existed here, as in all these other states that had been admitted with it existent. What the North tried to do was to abolish slavery where it had *already* existed, legally, and under the full permission of the Constitution. All of the Louisiana Purchase had slavery when we bought it, and under the Constitution Congress could not legislate slavery *out* of it."

The younger men of the party listened to him gravely, even eagerly. Regarding the personal arbitrament of arms which they now faced, they were indifferent; but always they were ready to hear the arguments pro and con of that day, when indeed this loosely organized republic had the giant wolf of slavery by the ear.

"But they claimed the right of the moral law!" said Dunwody finally.

"The moral law! Who is the judge of that? Governments are not run by that. If we overthrow our whole system of jurisprudence, why, I've nothing to say. That's anarchy, not government. The South is growing faster relatively than the North. The politicians on both sides are scared about the balance of power, and they're simply taking advantage of this cry of morality. They're putting the moralists out as cat's-paws to the fire!" Judge Clayton almost abandoned his usual calm.

"I imagine," ventured Doctor Jamieson, "that Missouri had as good a right to come in unrestricted as Louisiana had in 1812, or Arkansas in 1836."

"That argument was admitted by statesmen, but it was denied by politicians: I make a distinction between the two," commented Dunwody.

"Yes," rejoined Judge Clayton. "The politicians of the House, controlled by the North, would not give up the intention to regulate us into a place where it could hold us down. 'Very well,' said the Senate—and there were a few statesmen in the Senate the—'then you shall not have Maine admitted on your own side of the line!' And that was how Missouri sneaked into this Union— this state, one of the richest parts of the Union—by virtue of a compromise which even waited until Maine was ready to come in! Talk of principles—it was *politics*, and nothing less. That's your Missouri Compromise; but has the North ever considered it so sacred? She's stuck to it when it was good politics, and forgotten it when that was more to her interest. The Supreme Court of the United States will declare the whole Missouri Compromise unconstitutional at no late date. And what it is going to do with Mr. Clay's compromise, of this year, the Lord only knows."

It was young Yates who at length ventured to interrupt in his soft and drawling tones, "I don't see how the No'th can charge us up with much. Whenever they get into trouble and want help in a trade, or a fight, or a argument, why, they come south!"

Doctor Jamieson calmly took snuff. "Time was, when we first came in as a state," said he, "that we didn't take these attempts of the North to regulate us any too tamely."

[Illustration: Doctor Jamieson calmly took snuff.]

"I don't know about that," commented Judge Clayton. "Your 'moral law,' your 'higher law,' gentlemen, I don't find in my legal reading. It was personal liberty that took every man west, but we've stood and stickled for the actual law, and we've been robbed under it: robbed as a state, and now they want to rob us as individuals. Gentlemen, these men are carrying off a girl of mine worth, say fifteen hundred to two thousand. I say deliberately that, when these armed invaders come to cross this state with purposes such as that, there is

95

full process of law under which they can be turned back. For instance, you, Colonel Dunwody, are a United States marshal. I've the honor to represent the Judiciary of this state. We haven't time now to put the matter in the hands of the courts or of the legislature. But it seems to me—"

"Men," said young Desha tersely, "we're wastin' time. We've made our medicine. Let's hit the war trail."

Dunwody smiled at him. "You boys are hot-headed," said he.

"To hell with the Constitution!" exclaimed the Honorable William Jones suddenly.

"Well, it's one Constitution against the other, anyhow," said Clayton. "You can see the intent of the North now plainly enough. Indiana openly says she's going to make the Fugitive Slave Act impossible of enforcement. All over the North they call it immoral and unchristian—they reserve the right of interpreting both the Bible and the Constitution for us—as though we weren't grown men ourselves. That's the sort of law there is back of this boat load of fools down there."

"Men, we're wastin' time!" repeated young Desha.

"Get the horses!" ordered Dunwody of the nearest black.

CHAPTER XV

THE ARBITRAMENT

It was twilight when the little cavalcade from Tallwoods arrived at the old river town of St. Genevieve. The peaceful inhabitants, most of them of the old French strain, looked out in amazement at the jaded horses, the hard-faced men. By this time the original half dozen riders had received reinforcements at different plantations, so that a band of perhaps thirty armed men had assembled. It had needed little more for the average listener than a word telling the news.

Brief inquiry at St. Genevieve informed them that the little steamer *Helen Bell* had passed the town front that day soon after noon. As she depended almost as much upon poles and lines for her up-stream progress as upon her steam, it was thought likely she would tie up for the night at some point not more than ten or twelve miles up-stream. Dunwody therefore determined to ride across the river bed at its shortest distance, in the attempt to intercept the steamer, relying upon chance to secure small boats near at hand should they be necessary. His men by this time were glad enough to dismount and take some sort of refreshment before this last stage of their journey.

It was dark when again they mounted, and the old river road, full of wash-outs, stumps and roots, made going slow after the moon had sunk. They had, however, no great distance to ride. At a point ten miles up the river they came upon a small huddle of fishermen's huts. At one of these Dunwody knocked, and the frightened tenant, at first almost speechless at the sight of so many armed men, stammeringly informed him that the steamer had passed late that evening and was, in his belief, tied up at a little towhead island not more than half a mile up-stream.

"What boats have you got here?" demanded Dunwody.

"No boat at all, Monsieur," rejoined the habitant.

"Maybe so four, five feesh boat, that's hall."

"Bring them out!" was the terse order.

They dismounted and, leaving their horses tied in the wood at the roadside, they went to the water's edge and presently embarked, a half dozen men in each of as many long river skiffs, of the type used by the fishermen in carrying out their nets. Dunwody and Clayton were in the foremost boat and each pulled an oar. The little flotilla crawled up-stream slowly, hugging the bank and keeping to the shadows. At last they were opposite a low, willow-covered island, and within a narrow channel where the water, confined between two banks, flowed with swifter current. At length, at Dunwody's quiet signal, all the boats paused, the crews holding fast to the overhanging branches of the trees on the main shore of the river.

"She's out there, just across yonder island," he whispered. "I think I can see her stack now. She must be tied up close. We can slip in on this side, make a landing and get aboard her before she can stop us, if we're careful. Keep perfectly quiet. Follow us, boys. Come on, Clayton."

Silently they all cast loose and, each boat taking its own time, crossed the narrow channel, heading upstream, so as to make the landing as nearly opposite the steamer as possible. They crawled out through the mud, and hauled up their boats to safe places along shore. Then, each man looking to his own weapons, they came together under the cover of the willows. Dunwody again addressed them.

"We must slip across there, seventy or eighty yards or so, and get under the side of her before they know we're here," he said in low tones. "Let no one fire a shot until I order it. If there's going to be any shooting, be sure and let them begin it. When we get across and leave cover, you'd better spread out a little. Keep down low, and don't shoot unless you have to. Remember that. Come on, now."

Inside the first fringe of the tangled and heavy willows, the mud lay deep in a long, half-drained pool of water which stood in the middle of the willow-covered fiat. Into this, silently as they could, they were obliged to plunge, wading across, sometimes waist deep. In spite of the noise thus made there was no challenge, and the little body of men, re-forming into an irregular line, presently arrived at the outer edge of the willow flat. Here, in the light which hung above the river's surface, they could see the bulk of the steamer looming almost in their faces. She had her landing planks out, and here and there along the narrow sand beach a smouldering ember or so showed where little fires had been made. As a matter of fact, more than half of the men of the boat had preferred to sleep on shore. Their muffled bodies, covered in their blankets, might even now be seen here and there.

Although the sound of splashing and struggling in the water and mud had not raised any of these sleepers, now all at once, as though by some intuition, the whole bivouac sprang into life. The presence of so many men could not be concealed.

"Who goes there?" came a military call from the boat. "Halt! Halt!" came from the line of sleepers suddenly awakened. In an instant both parties were under arms.

It spoke well for the temper of the men with Dunwody, perhaps better for his serious counsel of them, that none of them made any answer. Silently, like so many shadows, they dropped down to the ground.

"What was that, Kammerer?" cried a voice on the boat, calling down to some one on the shore.

"There are men here," was the answer. "Somebody's out there."

The night was now astir. Men half clothed, but fully armed, now lined up along the beach, along the gunwale of the boat. Apparently there were some twenty or more of them in all.

"River pirates, likely," said the leader, who had now come down the gang-plank. "Fall in, men! Fall in!" His voice rang sharp and clear, like that of an officer.

"Line up along this beach, and get down low!" he commanded. "Hold your fire! Hold!—What do you mean?—What are you doing?" His voice rose into a scream.

Some one had fired a shot. At once the thicket was filled with armed men. Some unknown member of the boat party, standing on the deck behind the leader, had fired at a movement seen in the willows twenty yards away. The aim was true. A groan was answer to the shot, even before the exclamation of the leader was made. Young Desha fell back, shot through the body. His friends at first did not know that any one had been hurt, but to lie still under fire ill suited their wild temper. With a common impulse, and without order, they emptied their guns into the mass of dark figures ranged along the beach. The air was filled with shouts and curses. The attacking party advanced. The narrow beach of sand and mud was covered with a struggling mass of fighting men, of which neither party knew the nature of the other, and where the combatants could scarce tell friend from foe.

"Get in, men!" cried Dunwody. "Go on! Take the boat!" He pressed on slowly, Judge Clayton at his side, and they two passed on up the gang-plank and into the boat itself. The leader of the boat forces, who had retired again to the steamer deck, faced them here. It was Dunwody himself who reached out, caught him in a fell grip and took away from him his rifle.

"Call your men off!" he cried. "Do you all want to get killed?"

"You pirates!" exclaimed the boat leader as soon as he could get his breath. "What do you mean by firing on us here? We're peaceable men and on our own business."

Dunwody stood supporting himself on his rifle, the stock of it under his arm. "You call this peace!" he said. "We didn't intend to attack you. We're after a fugitive slave. I'm a United States marshal. You've killed some of our men, and you fired, first. You've no right—Who are you?" he cried, suddenly pushing closer to his prisoner in the half light. "I thought I knew your voice! You—Carlisle—What are you doing here?"

[Illustration: "Who are you?" he cried suddenly.]

"I'm about my business," rejoined that young officer curtly. "I've been on your trail."

"Well, you've found me," said Dunwody grimly. "You may wish you hadn't."

The Northerner was not in the least subdued, and remained fearless as before. "That's fine talk!" he said. "Why haven't we a right here? We're on a navigable stream of the United States, in free waters and in a free country, and we're free to do as we propose. We're under a free flag. What do you mean by firing into us?"

"You're not navigating the river at all," retorted Judge Clayton. "You're tied up to Missouri soil. The real channel of the river is away out yonder, and you know it. We're inside our right in boarding you. We want to know who you are and what you are doing here, an army officer, at the head of men armed in this way. We're going to search this boat. You've got property of mine on board, and we've the legal right to take it, and we're going to take it. You've killed some of our posse."

"You're pirates!" reiterated the northern, leader. "You're border ruffians, and you want to take this boat. You'll have to account for this."

"We are ready to account for it," said Dunwody. "Throw down your arms, or we will kill every man of you. At once!"

He swung heavily back on his support as he spoke. Clayton caught him by the arm. "You're hit, Dunwody!" he said in a low voice.

"Yes, a little," answered the other. "Don't say anything." Slowly he pushed on, directly up to Carlisle, who faced him fearless as ever. "Tell your men to throw down their guns!" demanded Dunwody once more.

"Attention, company!" called out the young Northerner. "Stack arms!"

Silently, in the dark, even in the confusion, the beleaguered men grouped together and leaned their rifles against this or that support. Silently they ranged themselves, some on the deck, some still upon the shore.

"Get lights now, at once!" commanded Dunwody. "We've got men hurt here. We'll have to do something at once. Jamieson!" he cried out. "Are you hurt?"

"I'm all right," answered Doctor Jamieson out of the darkness. "Not a scratch. But there's a lot of our fellows down."

"Take care of them," said Dunwody. "We'll attend to the rest of this business after that."

CHAPTER XVI

A dismal sight enough was presented when finally a few half-hearted torches were pressed into use to produce a scant illumination. What had been a commonplace scene now was become one of tragedy. The bank of this willow-covered island had assumed the appearance of a hostile shore. Combat, collision, war had taken the place of recent peace and silence. The night seemed ominous, as though not even these incidents were more than the beginning of others yet more serious soon to come.

Out of the confusion at last there might have been heard the voice of Dunwody, calling again for Jamieson. There was work for the surgeon when the dead and injured of both sides at last were brought aboard the little steamer and ranged in a ghastly common row along the narrow deck. "Take care of them, Jamieson," said Dunwody shortly. He himself leaned against the rail.

"You're hurt yourself, Dunwody," exclaimed Jamieson, the blood dripping from his fingers when he half rose. "What's wrong?"

"Nothing—I got a nick in my leg, I think, but I'm all right. See to the others."

Jamieson bent over the body of young Desha, who had been first to suffer here on the debated ground of Missouri. He had been shot through the upper body and had died with little suffering. Of the assailing party two others also were beyond aid, one a young planter who had joined the party some miles back beyond St. Genevieve, the other a sallow example of the "poor white trash" who made a certain part of the population of the lower country. Of these both were shot through the head, and death did not at once relieve them. They both lay groaning dully. Jamieson passed them swiftly by. The tally showed that of the Missourians three had been killed, four badly wounded, besides the slight wound of Dunwody and that of a planter by the name of Sanders, who had been shot through the arm.

Of the boat party, smaller in the first place though well armed, the loss had been slightly less. Two men had been killed outright and three others badly wounded, of these one, probably, fatally hurt. To all of these Jamieson ministered as best he might. The deck was wet with blood. Silent and saddened spectators, the attacking party stood ranged along the rail on the side next to the shore. On the opposite side were the sullen defenders.

Carlisle, the leader of the boat party, stood silent, with lips tightly compressed, not far from where Dunwody leaned against the rail. He made no comment on the scene and was apparently not unused to such spectacles. Occasionally he bent over, the better to observe the results of the surgeon's work, but he ventured no comment and indulged in no recriminations. His slight but erect figure was military now in its formality. His face was not handsome, but the straight eyes showed fearless. The brow was strong, the nose straight and firm. Once he removed his "wideawake" hat and passed a hand through the heavy tangle of his reddish hair. The face was that of a fanatic. It was later not unknown in yet bloodier fighting.

The night faded after all, at last. Along the level of the water's surface came some glints from the eastern sky. The horizon paled slightly. At last a haggard dawn came to light the scene. The shadows of the willow flat opened, and there lay exposed what now was a coast possessed by embattled forces.

"Captain," began Dunwody at last, turning to the commander of the boat forces. "We will be leaving before long. As to you, you will have to turn back. You will take your boat down-stream, if you please."

"It's not as I please," rejoined the other. "You order us back from our journey at your own peril."

"Why argue the matter?" said Dunwody dully. "It would do no good. We're as much in earnest as you are about it, and we have beaten you. You belong to the army, but these are not enlisted men, and you're not carrying out any orders."

"That part of the argument is plain," rejoined the young officer. "But you are mistaken if you think you can order me. I'm an officer, and I'm on my own way, and I am, therefore, under orders. I was following a prisoner late in my charge when I fell in with this party bound up the river, to the Kansas front."

"The courts may take all that up. This is Missouri soil."

"It's no case for courts," answered the other sternly. "This will come before the court of God Himself."

A bitter smile played over the face of the Missourian. "You preach. Yet you yourself are lawless as the worst law-breakers. Who made our laws—you, or the whole people of this country? And if God is your court, why did you have no better aid to-night. It's the long arm wins. You see, we will fight."

"That I agree. It's force that wins, but not brute force. You will see."

"Argument!" exclaimed Dunwody. "The answer is here at our feet—it's in blood."

"So be it then!" said the other solemnly. "If it means war, let it be war. I admit that we have a fugitive slave on board—a young woman—I suppose that was the excuse for your attack."

"It was the cause of it; and we intend to take her," answered Dunwody. "We didn't intend to use violence unless it was necessary. But as to you, will you take your boat below and out of this country?"

"I will not."

"Very well, then, we'll take you from your own boat, and we'll make her pay the penalty."

"By what right?"

"By the right of the long arm, since you insist."

"You would make us prisoners—without any process of law whatever!"

"You can thresh that out in your own courts later, if you like," said Dunwody. "Meantime, we'll see if I can't find a place that will hold you."

"Jamieson," he called out an instant later; "Clayton; come here. Take the roll of these men," he went on. "If any of them want to drop the thing at this point and go back, let them give parole. They'll have to agree to leave and never come back here again."

"That's an outrage!" broke out the northern leader. "You and your band of ruffians—you talk as though you owned this state, as though this river weren't made as a highway of this continent. Don't you know that not even a river can be owned by an entire state?"

"We own this part of it to-day," rejoined Dunwody simply. "This is our judiciary. These are our legislators whom you see." He slapped his rifle stock, touched a revolver butt at his belt. "You left the highway when you tied up to our shores. The temper of my men is such that you are lucky to have a parole offered to you. You deserve not the treatment of soldiers, but of spies. You disgrace your uniform. These men are only fools. But what do they say, Clayton?" he demanded turning to the latter as he finally returned.

"They consider the expedition at an end," returned the Judge. "Three of them want to go on home to St. Louis. Yates yonder is in favor of hanging them all. The boys are bitter about losing Desha."

Dunwody looked the young leader calmly in the face. "You hear," said he. "But you shall see that we are not such ruffians at heart, in spite of all. It's my intention to conclude this matter as decently as possible."

"The others are willing to return," continued Judge Clayton. "They want to know what their captain intends."

"Their captain does not intend to surrender," rejoined the latter fearlessly. "Let those desert who like."

"I am with you, Captain," quietly said a tall young man, of German accent, who had been foremost in the fighting.

[Illustration: "I am with you, Captain."]

"Good, Lieutenant Kammerer, I knew you'd stick," commented the leader.

"As to the boat, Judge Clayton," resumed Dunwody, "what shall we do with her?"

"Burned boats tell no tales," here called out young Yates sententiously.

"You hear," said Dunwody. "My men are not children."

"It's piracy, that's all," rejoined the young leader,

"Not in the least, sir," broke in Judge Clayton. "We'll burn her here, tied to this bank on Missouri soil. The river fell during the night—some inches in all —she's hard aground on the shore."

"Fall in, men!" commanded Dunwody suddenly. "Jamieson, fix up my leg, the best you can. It'll have to take its chances, for we're in a hurry. About the paroled men, get them in the rowboats and set them loose. Get your crippled men off the boat at once, Jamieson. This couple of prisoners I am going to take home with me. The rest can go.

"But there's one thing we've forgotten—where's that girl?" He turned to the northern leader.

"She's below, in the cabin."

"Go get her, Clayton," commanded Dunwody. "We'll have to be quick now."

Clayton found his way down the narrow companionway and in the darkness of the unlighted lower deck fumbled for the lock of the cabin. When he threw open the door he found the interior dimly lighted by the low window. At first he could make out nothing, but at last got a glimpse of a figure at the farther side of the little room. "Who's there!" he demanded, weapon ready.

There was no answer, but slowly, wearily, with unspeakable sadness in every gesture, there rose the figure of the girl Lily, around whose fortunes had centered all these turbulent scenes.

In the confusion which followed, no one had a clear conception of all the events which concluded this tragic encounter. Dunwody, Jamieson and Clayton cleared the men from the decks of the boat. The wounded hobbled to a place of shelter. The dead were laid out in a long and ghastly row at the edge of the willow grove. Meantime, busy hands brought dried brush and piled it up against the side of the boat as she lay against the bank, the leader in this being the Honorable William Jones, who now mysteriously reappeared, after a temporary absence which had not been noted. The faint light of a match showed in the dim dawn. There came a puff of smoke or so, a tiny crackling. A denser burst of smoke pierced through the light flames. Soon the fire settled to its work, eating in even against the damp planking of the boat. The drier railings caught, the deck floors, the sides of the cabin. In half an hour the *Helen Bell*, early border transport, was a mass of flames. In a quarter-hour more, her stacks had fallen overboard and the hulk lay consumed half to the water-line.

[Illustration: Soon the fire settled to its work.]

CHAPTER XVII

THE LADY AT TALLWOODS

The arrival of the four visitors at Tallwoods, and their departure so soon thereafter, were events of course not unknown to Josephine, but only conjecture could exist in her mind as to the real nature of the errand in either case. Jeanne, her maid, speculated as to this openly.

"That docteur also, he is now gone," said she, ruefully. "But yet, behold the better opportunity for us to escape, Madame. Ah, were it not for the injury of madame, I should say, let us at once set out—we could follow the road."

"But they will return!" exclaimed her mistress. "We can not tell how long they will be gone. And, Jeanne, I suffer."

"Ah, my poor angel! You suffer! It is criminal! We dare not start. But believe me, Madame, even so, it is not all misfortune. Suppose we remain; suppose Monsieur Dunwodee comes back? You suffer. He has pity. Pity is then your friend. In that itself are you most strong. Content yourself to be weak and helpless for a time. Not even that brute, that assassin, that criminal, dare offend you now, Madame. But—of course he is impossible for one like madame; yet I have delight to hear even a brute, an assassin, make such love! *Ah, mon Dieu!*"

Jeanne pursed a lip impartially. "*Mon Dieu!* And he was *repressed*, by reason of my presence. He was restrained, none the less, by this raiment here of another, so mysterious. Ah, if he—"

"*Tais-toi donc*, Jeanne!" exclaimed her mistress. "No more! We shall stay until to-morrow, at least."

And so the day passed. The sleepy life of the old plantation went on about them in silence. As a wild animal pursued, oppressed, but for the time left alone in some hiding-place, gains greater courage with each moment of freedom from pursuit, so Josephine St. Auban gained a groundless hope with the passing of the hours. Even the long night at length rolled away. Jeanne slept in her mistress' room. Nothing occurred to disturb their rest.

It was evening of the second day, and the shadows again were lying long across the valley, when there came slowly filing into view along the turn of the road the band of returning riders. At their head was the tall form of Dunwody, the others following, straggling, drooping in their saddles as though from long hours of exertion. The cavalcade slowly approached and drew up at the front door. As they dismounted the faces of all showed haggard, worn and stern.

"There has been combat, Madame!" whispered Jeanne. "See, he has been hurt. Look—those others!"

Dunwody got out of his saddle with difficulty. He limped as he stood now. A slender man near him got down unaided, a tall German-looking man followed suit. The group broke apart and showed a girl, riding, bound. Some one undid the bonds and helped her to the ground.

All of these things were apparent from the vantage ground of the upper story window, but Josephine, unwilling to play at spying, saw none of it. At last, however, an exclamation from Jeanne caused her to hasten to the window. "*Mon Dieu*, Madame! Madame, look—it is that officer—it is Monsieur le Capitaine Carlisle! Look! why then—"

[Illustration: An exclamation from Jeanne caused her to hasten.]

With no more than a glance, her mistress turned, flung open the door of the room, hurried down the stair, passed out of the hall and so fronted these newcomers at the gallery. They stood silent as they saw her. She herself was first to speak.

"What are you doing with that woman?" she demanded.

They all stood in silence, looking at her, at this apparition of a woman—a young and beautiful woman—here at Tallwoods, where none had known of any woman these many years. Clayton himself made no comment. The Honorable William Jones smiled broadly. Dunwody removed his hat. "Gentlemen," said he, "this is the Countess St. Auban, who has come to see these parts of our country. Madam," he added, "this is Judge Clayton. He was on the *Mount Vernon* with us. Lieutenant Kammerer, I think, is the name of this gentleman who came down here to teach us a few things. There has been some fighting. Mr. Yates—Mr. Jones. And this gentleman"—he stepped back so that Carlisle might come into view—"I think you already know."

"I knowed it! I knowed it!" broke in the Honorable William Jones. "I seen all along there was a woman in this house. I said—"

Josephine turned to him a swift glance. "There is a lady in this house."

"Yes," broke out Carlisle, "and all of you remember it. Don't I know! Madam, what are you doing here?"

"Kind words from my former jailer? So!" She rewarded him none too much for his quick sympathy. Then, relenting; "But at least you were better than this new jailer. Are you, too, a prisoner? I can't understand all this."

"But you're hurt. Madam," began Carlisle. "How is that? Have you also been attacked by these ruffians? I did not dream Dunwody was actually so much a ruffian."

"Madam," said Dunwody slowly turning to her, "I can't exchange words now. There has been an encounter, as I said. There have been men killed, and some of us have been hurt. The northern abolitionists have made their first attack on southern soil. This gentleman is an army officer. I'm a United States marshal, and as a prisoner he's safe in talking. He has come here on his own moral initiative, in the interest of what you call freedom. You two should be friends once more. But would you mind helping me make these people comfortable as we can?"

"You are hurt, yourself, then!" she said, turning toward him, seeing him wince as he started up the step.

"No;" he said curtly, "it's nothing."

"That girl yonder—ah! she has been whipped! My God in Heaven. What is to be next, in this wilderness! Is there indeed here no law, no justice?"

The deep voice of the German, Kammerer, broke in. "Thank God in Heaven, at least you are a woman!" he said, turning to her.

"A woman! Why thank God for that? Here, at least, a woman's sole privilege is insult and abuse."

The others heard but did not all understand her taunt. Tears sprang to the eyes of young Carlisle. "Don't talk so!" was all he could exclaim, feeling himself not wholly innocent of reproach. Dunwody's face flushed a deep red. He made no answer except to call aloud for the old house servant, Sally, who presently appeared.

"Madam," said Dunwody, in a low voice, limping forward toward Josephine, "you and I must declare some sort of truce. The world has all gone helter-skelter. What'll become of us I don't know; but we need a woman here now."

She gazed at him steadily, but made no reply. Growling, he turned away and limped up the steps, beckoning the others to follow into the hall.

They entered, awkward, silent, and stood about, none knowing what was best to do. Dunwody, luckless and unhappy as he was, still remembered something of his place as host, and would have led them, friends and enemies, into the dining-room beyond in search of some refreshment. He limped forward, without any support. In the door between the hall and the farther room there lay a mounted rug, of a bear skin. He tripped at its edge and fell, catching vainly at the door. A sharp exclamation escaped him. He did not at once rise.

It was the arm of his prisoner, Carlisle, who aided him. "You are hurt, sir."

"No, no, go away!" exclaimed Dunwody, as he struggled to his feet.

"One bone's gone," he said presently in a low tone to Clayton. "I broke it when I fell that time."

A curious moment of doubt and indecision was at hand. The men, captors and captives, looked blankly at one another. It was the mind of a woman which first rose to this occasion. In an instant Josephine, with a sudden exclamation, flung aside indecision.

"Jeanne' Sally!" she called. "Show these gentlemen to their rooms," naming Clayton and Jones. "Sir," she said to Dunwody, whose injury she did not guess to be so severe, "you must lie down. Gentlemen, pass into the other room, there, if you please." She motioned to the two prisoners, and stepped to Dunwody's side.

"I can't have this," he broke out suddenly. "You're hurt, yourself. Go to your room. I tell you, it's nothing."

"Be quiet," she said, close at his ear. "I'm not afraid of you now."

CHAPTER XVIII

In this strange house party, a truce was tacitly agreed. It seemed sufficient that the future for the time should take care of itself. Dunwody's injury left Clayton practically leader of the Missourians. His party gravitated toward him, while opposite sat the two prisoners, Carlisle and Kammerer, composed and silent, now and then exchanging a glance with each other, but making no spoken comment.

Dunwody, in his own room, was looking into the seriousness of his injury, with the old trapper Eleazar, once more summoned as readiest physician. Eleazar shook his head when he had stripped off the first bloody bandages from the limb. "She'll been broke," was his dictum. "She'll been bad broke. We mus' have docteur soon." For half an hour the old man did the best he could, cleansing and rebandaging.

"We *mus'* have *docteur!*" complained he, mindful of Jamieson, far away, busy with cases as bad as this.

For half an hour or so Josephine remained in her own room above, having done all she could to establish some sort of order. All at once to her strained senses there seemed to flash some apprehension of a coming danger. She rose, tiptoed to her door, looked down. A moment later she turned, and caught up an old pistol which hung on the wall near the door in the narrow hallway. Silently and swiftly she stepped forward to the head of the stair.

What she saw now was this: Carlisle and Kammerer, themselves now armed with weapons carelessly left in the lower hall, had passed unnoticed from the dining-room, and now were tiptoeing down the hall toward the door of Dunwody's apartment. Clayton and his men, dulled with loss of sleep, had allowed them to leave the main room, and these two, soldiers by training, had resolved to turn the tables and take possession of the place. Their plans were at the point of success. They had almost reached the door of Dunwody's room, weapons in hand, when from above they heard a sharp command.

"Halt, there!" a woman cried to them.

They turned and looked up, arrested by the unmistakable quality in the tones. They saw her leaning against the baluster of the stair, one arm bound tightly to her side, the other resting a revolver barrel along the baluster and glancing down it with a fearless eye. She took a step or two lower down the stair, sliding the weapon with her. "What are you doing there?" she demanded.

A half-humorous twist came to the mouth of Carlisle. He answered quietly, as he raised a hand for silence:

"Just about what you might expect us to do. We're trying to take care of ourselves. But how about yourself? I thought you were with us, Madam. I had heard that you—"

"Come," she answered, lowering the weapon and stepping swiftly down the stairs. "Come outside, where we can talk."

The three now passed out the open front door to the wide gallery, which lay in the dim twilight untenanted. Kammerer kept his eyes still on the muzzle of the revolver. Carlisle laughed. "That's right, Kammerer," said he. "Be careful when a woman gets the drop on you. She'll shoot quicker than a man, because she doesn't know any better. I don't doubt you had a reason for stopping us, Madam," said he; "but what?—that puzzles me."

"How came you here?" she demanded. "You left me. I don't know anything about what's going on. I'm all at sea."

"So are we all, Madam. But I'll tell you all I know. I left you for several reasons. I knew my main errand with you was done. My post is out beyond, up the Missouri. I was on my way there when I got orders to take you with me, as you know. I concluded to drop off and send a telegraphic report to Washington, and to ask consent to go on out to my post. I saw your note to Dunwody. You had then chosen a new jailer. I thought, since he was better known in this country than myself, your reputation would be safer in his hands than mine. But as soon as I left, I began to think it over, and I resolved to follow after you, not as a jailer but as a friend. I met a little party of northern men, going out to the Kansas country; and I knew Lieutenant Kammerer, here, at St. Louis. We all thought alike. That girl yonder pleaded so hard that we took her on with us, at Cairo. She was bound to get away. When we tied up for the night, above St. Genevieve, we were attacked by these Missourians here. I had intended to leave the boat, for now I knew where you were. Lily told me you were taken—handled rudely—like a slave—that you—Well then, I knew it was Dunwody.

"Of course, I was going to kill him. In the night none of us knew who made up the party that fired on us. There were half a dozen men killed, more than that many wounded, and we are prisoners here, as you see. I suppose that's about all. But then, good God! Madam, why break up our attempt to escape? Aren't you with us? And how did you get hurt?"

She told him, simply, there had been accident.

"Are you of the revolutionists, Madam?" demanded the big German suddenly.

"Yes!" she wheeled upon him. "I am from Europe. I am for liberty."

"Come, then," said Kammerer, quietly reaching out and taking away the revolver from her hand. "We're friends. How came you to be in this country, here?"

She smiled at him bitterly. "Because of my zeal. There were powers who wanted me out of Washington. Ask Captain Carlisle as to that. But this man I met later on the boat, as you know. He—brought me here—as you have heard!"

"It iss outrage!" broke in Kammerer. "It iss crime!"

"We'll call him to account," interrupted Carlisle. "Why did you stop us? We'd have killed him the next minute. I'll kill him yet."

"I was afraid you *would* kill him," she said simply.

"Well, why not? What has he done to us,—our men,—to you?"

"I could not see it done."

"You'll see worse done. We'll do it yet. You must not stand in our way." His hand closed over his own revolver butt, and he made a half motion forward.

"No!" she said, and stepped before him.

Carlisle would have put her aside. "What do you mean? They'll be out here in a minute,—we'll have to fight if they catch us here. Do you want to see us killed? Quick! Out of the way!" His voice, raucous in anger, rasped at her ears, low as it was pitched.

"No," she still replied. "Let me do the thinking. Keep quiet! I'll get you out. There's been blood enough shed now."

"You are magnificent, Madam!" said Carlisle. "But you are visionary. Get out of our way. I claim him. Leave him to me."

"No, I claim him myself. Leave him to me!"

"In God's name, what next!" exclaimed the young Northerner bitterly. "Are we all mad? Haven't you had trouble enough already with this man? You don't make yourself clear. What do you want of him?"

"I'm entirely clear about it myself. I can't get away from here now, but I'm safe here now. For all of you to stay would mean trouble, certainly. If those men knew you were planning escape there would be more men killed. But you don't belong here. Very well. I'm obliged to stay for a time. So, I'm just going to take the position of commander. I'm just going to parole you two. You're free to go if you like!"

113

Carlisle turned toward the big German, Kammerer, and broke into a laugh. "Did you ever see anything like this?" he demanded. But the assent of the other shone in his eyes.

"The lady hass right," he said. "What she said iss wise, if it can be done."

"But, Madam, what will become of *you*?" said Carlisle at last. Her answer was instant. She turned back to the door.

"Judge Clayton!" she called out, loud and clear. "Mr. Yates! All of you, come here!"

The inner doors opened, and they ran out at her call. Some of them had been asleep, leaning back in their chairs against the wall. The confusion of their approach now aroused all the house. There appeared also the tall form of Dunwody himself, leaning on a rifle barrel for a crutch. All these paused in the hall or on the gallery, close to the great door. Dunwody's frown was unmistakable enough, when he saw the three grouped outside, the two prisoners armed.

"There's been plotting here!" he cried. "What's up? Get your arms, men! Cover them, quick!"

"Wait!" said Carlisle quietly. "We're armed, and we've got you covered." His weapon and that of Kammerer shone gray in the half light. Dunwody threw himself against the doorpost with a growl of anger.

"You've been plotting against us!" he said to Josephine grimly. "Well!"

"You are unjust, as usual, Sir," said Carlisle hotly. "On the contrary, she just kept us from killing you—which by all the rights of God and man we ought to have done,—and will do, some day."

"What do you mean?" demanded Dunwody dully. "You—she saved—"

"It iss the truth," assented Kammerer, in his turn. "It wass the lady who hass saved you. She hass spoken for peace and not for bloodshed. You owe to her your life."

"My life!" he said, turning toward her. "You—"

"I've assumed command here," interrupted Josephine calmly. "I've paroled these gentlemen."

"Indeed!" said Dunwody sarcastically. "That's very nice, for them!".

She went on unperturbed. "I'm going to set them free. Judge Clayton and Mr. Jones and you others, too, must go on home. You will have to surrender to the courts. These men are going to leave the state. All of you must disperse—at once."

"And you yourself,—" began Dunwody grimly; "what do you plan?"

"I remain. I am a hostage. It will now be known where I am. You will be responsible for me, now. I fancy that will suit Washington as well as to detain Captain Carlisle as my jailer any longer. If I thought I needed him, I would not let him go. We are all of us going to be under parole, don't you see?"

"Is it your wish that we should give parole in these circumstances, Dunwody?" Judge Clayton himself smiled rather sardonically.

"I don't see why not, after all," said Dunwody, at length, slowly. "I don't see why that isn't about as wise as anything we can do. The law will do the rest of this work, and we must all be ready for it, as she says. Only one thing, gentlemen, before we part. As to this young lady here, I'll kill the first man, friend or foe, who raises a breath against her. Do I make myself plain? Put down your guns, then. I won't turn any man away, not even an enemy. Have you eaten, gentlemen? Are you rested enough to go to-night?"

An hour later clattering hoofs once more resounded along the Tallwoods road.

CHAPTER XIX

Leaning against the pillar of the gallery, Dunwody watched them all, old friends, late foes, depart. Josephine St. Auban stood not far away. He turned to her, and her gaze fell upon his face, now haggard and gaunt. He had ridden sixty miles since the previous sun, half the distance wounded as he was; had been without sleep for thirty-six hours, without food for almost as long, and now was suffering with an aggravated wound.

"You are ill," she said to him impulsively. "You're badly hurt."

"Aren't you glad to see me suffer?" he asked grimly.

"I am not glad to see any one suffer."

"Well, never mind about me. But now, you, yourself. Didn't I tell you to go to your room and rest?"

She was pale, the corners of her mouth were drawn, her eyes were duller. Neither had she slept. She also suffered, even now. Yet her courage matched his own. She smiled.

"It makes me crawl, all the way through, to see a woman hurt that way. Why did you try to climb out of that window? You weren't walking in your sleep."

"I was trying to get away from you. I thought you were coming. I thought I heard you—at the door." She looked him full in the face, searching it for sign of guilt, of confusion. "Was it not enough?" she added.

The frown on his face only deepened. "That was not true," said he. "I never came to your door. It was Sally you heard. I'll confess—I sent her, to get away those—those clothes you saw. I didn't want—you to see them."

"I believe you!" she said, low, as if she spoke to herself. "Yes, I understand now."

"Why don't you say I'm lying to you?"

"Because you are not lying. Because you tell me the truth, and I know it. I was mistaken."

"How do you know? Why forgive me? I don't want you to forgive me. You don't understand the madness—"

"What hope could there be in a particular madness such as that?" He could

116

see her eyes turned on him steadily. He turned away, sighing.

"I am degraded for ever."

"Tell me," she flashed out upon him suddenly; "what did you think then of *me*, there on the boat? How did you dare—"

"I don't think I had any conclusion—I only wanted you. I just couldn't think of your going away, that was all. I'd never seen a woman like you, I'll never hope to see another your equal in all my life. And you sent for me, told me to come, said you needed help. I didn't know what you were. But I didn't care what you were, either. I don't care now. Your past might be what you liked, you might be what you are not, and it would make no difference to me. I wanted you. I'll never in all my life cease to want you. Who you are or what you are is nothing to me."

[Illustration: "I'll never in all my life cease to want you."]

"But what is the right thing to do now?" he resumed, after a time. "Parole? Hostage? I don't need to tell you I'm the prisoner now. My future, my character, are absolutely in your hands. The fact that I have insulted a woman can be proved. It is with you, what revenge you will take. As a lawyer, I point out to you that the courts are open. You easily can obtain redress there against Warville Dunwody. And your relatives or friends will of course hold me accountable."

"Then you fear me?"

"No. What comes, comes. I am afraid of no one in the world but my own self. I fear only the dread of facing life—of looking about me here, in my own home, and not seeing, not hearing you.

"But you haven't told me what you wish," he added; raising his eyes at last; "nor what you intend to do. Tell me, when will your lawyers call on me?"

"Never at all," she answered at last.

"What do you mean?" he demanded. "To set me quit so easily? Oh, no."

"Never fear. You shall pay me ransom, and heavily."

"Ransom? Parole? Hostages? How do you mean?"

"What ransom you pay me must be out of yourself, out of your own character. I shall exact it a hundredfold, in shame, in regret, of you. Do you hold any of that ready to pay your debtor?"

He shook his head. "No, I'll never regret. But you don't know me, do you? My fortune is adequate."

"So is mine," she rejoined. "I could perhaps buy some of your property, if it were for sale. But I want more than money of you."

"Who are you?" demanded he suddenly, reverting to the old puzzle regarding her.

A sadness came upon her averted face. "Only a bit of flotsam on the human wave. How small we all are, any of us! And there's so much to be done!"

Half stumbling, he shifted his position, leaning his weight against the tall pillar of the gallery. He could see her plainly. In the light from the hall half her features were now thrown into Rembrandt lighting. The roll of dark hair framed her face, highbred, aristocratic, yet wholly human and sweet. Gravity sat on all her features; a woman for thought, said they. A woman for dreams; so declared the fineness of brow and temple and cheek and chin, the hand— which, lifted now for an instant, lingered at her throat. But a woman for love! so said every throb of the pulse of the man regarding her. And now, most of all, pity of her just because she was woman was the thought first in his soul. Already he was beginning to pay, and as she had said!

"You don't answer me," said he, at length, gently. "I can imagine your ambitions; but I don't learn enough of *you*."

"No," said she, with a deep breath. "As you said, we part, each with secrets untold. To you, I am of no consequence. Very well. I was born, no matter where, but free and equal to yourself, I fancy. I came here in the pursuit of life and liberty, and of the days of my remaining unhappiness. I suppose this must be your answer."

"You speak, at least, as though you had studied life—and history."

"I have lived. And I have seen some history made—for a cause. Sir, a great cause. Men will fight for that again, here, on this soil, not under man-made laws, but under a higher and greater law. You love my body. You do not love my mind. I love them, both. Yes, I am student of the law. Humanity! Is it not larger than we? Is this narrow, selfish life of yours all you can see—of life— of this law?"

"Yes," said Dunwody, grinning painfully. "I reckon maybe it was one of those 'higher law' abolitionists that shot me!"

"Shot? What do you mean?" Forgetting philosophy, she turned swiftly. Yet even as she spoke she now for the first time caught sight of the dark rimmed rent in his trousers leg, noted the uneasy fashion in which he held his weight.

"No one told me you were hurt—I thought you only tired, or perhaps bruised by some accident—when you fell, in there."

"No; shot," he replied. "Shot right in here, through the edge of the bone. When I tripped and fell, there in the hall, I broke the bone short off—it was only nicked at first."

"And you have been standing here, talking to me, with *that*?" She stepped to him swiftly and placed a hand under his arm. "You must go in. Come. Can you walk?"

Through his nerves, racked as they were, there swept a flood of joy, more sweet than that of any drug. He could see the blown hair about her ears, see the round of her neck, the curve of her body as she bent to aid him, putting her free arm under his, forgetful of everything in her woman's wish to allay suffering, to brood, to protect, to increase life. They passed through the door toward the foot of the stairs. Here she turned to him.

"The pain is very great?" she inquired.

"The pain at thinking of your going away is very great," he answered. One hand on the newel post, he bent down, his head on his arm for an instant. "Oh, you're making me *pay*!" he groaned. But the next moment he turned on her defiantly. "I'll not learn! If this was the only way for me to meet you, then I'll not regret a single thing I've done. I'll not! I'll not! I'll not pay! It all comes back to me, just what I said before. What couldn't we do, *together*?—I need you—I need you!"

"You must go to your room. You've been standing for an hour."

"But I've been with you. I can't hope for another hour like this. You'll be leaving me. But I'd live the hour over again—in hell with you!"

"I told you, when we all gave parole, that I would exact my price of you, in regret, in remorse."

"You shall not have it in regret, I'll not regret. But I'm paying!
See, I'm telling you you may go, that you must go—away from me."

CHAPTER XX

Eleazar proved a faithful messenger once more. Before the evening shadows had greatly lengthened, three figures appeared at the lower end of the approach to Tallwoods mansion house. Jeanne, as usual looking out from their window, saw these.

"It is the old man, Madame," she commented. "And yes, *Monsieur le Docteur* at last—thank the *Bon Dieu*! But one other—who is that?"

[Illustration: "It is the old man, Madame," commented Jeanne.]

It was a very worn and weary doctor who presently swung out of his saddle at the gallery step. His clothing was stained with mud, his very shoulders drooping with fatigue. In the past few days he scarcely had slept, but had been here and there attending to the wants of surviving sufferers of the boat encounter. None the less he smiled as he held out his hand to Josephine.

"How is my patient?" he inquired. "Plumb well, of course. And how about this new one—I thought I fixed him up before he came home. I've been grunting at Eleazar all the way, telling him it's all foolishness, my coming away out here—he could have fixed Dunwody's leg up, somehow. I suppose you know the old man's son, Hector. He came along for good measure, I reckon."

The young man referred to now advanced, made a leg and pulled a black forelock. He was a strapping youth, attired in the latest fashion of French St. Genevieve. He bowed to this lady; but at the same time, the glance he cast at her French waiting-maid was evidence enough of the actuating cause of his journey. He had heard somewhat of these strangers at Tallwoods house.

"I'll been forget to tell the *docteur* h'all about Mr. Dunwodee," began Eleazar.

"What business have you to forget!" demanded Jamieson sternly. "Has anything gone wrong?"

"*Mon pere*," began Hector, "I'll tol' him, if he didn't tell the *docteur* about how Monsieur Dunwodee he'll broke it his leg some more—"

"What's that?" The doctor whirled upon him.

"It's quite true," said Josephine. "He had a fall, here in the house. He thinks he has broken the injured bone. I didn't know for a long time that he had been shot. He stood out here last night talking to me."

"*Stood* out here—*talking* to you—with his leg broken through—the front bone? Couldn't you have any mercy? You didn't have to *use* that broken wrist, but he—standing around—"

"He did not tell me, until the last moment. He said he thought he had a little fever and believed he would take a little quinine."

"Oh, quinine—a Missourian would take that to save his immortal soul—and quite as well as to take it for a broken bone like that. I did the best I could with it—out there in the dark, but it wasn't half dressed. Come—" He motioned Josephine to follow him to Dunwody's room.

Eleazar had slunk away about the house, but Hector, left alone with Jeanne, improved the shining hour. In a few moments he had informed her that he was most happy to see one so beautiful, one, moreover, who spoke his own tongue —although perhaps, it was true, not quite as that tongue was spoken in Canada. As for himself, he was a cooper, and had a most excellent business, yonder at St. Genevieve. But the society of St. Genevieve—ah, well! And so on, very swimmingly.

In the sick chamber Jamieson advanced with one glance at Dunwody's fevered face. "What's up, Dunwody?" said he. "What has gone wrong? Easy now, never mind."

He shook his head over the results of his first scrutiny. He turned to Josephine, "Have you ever seen anybody hurt?"

"I've been on two battlefields," said she. "I've nursed a little."

Dunwody turned to her a face whose eyes now were glazed with suffering. He nodded to Jamieson without any word.

"Sally, get some hot water, quick!" called out Jamieson in the hall. "So, now, old man, let's see."

He stripped the covering quite down and bared the lower limb, removing the bandage which he had originally applied. For a moment he looked at the angry wound. Then he pulled back the covering, and turned away.

"Well, well, what is it?" croaked Dunwody hoarsely, half-rising on his crumpled pillow. Jamieson did not reply. "I fell, out there in the hall. Weight must have come on the bad place in the leg. I think the bone snapped."

"I think so too! That mightn't have been so bad—but then you stood a while on that bad leg, eh? Now look here, Dunwody; do you know what shape you are in now?"

"No, I only know it hurts."

"If that leg were mine, do you know what I'd do with it?"

"No; but it isn't yours."

"Well, I'd have it off—as quick as it could come, that's all. If you don't, you'll lose your life."

"You don't mean that?" whispered Dunwody tensely, after a time. "You don't mean that, Doctor?"

"I mean every word I say. It's blood poisoning."

The only answer his patient made was to reach a slow hand under his pillow and draw out a long-barreled revolver, which he laid upon the bed beside him.

"I didn't think you such a coward," ruminated Jamieson, rubbing his chin.

"If you think I'm afraid of the hurt of it, I'll let you do your work first, and I'll do mine afterward," gasped Dunwody slowly. "But I'm not going to live a cripple. I'll not be maimed."

They looked each other firmly in the face.

"Is it so bad as all that, Doctor?" demanded Josephine. Her answer was a sad look from the gray old eyes. "Blood poison. Some kind of an aggravation. It's traveling fast."

Josephine gazed down at the bulky figure lying there prone, so lately full of rugged ferocity, now so weak and helpless. Her eye fell on the weapon lying on the bed. She gently removed it.

"That was what he preferred to my skill," commented Jamieson.

Dunwody turned, his gaze on Josephine now. "You don't belong here, now," said he at length. "You'd better go away."

"This is just where she *does* belong!" contradicted Jamieson. "If she has courage to stay here, I want her. I've got to have help. She'll do her duty, and with one hand tied! Can't you do as much? Haven't you any idea of duty in the world?"

"Duty!" Dunwody's lips met in a bitter smile.

"Listen here, Mr. Dunwody," began Josephine, "I've seen worse wounds than that, seen weaker men survive worse than that. There's a chance perhaps— why don't you take it like a man? I exact it of you. I demand it! Your duty to me is unpaid. Come. We must live, all of us, *till all our debts are paid.*"

He made no answer at first save to look her straight in the face for a moment. "Maybe there is such a thing as duty," said he. "Maybe I do owe it—to you. I've—not yet—paid enough. Very well, then."

"Come," cried out Jamieson suddenly, "out you go on the table. Get a hand under there, girl."

There was no word further spoken. Gently they aided the injured man to his feet and helped him hobble through the hall and into the great dining-room beyond, where stood the long table of polished mahogany. Dunwody, swaying, leaned against it, while Jamieson hurried to the window and threw up the curtains to admit as much as possible of the light of late afternoon. Returning, he motioned Dunwody to remove his coat, which he folded up for a pillow. The remainder of his preparations necessarily were scant. Hot water, clean instruments—that was almost all. An anaesthetic was of course out of the question.

"Dunwody, we're going to hurt you a little," said Jamieson, at last. "You've got to stand it, that's all. Lie down there on the table and get ready."

He himself turned his back and was busy near by at a smaller table, arranging his instruments. What then represented surgical care would to-day be called criminal carelessness. Next he went out to the front door and called aloud for Eleazar.

"Come here, man," commanded Jamieson, after he had the old trapper in the room. "Take hold of this good leg and hold it still. Madam, I want you at the foot on the other side. You may get hold of the edge of the table with your hands, Dunwody, and hold still, if you can. I won't be very long."

Swiftly the doctor cut away the garments from the wounded limb, which lay now exposed in all the horrors of its inflammation.... . The next instant there was a tense tightening of the muscles of the man on the table. There was a sigh of deep, intaken breath, followed, however, by no more than a faint moan as the knife went at its work.... .

"I'm not going to do it!" came back from under the surgeon's arm. "There's half a chance—I'm going to try to save it! Hold on, old man,—here's the thing to do—we're going to try—"

He went down now into the quivering tissues and laid bare the edge of the broken bone, deep to the inner lines. Thus the front of the shattered bone lay exposed. The doctor sighed, as he pushed at this with a steady finger, his eyes frowning, absorbed. The bullet wound in the anterior edge was not clean cut. Near it was a long, heavy splinter of bone, the cause of the inflammation—something not suspected in the hurried dressing of the wound in the half darkness at the river edge. This bone end, but loosely attached, was broken free, thrust down into the angry and irritated flesh.

For an instant Jamieson studied the injury. The silence of death was in the room. The tense muscles of the patient might have been those of a lifeless man. Only the horrid sound of the dripping blood, falling from the table upon the carpet, broke the silence.

"I had a coon dog once," began Doctor Jamieson cheerfully—"I don't know whether you remember him or not, Dunwody. Sort of a yellow dog, with long ears and white eye. Just wait a minute." He hastened over to the side of the table and bent again over his case of instruments.

"There's been all kinds of coon dogs in these bottoms and hills, I suppose, ever since white folks came here, but Dunwody, I'm telling you the truth, that dog of mine—"

By this time he had fished out from his case a slender probe, which he bent back and forth as he once more approached the table.

"There's wasn't anything he wouldn't run, from deer to catamount; and, one day, when we were out back here in the hills—I don't know but Eleazar here might remember something about that himself.... . *Hold on, now, old man!*"

The old doctor's forehead for the first time was beaded. He wanted silver wire. He would have accepted catgut. He had neither. For one moment, in agony himself, he looked about; then a look of joy came to his face. An old fiddle was lying in the window. A moment, and he had ripped off a string. In two strides he was back at the dripping table, where lay one marble figure, stood a second figure also of marble.

"We were just trailing along, not paying much attention to anything, when all at once that *dog*..."

Doctor Jamieson's story of his famous coon dog was never entirely completed. His voice droned away and ceased now, as he bent once more over his work.

What he did, so far as he in his taciturn way ever would admit, was in some way to poke the catgut violin string under the bone, with the end of the probe, and so to pass a ligature around the broken bone itself. After that, it was easier to fasten the splinter back in place where it belonged.

Doctor Jamieson used all his violin string. Then he cleaned the wound thoroughly, and with a frank brutality drenched it with turpentine, as he would have done with a horse or a dog; for this burning liquid was the only thing at hand to aid him. His own eyes grew moist as he saw the twitching of the burned tissues under this infliction, but his hand was none the less steady. The edge of the great table was splintered where Dunwody's hands had grasped it. The flesh on the inside of his fingers was broken loose under his grip. Blood dripped also from his hands.

"I'm only a backwoods doctor, Dunwody," said Jamieson at length, as he began rebandaging the limb. "I reckon there's a heap of good surgeons up North that could make a finer job of this. God knows, I wish they'd had it, and not me. But with what's at hand, I've done the best I could. My experience is, it's pretty hard to kill a man.

"Wait now until I get some splints—hold still, can't you! If we have to cut your leg off after a while, I can do a better job than this, maybe. But now we have all done the best we could. Young lady, your arm again, if you please. God bless you!"

The face of Josephine St. Auban was wholly colorless as once more she assisted the doctor with his patient. They got him upon his own bed at last. To Dunwody's imagination, although he could never settle it clearly in his mind, it seemed that a hand had pushed the hair back from his brow; that some one perhaps had arranged a pillow for him.

Jamieson left the room and dropped into a chair in the hall, his face between his hands. "Sally," he whispered after a time, "whisky—quick!" And when she got the decanter he drank half a tumblerful without a gasp.

"Fiddle string in his leg!" he grinned to himself at last. "Maybe it won't make him dance, but I'll bet a thousand dollars he'd never have danced again without it!"

When at last Josephine found her own room she discovered her maid Jeanne, waiting for her, fright still in her face.

"Madame!" exclaimed Jeanne, "it is terrible! What horrors there are in this place. What has been done—is it true that Monsieur has lost both his legs? But one, perhaps? For the man with one leg, it is to be said that he is more docile, which is to be desired. But both legs—"

"It is not true, Jeanne. There has been surgery, but perhaps Mr. Dunwody will not even be a cripple. He may get well—it is still doubtful."

"How then was it possible, Madame, for you to endure such sights? But is it not true, how the *Bon Dieu* punishes the wicked? For myself, I was in terror —even though I was some distance away; and although that young gentleman, Monsieur Hector, was so good as to hold my hand."

CHAPTER XXI

Doctor Jamieson did not at once return to his other duties. He knew that in this case care and skill would for a time continue in demand. Little sleep was accorded him during his first night. Ammonia—whisky—what he had, he used to keep his patient alive; but morning came, and Dunwody still was living. Morphine now seemed proper to the backwoods physician; after this had done its work, so that his patient slept, he left the room and wandered discontentedly about in the great house, too tired to wake, too strained to sleep.

"Old—old—it's an old, tumble-down ruin, that's what it is," he grumbled. "Everything in sixes and sevens—a man like that—and an ending like this to it all."

He had called several times before he could get any attendance from the shiftless blacks. These, quick to catch any slackening in the reins of the governing power which controlled their lives, dropped back into unreadiness and pretense more and more each hour.

"What it needs here is a woman," grumbled Jamieson to himself. "All the time, for that matter. But this one's got to stay now, I don't care who she is. There must be some one here to run things for a month or two. Besides, she's got his life in her two hands, some way. If she left now, might as well shoot him at once. Oh, hell! when I die, I want to go to a womanless world. No I don't, either!"

His decision he at last announced to Josephine herself when finally the latter appeared to make inquiry regarding the sick master of Tallwoods.

"My dear girl," said he, "I am a blunt man, not a very good doctor maybe, and perhaps not much of a gentleman, I don't know—never stopped to ask myself about it. But now, anyhow, I don't know how you happened to be here, or who you are, or when you are going away, and I'm not going to ask you about any of those things. What I want to say is this: Mr. Dunwody is going to be a very sick man. He hasn't got any sort of proper care here, there's no one to run this place, and I can't stay here all the time myself. Even if I did stay, all I could do would be to give him a dose of quinine or calomel once in a while, and that isn't what he needs. He needs some one to be around and watch after things—this whole place is sick, as much as the owner of it. I reckon you've got to help me, my dear."

She looked at him, her large, dark eyes slightly contracting, making neither protest nor assent. He drew a long breath of satisfaction.

"Of course you'll stay," he said; "it's the right thing to do, and we both know it. You don't want to kill a man, no matter how much he desires or deserves it. Doctors and women—they sometimes are fatal, but they don't consciously mean to be, now do they? We don't ask many questions out here in these hills, and I will never bother you, I feel entirely free to ask you to remain at least for a few days—or maybe weeks."

[Illustration: Doctors and women—they sometimes are fatal.]

Her eyes still were on his face. It was a face fit for trust. "Very well," said she at length, quietly. "If you think it is necessary."

It was thus that Josephine St. Auban became the head of Tallwoods household. Not that week did she leave, nor the next, nor the one thereafter. The winter advanced, it was about to wane, and still she remained. Slowly, the master advanced toward recovery. Meantime, under charge of the mistress, the household machine fell once more into proper ways. The servants learned obedience. The plans for the work of the spring somehow went on much as formerly. Everywhere there became manifest the presence of a quiet, strong, restraining and self-restrained influence.

In time the doctor became lighter in his speech, less frequent in his visits. "You're not going to lose that musical leg, Dunwody," said he. "Old Ma Nature beats all us surgeons. In time she'll fill you in a nice new bone along there maybe, and if you're careful you'll have two feet for quite a while yet to come. You've ruined old Eleazar's fiddle, though, taking that E string! Did I ever tell you all about that coon dog of mine I had, once?"

Dunwody at last reached the point of his recovery where he could grin at these remarks; but if anything, he had grown more grim and silent than before. Once in a while his eyes would linger on the face of Josephine. Little speech of any kind passed between them. There were no callers at Tallwoods, no news came, and apparently none went out from that place. It might have been a fortress, an island, a hospital, a prison, all in one.

At length Dunwody was able safely to leave his room and to take up a resting place occasionally in the large library across the hall. Here one day by accident she met him. He did not at first note her coming, and she had opportunity now carefully to regard him, as he stood moodily looking out over the lawn. Always a tall man, and large, his figure had fined down in the confinement of the last few weeks. It seemed to her that she saw the tinge of gray crawling a little higher on his temples. His face was not yet thin, yet in some way the lines of the mouth and jaw seemed stronger, more deeply out. It was a face not sullen, yet absorbed, and above all full, now, of a settled melancholy.

"Good morning," said he, smiling, as he saw her. "Come in. I want to talk to you. But please don't resume our old argument about the compromise, and about slavery and the rights of man. You've been trying—all these weeks when I've been down and helpless and couldn't either fight or run away—to make me be a Bentonite, or worse, an abolitionist—trying, haven't you? to make me an apostate, faithless to my state, my beliefs, my traditions—and I suppose you'd be shrewd enough to add, faithless to my material interests. Please don't, this morning. I don't want subjective thought. I don't want algebra. I don't want history or law, or medicine. I want—"

She stood near the window, at some distance removed from him, even as she passed stopping to tidy Up a disarranged article on the tables here or there. He smiled again at this. "Where is Sally?" he asked. "And how about your maid?"

"Some one must do these things," she answered. "Your servants need watching. Sally is never where I can find her. Jeanne I can always find—but it is with her young man, Hector!"

He shook his head impatiently. "It all comes on you—work like this. What could I have done without you? But yourself, how are you coming on? That arm of yours has pained me—"

"It ceased to trouble me some time since. The doctor says, too, that you'll be quite well, soon. That's fine."

He nodded. "It's wonderful, isn't it?" said he. "You did it. Without you I'd be out there." He nodded toward the window, beyond which the grass-grown stones of the little family graveyard might be seen. "You're wonderful."

He wheeled painfully toward her presently, "Listen. We two are alone here, in spite of ourselves. Face to face again, in spite of all, and well enough, now, both of us, to go back to our firing lines before long. We have come closer together than many men and women get to be in a good many years; but we're enemies, and apart, now. At least you have seen me pretty much as I am —a savage—not much more. I've seen you for what you are—one woman out of hundreds, of thousands. There isn't going to be any woman in my life, after you.—Would you mind handing me that paper, please?"

He passed the document to her opened. "Here's what I meant to do if I didn't come through. It wasn't much. But I am to pay; and if I had died, that was all I could pay. That's my last will and testament, my dear girl. I have left you all I have. It is a legal will. There'll never be any codicil."

She looked at him straight. "It is not valid," she said. "Surely you are not of sound mind!"

He looked about him at the room, for the first time in his memory immaculately neat. From a distance there came the sound of a contented servant's voice. An air of rest and peace seemed in some way to be all about him. He sighed. "I never will be of sound mind again, I fear."

"Make this paper valid!" he suddenly demanded. "Give me my sound mind too. You've given me back my body sound."

Her lips parted in a smile sufficient to show the row of her white and even teeth, "You are getting well. It is time for me to go. As to this—" She handed him back the paper folded.

"You think it's only an attempt to heal the soreness of my conscience, don't you?" he said after a time, shaking his head. "It was; but it was more. Well, you can't put your image out of my heart, anyhow. I've got that. So you're going to leave me now? Soon? Let it be soon. I suppose it has to come."

"My own affairs require me. There is no possible tenure on which I could stay here much longer. Not even Jeanne—"

"No," said he, at length, again in conviction, shaking his head. "There isn't any way."

"You make it so hard," said she. "Why are you so stubborn?"

"Listen!" He turned, and again there came back to his face the old fighting flush. "I faced the loss of a limb and said I couldn't stand that and live. Now you are going to cut the heart out of me. You ask me to live in spite of that. How can I? Were you ever married, Madam?" This last suddenly.

"You may regard it as true," said she slowly, after long hesitation. "Were you?"

"You may regard that also as true!" He set his jaw, and looked at her straight. Their eyes met, steadily, seeking, searching. They now again, opposed, stood on the firing lines as he had said.

"But you told me,—" she began.

"I told you nothing, if you will remember. I only said that, if you could feel as I did, I'd let the heavens fold as a scroll before I'd ask a word about your past. I'd begin all the world all over again, right here. So far as I am concerned, I wouldn't even care about the law. But you're not so lawless as I am. And somehow, I've got to thinking—a little—of your side of things."

"The law does not prevent me from doing as I like," she replied.

129

It was agony that showed on his face at this.

"That demands as much from me, if I play fair with you," he said slowly. "Suppose there was some sort of law that held me back?"

"I have not observed any vast restraint in you!"

"Not at first. Haven't you gained any better opinion?"

She was one of those able to meet a question with silence. He was obliged to continue.

"Suppose I should tell you that, all the time I was talking to you about what I felt, there was a wall, a great wall, for ever between us?"

"In that case, I should regret God had made a man so forgetful of honor. I should be glad Heaven had left me untouched by anything such a man could say. Suppose that?—Why, suppose I had cared, and that I had found after all that there was no hope? There comes in conscience, Sir, there comes in honor."

"Then, in such case—"

"In such case any woman would hate a man. Stress may win some women, but deceit never did."

"I have not deceived you."

"Do you wish to do so now?"

"No. It's just the contrary. Haven't I said you must go? But since you must go, and since I must pay, I'm willing, if you wish, to bare my life to the very bone, to the heart before you, now—right now."

She pondered for a moment. "Of course, I knew there was something. There, in that room—in that wardrobe—those were her garments—of another—another woman. Who?"

"Wait, now. Go slow, because I'm suffering. Listen. I'll not hear a word about your own life—I want no secret of you. I'm content. But I'm willing now, I say, to tell you all about that—about those things.

"I didn't do that at first, but how could I? There wasn't any chance. Besides, when I saw you, the rest of the world, the rest of my life, it was all, all wiped out of my mind, as though some drug had done it. You came, you were so sweet, my lack was so horrible, that I took you into my soul, a drug, a balm, an influence, a wonderful thing.

"Oh, I'm awake now! But I reckon maybe that doesn't mean that I'm getting out of my dream, but only into it, deeper yet. I was mad for you then. I could feel the blood sting in my veins, for you. Life is life after all, and we're made as we are. But later, now, beside that, on top of that, something else—do you think it's—do you suppose I'm capable of it, selfish as I am? Do you reckon it's love, just big, worthy, *decent* love, better than anything in the world? Is that—do you reckon, dear girl, that that's why I'm able now to say good-by? I loved you once so much I could not let you go. Now I love so much I can not let you stay! I reckon this is love. I'm not ashamed to tell it. I'm not afraid to justify it. And I can't help it."

It was any sort of time, a moment, an hour, before there was spoken speech between them after that. At last they both heard her voice.

"Now, you begin to pay. I am glad. I am glad."

"Then it is your revenge? Very well. You have it."

"No, no! You must not say that. Believe me, I want you to feel how—how much I admire—no, wait,—how much I admire any man who could show your courage. It's not revenge, it's not vanity—"

He waited, his soul in his eyes, hoping for more than this; but she fell silent again.

"Then it is the end," he said.

He held up his fingers, scarred to the bone.

"That's where I bruised my hands when I clenched on the table, yonder. You wouldn't think it, maybe, but I love pictures. I've spent a lot of time looking for them and at them. I remember one collection—many pictures of the martyrs, horrors in art, nightmares. Here was a man disemboweled—they wound his very bowels about a windlass, before his eyes, and at each turn—I could see it written in the picture—they asked him, did he yield at last, did he agree, did he consent... . Then they wound again. Here another man was on an iron chair, flames under him. Now and then they asked him. Should they put out the flames and hear him say he had foresworn his cause? Again, there was a man whom they had shot full of arrows, one by one, little by little, and they asked him, now and then, if he foreswore his faith... . But I knew he would not—I knew these had not... .

"That's the way it is," he said slowly. "That's what you're seeing now. These scars on my fingers came cheap. I reckon they've got to run deeper, clean down into my heart. Yet you're saying that now I begin to pay. Yes. When I pay, I'm going to *pay*. And I'm not going to take my martyrdom for immediate sake of any crown, either. There is none for me. I reckon I sinned too far against one of God's angels. I reckon it's maybe just lasting hell for me, and not a martyrdom with an end to it some time. That's how *I've* got to pay.

"Now, do you want me to tell you all the rest?"

She would not answer, and he resumed.

"Do you want me to tell what you've maybe heard, about this house? Do you want me to tell whose garments those were that you saw? Do you want my past? Do you want to see my bowels dragged out before your eyes? Do you want to turn the wheel with your own hands? Do you want me to pay, that way?"

She went to him swiftly, put a hand on his arm.

"No!" said she. "What I want you to believe is that it's *life* makes us pay, that it's *God* makes us pay.

"I want you to believe, too," she went on after a time, "that we need neither of us be cheap. I'm not going to ask you one thing, I'm not going to listen to one word. You must not speak. I must go. It's just because I must go that I shall not allow you to speak."

"Is my debt to you paid, then?" His voice trembled.

"So far as it runs to me, it is paid."

"What remains?"

"Nothing but the debt of yourself to yourself. I'm going to look back to a strange chapter in my life—a life which has had some strange ones. I'm not going to be able to forget, of course, what you've said to me. A woman loves to be loved. When I go, I go; but I want to look back, now and then, and see you still paying, and getting richer with each act of courage, when you pay, to yourself, not me."

"Ah! fanatic. Ah! visionary. Ah! dreamer, dreamer. And you!"

"That is the rest of the debt. Let the wheel turn if need be. Each of us has suffering. Mine own is for the faith, for the cause."

"For what faith? What cause do you mean?"

"The cause of the world," she answered vaguely. "The cause of humanity. Oh, the world's so big, and we're so very little. Life runs away so fast. So many suffer, in the world, so many want! Is it right for us, more fortunate, to take all, to eat in greed, to sleep in sloth, to be free from care, when there are thousands, all over the world, needing food, aid, sympathy, opportunity, the chance to grow?

"Why," she went on, "I put out little plants, and I love them, always, because they're going to grow, they're going to live. I love it—that thought of life, of growth. Well, can I make you understand, that was what I felt over yonder, in that revolution, in mid-Europe. I felt it was just like seeing little plants set out, to grow. Those poor people! Those poor people! They're coming over here, to grow, here in America, in this great country out here, in this West. They'll grow, like plants extending, like grass multiplying, going out, edging westward, all the time. Ah, thousands of them, millions yet to come, plants, little human plants, with the right to live born with them. I don't so much mind about their creed. I don't so much mind about race—their color, even. But to see them grow—why, I suppose God up in His Heaven looks down and smiles when He sees that. And we—we who are here for a little time—we who sometimes are given minds and means to fall in tune with God's smile— why, when we grow little and selfish, instead of getting in tune with the wish of God—why, we fail. Then, indeed, we do not pay—we repudiate our debt to ourselves."

"You are shaming me," he said slowly. "But I see why they put you out of Washington."

"But they can not put God out of Heaven! They can not turn back the stars! They can not stop the rush of those westbound feet, the spread of the millions, millions of blades of grass edging out, on. That is what will make you see this 'higher law,' some time. That is big politics, higher than what you call your traditions. That will shame little men. Many traditions are only egotism and selfishness. There is a compromise which will be final—not one done in a mutual cowardice. It's one done in a mutual largeness and courage.

"Oh,"—she beat her hands together, as was sometimes her way—"America, this great West, this splendid country where the feet are hurrying on so fast, fast—and the steam now carries men faster, faster, so that it may be done—it may be done—without delay—why, all this America must one day give over war and selfishness—just as we two have tried to give over war and selfishness, right here, right now. Do you suppose this world was made just to hold selfishness and unhappiness? Do you think that's all there ever was to the plan of life? Ah, no! There's something in living beyond eating and drinking and sleeping and begetting. Faith—a great faith in something, some plan ahead, some *purpose* under you—ah, *that's* living!"

"But they banished you for that?"

"Yes, that's why they put me out of Washington, I suppose. I've been twice banished. That is why I came here to this country. Maybe, Sir, that is why I came to you, here! Who shall say as to these things? If only I could feel your faith, your beliefs to be the same as mine, I'd go away happy, for then I'd know it had been a plan, somehow, somewhere—for us, maybe."

133

His throat worked strongly. There was some struggle in the man. At last he spoke, and quietly. "I see what separates us now. It is the wall of our convictions. You are specifically an abolitionist, just as you are in general a revolutionist. I'm on the other side. That's between us, then? An abstraction!"

"I don't think so. There are *three* walls between us. The first you put up when you first met me. The second is what you call your traditions, your belief in wasting human life. The third—it's this thing of which you must not speak. Why should I ponder as to that last wall, when two others, insurmountable, lie between?"

"Visionary, subjective!"

"Then let us be concrete if you like. Take the case of the girl Lily. She was the actual cause of your getting hurt, of many men being killed. Why?"

"Because she was a runaway slave. The law has to be enforced, property must be protected, even if it costs life sometimes. There'd be no government otherwise. We men have to take our chances in a time like that. The duty is plain."

"How utterly you fail of the truth! That's not why there was blood spilled over her. Do you know who she is?"

"No," he said.

"She is the daughter of your *friend*, Judge Clayton, of the bench of justice in your commonwealth. *That* is why she wants to run away! Her father does not know he is her father. God has His own way of righting such things."

"There are things we must not talk about in this slavery question. Stop! I did not, of course, know this. And Clayton did not know!"

"There are things which ought not to be; but if you vote for oppression, if you vote yonder in your legislature for the protection of this institution, if you must some day vote yonder in Congress for its extension, for the right to carry it into other lands—the same lands where now the feet of freedom-seekers are hurrying from all over the world, so strangely, so wonderfully—then you vote for a compromise that God never intended to go through or to endure. Is that your vote? Come now, I will tell you something."

"You are telling me much."

"I will tell you—that night, when Carlisle would have killed you in your room there, when I afterward put you all on parole—"

"Yes, yes."

"I saved you then; and sent them away. Do you know why?"

"I suppose it was horror of more blood."

"I don't think so. I believe it was just for this—for this very talk I'm having now with you. I saved you then so that some day I might demand you as hostage.

"I want you to vote with me," she continued, "for the 'higher law.' I want you to vote with the west-bound wheels, with God's blades of grass!"

"God! woman! You have gift of tongues! Now listen to me. Which shall we train with, among your northern men, John Quincy Adams or William Lloyd Garrison, with that sane man or the hysterical one? Is Mr. Beecher a bigger man than Mr. Jefferson was?"

"I know you're honest," she said, frowning, "but let us try to see. There's Mr. Birney, of Alabama, a Southerner who has gone over, through all, to the abolitionists as you call them. And would you call Mr. Clay a fool? Or Mr. Benton, here in your own state, who—"

"Oh, don't mention Benton to me here! He's anathema in this state."

"Yet you might well study Mr. Benton's views. He sees the case of Lily first, the case of the Constitution afterward. Ah, why can't *you*? Why, Sir, if I could only get you to think as he does—a man with your power and influence and faculty for leadership—I'd call this winter well spent—better spent than if I'd been left in Washington."

"Suppose I wanted to change my beliefs, how would I go about it?" He frowned in his intent effort to follow her, even in her enthusiasm. "Once I asked a preacher how I could find religion, and he told me by coming to the Saviour. I told him that was begging the question, and asked him how I could find the Saviour. All he could say was to answer once more, 'Come to the Saviour!' That's reasoning in a circle. Now, if a man hasn't *got* faith, how's he going to get it—by what process can he reach out into the dark and find it? What's the use of his saying he has found faith when he knows he hasn't? There's a resemblance between clean religion and honest politics. The abolitionists have never given us Southerners any answer to this."

"No," said she. "I can not give you any answer. For myself, I have found that faith."

"You would endure much for your convictions?" he demanded suddenly.

"Very much, Sir."

"Suffer martyrdom?"

"Perhaps I have done so."

"Would you suffer more? You undertake the conversion of a sinner like myself?"

The flame of his eye caught hers in spite of herself. A little flush came into her cheek.

"Tell me," he demanded imperiously, "on what terms?"

"You do not play the game. You would ask me to preach to you—but you would come to see the revival, not to listen to grace. It isn't playing the game."

"But you're seeking converts?"

"I would despise no man in the world so much as a hypocrite, a turn-coat! You can't purchase faith in the market place, not any more than—"

"Any more than you can purchase love? But I've been wanting not the sermon, but the preacher. You! You! Yes, it is the truth. I want nothing else in the world so much as you."

"I'd never care for a man who would admit that."

"There never was a woman in the world loved a man who did not."

"Oh, always I try to analyze these things," she went on desperately, facing him, her eyes somber, her face aglow, her attitude tense. "I try to look in my mirror and I demand of what I see there. 'What are you?' I say. 'What is this that I see?' Why, I can see that a woman might love her own beauty for itself. Yes, I love my beauty. But I don't see how a woman could care for a man who only cared for that,—what she saw in her mirror, don't you know?"

"Any price, for just that!" he said grimly.

"No, no! You would not. Don't say that! I so much want you to be bigger than that."

"The woman you see in your mirror would be cheap at any cost."

"But a man even like yourself. Sir, would be very cheap, if his price was such as you say. No turncoat could win me—I'd love him more on his own side yonder threefold wall, *with* his convictions, than on my side without them. I couldn't be bought cheap as that, nor by a cheap man. I'd never love a man who held himself cheap.

"But then," she added, casting back at him one of his own earlier speeches, "if you only thought as I did, what could not we two do together—for the cause of those human blades of grass—so soon cut down? Ah, life is so little, so short!"

"No! No! Stop!" he cried out. "Ah, now is the torture—now you turn the wheel. I can not recant! I can not give up my convictions, or my love, either one; and yet—I'm not sure I'm going to have left either one. It's hell, that's what's left for me. But listen! What for those that grow as flowers, tall, beautiful, there among the grass that is cut down—should they perish from the earth? For what were such as they made, tall and beautiful?—poppies, mystic, drug-like, delirium producing? Is that it—is that your purpose in life, then, after all? You—what you see in your mirror there—is it the purpose of *that* being—so beautiful, so beautiful—to waste itself, all through life, over some vague and abstract thing out of which no good can come? Is that all? My God! Much as I love you, I'd rather see you marry some other man than think of you never married at all. God never meant a flower such as you to wither, to die, to be *wasted*. Why, look at you! Look … at … you! And you say you are to be wasted! God never meant it so, you beauty, you wonderful woman!"

Even as she was about to speak, drawn by the passion of him, the agony of his cry, there came to the ears of both an arresting sound—one which it seemed to Josephine was not wholly strange to her ears. It was like the cry of a babe, a child's wail, difficult to locate, indefinite in distance.

"What was it?" she whispered. "Did you hear?"

He made no answer, except to walk to her straight and take her by the arms, looking sadly, mournfully into her face.

"Ah, my God! My God! Have I not heard? What else have I heard, these years? And you're big enough not to ask—

"It can't endure this way," said he, after a time at last. "You must go. Once in a while I forget. It's got to be good-by between you and me. We'll set to-morrow morning as the time for you to go.

"As I have a witness," he said at last, "I've paid. Good-by!"

He crushed her to him once, as though she were no more than a flower, as though he would take the heart of her fragrance. Then, even as she felt the heave of his great body, panting at the touch of her, mad at the scent of her hair, he put her back from him with a sob, a groan. As when the knife had begun its work, his scarred fingers caught her white arms. He bent over, afraid to look into her eyes, afraid to ask if her throat panted too, afraid to risk the red curve of her lips, so close now to his, so sure to ruin him. He bent and kissed her hands, his lips hot on them; and so left her trembling.

[Illustration: He bent and kissed her hands.]

137

CHAPTER XXII

It is the blessing of the humble that they have simplicity of mental processes. Not that Hector himself perhaps would thus have described himself. The curve of the black crow's wing on his somewhat retreating forehead, the tilt of his little hat, the swing of his body above the hips as he walked, all bespoke Hector's opinion of himself to be a good one. Valiant among men, irresistible among the women of St. Genevieve, he was not the one to mitigate his confidence in himself now that he found himself free from competition and in the presence of a fair one whom in sudden resolve he established in his affections as quite without compare. In short, Hector had not tarried a second week at Tallwoods before offering his hand and his cooper shop to Jeanne.

To the eyes of Jeanne herself, confined as they had been to the offerings of a somewhat hopeless class of serving persons here or there, this swaggering young man, with his broad shoulders, his bulky body, his air of bravado, his easy speech, his ready arm, offered a personality with which she was not too familiar, and which did not lack its appeal. With Gallic caution she made delicate inquiry of Hector's father as to the yearly returns and probable future of the cooperage business at St. Genevieve, as to the desirability of the surrounding country upon which the cooperage business must base its own fortunes. All these matters met her approval. Wherefore, the air of Jeanne became tinged with a certain lofty condescension. In her own heart she trembled now, not so much as to her own wisdom or her own future, but as to the meeting which must be had between herself and her mistress.

This meeting at last did take place, not by the original motion of Jeanne herself. The eye of her mistress had not been wholly blind all these days.

"Jeanne," she demanded one day, "why are you away so much when I desire you? I have often seen you and that young man yonder in very close conversation. Since I stand with you as your guardian and protector, I feel it my duty to inquire, although it is not in the least my pleasure. You must have a care."

"Madame," expostulated Jeanne, "it is nothing, I assure you. *Rien du tout— jamais de la vie*, Madame."

"Perhaps, but it is of such nothings that troubles sometimes come. Tell, me, what has this young man said to you?"

"But, Madame!—"

"Tell me. It is quite my right to demand it."

"But he has said many things, Madame."

"As, for instance, that you please him, that you are beautiful, that you have a voice and hand, a turn of the arm—that you have the manner Parisienne—Jeanne, is it not so?"

"But, yes, Madame, and indeed more. I find that young man of excellent judgment, of most discriminating taste."

"And also of sufficient boldness to express the same to you, is it not so, Jeanne?"

"Madame, the strong are brave. I do not deny. Also he is of an excellent cooperage business in St. Genevieve yonder. Moreover, I find the produce of the grape in this country to increase yearly, so that the business seems to be of a certain future, Madame. His community is well founded, the oldest in this portion of the valley. He is young, he has no entanglements—at least, so far as I discover. He has an excellent home with his old mother. Ah, well! Madame, one might do worse."

"So, then, a cooperage business so promising as that, Jeanne, seems more desirable than my own poor employment? You have no regard for your duty to one who has cared for you, I suppose? You desert me precisely at the time my own affairs require my presence in Washington."

"But, Madame, why Washington? Is that our home? What actual home has madame on the face of the earth? Ah, Heaven!—were only it possible that this man were to be considered. This place so large, so beautiful, so in need of a mistress to control it. Madame says she was carried away against her will. *Mon Dieu!* All my life have I dreamed—have I hoped—that some time a man should steal me, to carry me away to some place such as this! And to make love of such a warmness! Ah, *Mon Dieu!*

"Behold, Madame," she went on, "France itself is not more beautiful than this country. There is richness here, large lands. That young man Hector, he says that none in the country is so rich as Mr. Dunwodee—he does not know how rich he is himself. And such romance!"

"Jeanne, I forbid you to continue!" The eyes of her mistress had a dangerous sparkle.

"I obey, Madame, I am silent. But listen! I have followed the fortunes of madame quite across the sea. As madame knows, I do not lack intelligence. I have read—many romances, my heart not lacking interest. Always I have read, I have dreamed, of some man who should carry me away, who should oblige me—Ah, Madame! what girl has not in her soul some hero? Almost I was about to say it was the sight, the words, of the boldness, the audacity of this assassin, this brute, who has brought us here by force—the words of his love so passionate to madame, which stirred in my own heart the passion! That I might be stolen! It was the dream of my youth! And now comes this Hector, far more bold and determined than this Mr. Dunwodee. That assassin, that brute *began*, but hesitated. Ah, Hector has not hesitated! Seeing that he would in any case possess myself, would carry me away, I yielded, but with honor and grace, Madame. As between Monsieur Dunwodee and Hector—*il y a une différence*, Madame!"

"*Je crois qu' oui*, Jeanne—*Je le crois*! But it comes to the same thing, eh? You forsake me?"

"Madame, I confess sometimes in my heart there comes a desire for a home, for a place where one may abide, where one may cease to wander."

Josephine sat silent for a moment. In what direction might she herself now turn for even the humblest friendship? And where was any home now for her? The recreant maid saw something of this upon her face.

"Madame," she exclaimed, falling upon her knees in consternation. "To think I would desert you! In my heart resides nothing but loyalty for you. How could you doubt?"

But Josephine was wise in her own way. That night Jeanne kissed her hand dutifully, yet the very next morning she had changed her mind. With sobs, tears, she admitted that she had decided to leave service, no longer to be Jeanne, but Madame Hector Fournier. Thus, at the very time when she most would have needed aid and attendance, Josephine saw herself about to be left alone.

"But, Madame," said Jeanne, still tearful, returning after brief absence from the room, "although I leave now for St. Genevieve to stand before the priest, I shall not see madame left without attendance. See, I have asked of this Lily person,—*la voici*, Madame—if she could take service with madame. Madame plans soon to return to the East. Perhaps this Lily, then—"

"Ma'am, I want to work for you!" broke out Lily suddenly, stretching out her hands. "I don't want to go back home. I want to go with you. I cain't go back home—I'd only run away—again. They'd have to kill me."

Some swift arithmetic was passing through Josephine's mind at the time. Here, then, was concrete opportunity to set in practice some of her theories.

"Lily, would you like to come with me as my maid?" she demanded. "Could you learn, do you think, in case I should need you?"

"Of co'se I could learn, Ma'am. I'd do my very best."

It was thus that it was agreed, with small preliminary, that on the next morning Tallwoods should lose three of its late tenants. Josephine ventured to inquire of Dunwody regarding Lily. "Take her if you like," said he bruskly. "I will arrange the papers for it with Clayton himself. There will be no expense to you. If he wants to sell the girl I'll pay him. No, not a cent from you. Go on, Lily, if you want to. This time you'll get shut of us, I reckon, and we'll get shut of you. I hope you'll never come back, this time. You've made trouble enough already."

Thus, then, on the day of departure, Josephine St. Auban found herself standing before her mirror. It was not an unlovely image which she saw there. In some woman's fashion, assisted by Jeanne's last tearful services and the clumsy art of Lily, she had managed a garbing different from that of her first arrival at this place. The lines of her excellent figure now were wholly shown in this costume of golden brown which she had reserved to the last. Her hair was even glossier than when she first came here to Tallwoods, her cheek of better color. She was almost disconcerted that the trials of the winter had wrought no greater ravages; but after all, a smile was not absent from her lips. Not abolitionist here in the mirror, but a beautiful young woman. Certainly, whichever or whoever she was, she made a picture fit wholly to fill the eyes of the master of Tallwoods when he came to tell her the coach was ready for the journey to St. Genevieve. But he made no comment, not daring.

"See," she said, almost gaily, "I can put on both my gloves." She held out to him her hands.

"They are very small," he replied studiously. He was calm now. She saw he had himself well in hand. His face was pale and grave.

"Well," said she finally, as the great coach drove around to the door, "I suppose I am to say good-by."

"I'll just walk with you down the road," he answered. "We walked up it, once, together."

They followed on, after the coach had passed down the driveway, Dunwody now moody and silent, his head dropped, his hands behind him, until the carriage pulled up and waited at the end of the shut-in at the lower end of the valley. Josephine herself remained silent as well, but as the turn of the road approached which would cut off the view of Tallwoods, she turned impulsively and waved a hand in farewell at the great mansion house which lay back, silent and strong, among the hills.

[Illustration: She waved a hand in farewell.]

He caught the gesture and looked at her quickly. "That's nice of you," said he, "mighty nice."

In some new sort of half-abashment she found no immediate reply. He left her then, and walked steadily back up the driveway, saying nothing in farewell, and not once looking back. For a time she followed him with her gaze, a strange sinking at her heart of which she was ashamed, which gave her alike surprise and sudden fear.

It was a much abashed and still tearful though not a repentant Jeanne who embraced her mistress, after the simple little wedding of Jeanne and Hector, when they had repaired to the wedding feast at the *maison* Fournier.

"But come, Madame," said Jeanne. "Behold my new home. Is it not delightful? This is the mother of Hector, Madame, and this—ah, this is the home of Hector and myself. To-night also it is yours. I am rejoiced. Madame," she added, in an aside, while Lily, stupid and awkward, was for the time out of the way, "I can not bear to think of your going away with but that impossible niggaire there to care for you. Almost—were it not for Hector and for this home—could you take Hector also—I should forget all and go with you even yet. To-morrow I shall go with you to the boat."

But alas! in the morning Jeanne had again forgotten.

When at last the busy little steamer swung inshore, presently to churn her way out again into the current, Josephine went aboard with only the colored girl for her company. Her heart sank strangely, and she felt more lonely than ever in her life before. She leaned against the rail for a time, looking at the banks slip back across the turbid stream. The truth was coming into her heart that it was not with exultation she now was turning back to the East to take up her life again. Something was different now—was it the loss of Jeanne? Again surprise, terror, shame, withal wonder.

CHAPTER XXIII

Meantime, the storm dreaded as so immediate by the administration at Washington—the organization of a new political party, born of the unrest over the slavery question—had spent its force, and, temporarily, long since had muttered away in the distance, leaving scarce a trace behind it on the political sky. Austria, England, the Old World creeds of monarchies arrayed against popular governments, had their way at our capital, where the birth of an actual democracy impended. Active leadership by revolutionists trained in Europe was suppressed, removed; as in one instance we have seen. One abolitionist mass-meeting followed another in those days, but the results of all were much the same. Protests and declamation abounded, plan and leadership lacked. The strained compromise held. Neither war nor a new party came as yet, disunion was not yet openly attempted. Moreover, there was a deliberate intent upon an era of good feeling. Whig and Democrat alike forced themselves to settle down into the belief that peace had come. If men were slaves, why, let them be slaves. At that time the national reflex was less sensitive than it later became with increased telegraphic and news facilities. Washington was not always promptly and exactly advised of the political situation in this or that more remote portion of the country. This very fact, however, meant a greater stability in the political equilibrium. Upon the western borders the feeling of unrest now became most marked; and, more swiftly than was generally recognized, important matters there were going forward; but even in that direction, declared the prophets of peace, all now was more calm than it had been for years.

Six years before this time Mr. Wilkins, secretary of war, had proposed to organize Nebraska Territory and to extend thither the army posts; and in that same year Stephen A. Douglas, then of the House, had introduced a bill for the organization of Nebraska; but neither effort had had result. Two years later, Douglas, then in the Senate, once more sought to test the Squatter Sovereignty idea regarding the new western lands, but once more a cold silence met his attempts. Six months after that time the same bill, with the intent of attaching Nebraska to the state of Arkansas, was killed by Congress, because held to be dangerous. A third bill by Douglas, later in the same year, was also recommitted. The "Territory of the Platte" was the next attempt to be dropped. All these crude attempts were merged in the great Compromise of 1850. The might of party was brought to bear upon all questions of principle, and the country was commanded to be calm; indeed for a time was calm. It was the time of manacled hands and of manacled minds. Our government was not a real democracy. The great West had not yet raised its voice, augmented by new millions of voices pealing the paean of liberty and opportunity for man.

In this era of arrested activities, the energies of a restless people turned otherwise for interest. To relieve the monotony of political stagnation, popular attention was now turned toward the affairs of Hungary. We could not solve our own problems, but we were as ready to solve those of Europe as Europe was to offer us aid in ours. Therefore, instant interest attached to the news that a Hungarian committee of inquiry had landed upon our shores, with the purpose of investigating a possible invitation from our republic to the Hungarian patriot, Kossuth, then in exile in Turkey.

The leader of this mission was General Zewlinski, an officer of the patriot army of Hungary, who brought with him a suite of some dozen persons. These, late in the winter of 1850-51, arrived at Washington and found quarters of somewhat magnificent sort in one of the more prominent hotels of the national capital. At once political and journalistic Washington was on the *qui vive*. The Hungarians became the object of a solicitude, not to say a curiosity, which must at times have tried their souls.

The first formal action of the Hungarian committee took the shape of a return reception, to be held in the hotel parlors. The invitations, liberal as they were, were sought for quite in excess of the supply, and long before the doors were open, it was quite assured that the affair would be a crush. The administration, for which Mr. Webster, our secretary of state, had not hesitated to write in most determined fashion to the attache Hulsemann regarding the presumptuous Austrian demands upon our government, none the less was much in a funk regarding "European obligations." Not wishing to offend the popular fancy, and not daring to take decisive stand, the usual compromise was made. Although no member of the administration was sent officially to recognize these unofficial ambassadors, a long suffering officer of the navy, with his wife and one or two other ladies, were despatched quasi-officially to lend color to the occasion.

Such splendor as could be arranged had been provided for the setting of this event. A Hungarian orchestra, brought with these commissioners, discoursed its peculiar music beyond a screen of palms and flowers. One of the great parlors had been prepared for those of the young who could not resist the temptation to dance. At the head of the little line of these visitors, now themselves in effect hosts, stood the old Hungarian general, Zewlinski, an officer over six feet in height, with white hair and wide white mustaches, a distinguished figure in the brilliant Hungarian uniform. Those of his staff near by added additional vividness to the picture. The ladies of the party, half of whom spoke English, were costumed quite in keeping, and endeavored by the graciousness of their manner to add to the good impression already formed by their more brilliant companions. Here and there the more sober uniform of an American army or navy officer might have been seen, brought thither on demand of his lady. The ladies themselves were out in force, and in their most brilliant array. The doors had not been opened for a half hour before all prophecies were more than fulfilled. The rooms were packed with a struggling mass of humanity, all eager to grasp the hand of the representative of Hungary and of the members of his company. Patriotism, liberty, brotherly love were in the speech of all. Never has our country been more full of zeal for liberty than then, never more inconsistent, never more swiftly forgetful.

In these circumstances, the somewhat bewildered commissioners did what they could graciously to discover to all their friendly feeling toward this country. For more than an hour they stood in line, bowing, smiling, accepting hands, offering greetings, a little wondering perhaps, yet none the less well assured of the attitude of this people toward their own country, and hoping there might later be substantial financial proof of its sincerity.

It was at about this time that there entered at the door near the head of the receiving line a young woman, for the time apparently quite unattended. She was brilliantly robed, with jewels flashing at neck and wrists, clad like a queen and looking one. Of good height and splendid carriage, her dark hair and singularly striking features might at first have caused the belief that she was one of this party of foreigners, toward whom she now advanced. A second glance would have shown her beauty to be of that universal world-quality which makes its owner difficult to classify, although assured of approval in any quarter of the world.

[Illustration: Clad like a queen and looking one.]

That this lady was acquainted with social pageants might have been in the first instant quite evidenced by her comportment here. Many eyes turned toward her as she approached the head of the line. She was unconscious of all, lazily, half-insolently observant, yet wholly unconcerned. Some observers choked back a sudden exclamation. A hush fell in the great room, then followed a low buzzing of curious or interested, wise or ignorant human bees.

There were many in Washington social circles who knew by sight or by reputation Josephine, Countess St. Auban, no longer than six months ago pronounced by one journal of the capital to be the most beautiful and the most dangerous woman in Washington. Yet even the most hostile of these suddenly suspended judgment as they saw her advance met now by that of the old Hungarian general himself. With the enthusiasm of a boy he fell upon her, both his hands extended.

"Countess—my dear child—at last you are here!" he exclaimed. Taking her by the hand he led her back to the line of his official company, volleying rapid exclamations in his native tongue. Eager groups fell into line near at hand, seeking to know what was toward.

"You left us!" at length exclaimed the old general, politely speaking in his best English, since these others were thus bound to hear. "Where you had gone we did not know. It was as though the heavens had opened. See then, Sir,"—he addressed the naval officer who stood near at hand—"the Countess St. Auban was one of the most important members of our little company—she was to come in advance of us, who also are in advance of a greater number. For a time we heard from her, then all was silent! She had disappeared!—But now, at last, my dear Countess, you are here! We shall succeed, it is certain; henceforth you will be of our party. Is it not true?"

Political, social and journalistic Washington then and there begged a sudden though silent pardon of the Countess St. Auban. A few journalists left the room quickly. An attache of the Austrian legation also hurriedly took his leave.

"But where have you been, my dear?" again demanded General Zewlinski, his hand again affectionately grasping that of Josephine St. Auban. "We have so missed you."

"I have been visiting some of the more remote parts of this country," replied she in even tones.

"So, then, you have not forgotten our mission from Hungary! Well, now we shall surely have the invitation for our Kossuth to come? Is it not true?"

"Assuredly, my dear General. You will find this country eager to meet him. But alas! I fear that Kossuth himself will find problems also in this country."

"Our own problem—our cause, dear Countess?"

"Pardon, General, really it is also the cause of this country. We think that in Hungary democracy is in peril. It is not less so here."

"But, my dear child, you would not cast doubt upon our plans,—you have not become lukewarm to our cause so soon, my dear?"

"No, no, General. But Europe does not understand America. America does not understand herself. I ask only that the great men of that country shall see the great problems of this. There we could win freedom by sword and gun. Here also that must yet be done. The time for such means has not yet arrived. Yet here also evil cries aloud. Soon war must come, here also—bloody war.

We ask funds for Hungary. America soon will need funds for herself."

"Ah, you mean this problem of the North and South—of slavery." The face of the old general became grave. "I have talked with many," said he. "It seems incapable of solution. But have not your brilliant faculties, my dear Countess, suggested any solution? We learned to value your counsel over yonder."

"What could a mere woman do in a matter vast as this? My General, not all the wisdom of this country has suggested a remedy. I am but a woman and not wise. He who attempts to solve this slavery question must do what no statesman in all history has been able to do, what human wisdom here has failed to do for fifty years or more. America has spent thirty years of statesmanship on this one question, and is just where it started. This country, as Thomas Jefferson said so long ago, still has the wolf by the ear, but has not killed it and dare not let it go. Out there—where I have been—in the West—there the new battle must be fought. Now, my General, what difference, whether America shall help Europe. or Europe shall help America? The battle for democracy must be fought, in this generation, perhaps again in the next. What would be the result of that war, if either section won to the destruction of this Union? Ah! *there*, my General, is the danger to Hungary, the danger to Europe, to the cause of freedom and humanity. As I said, Kossuth will find things here to engage his best attention."

"I know your generosity," said Zewlinski, swiftly leading her apart and gazing her straight in the face as he spoke, in low tones none else might hear. "I know how you got your estates yonder—how wide handed you have been with your revenues. I know your strange, unhappy life, my dear. But have a care. Do not make that life more unhappy. Do not let your penitence, your devotion, your self-abnegation, carry you too far. Listen; times are very troublous abroad. The nations are banding against us—even France. He who gives may take. Let me tell you, be careful. Do not involve yourself. Do not jeopardize the good will of Louis Napoleon. Do not let your warm heart endanger your own good fortune."

She laughed almost gaily. "You suggest an idea, my General!" she said. "I still am rich. Since I advocate a measure, why should I not enforce it to the best of my ability? Let Louis Napoleon do as he likes with the widow of a man he murdered! Bring over our friend Louis Kossuth, General, as soon as you like! Meantime, I shall be busy here, seeking to set on foot certain little plans of my own."

"My child, you will be lost! Forget these matters. Come back with us to our own country. You are young, you are beautiful. You are a woman. As a patriot we love you, but you are a woman, and we would not rob you of your life. You are young. You did not love old St. Auban, who took you from your

American mother. You did not love him—but you will love some other—some young, strong man. Many have sought your hand, my dear."

"You call me a lost child, General? Ah, you remember the term! At many battles there is what is known as the forlorn hope—those whom the French call *Les enfants perdus*—The Lost Children. Perhaps they perish. But at the next battle, at the crucial time, they rise again from the dead. Always there is the band of the Lost Children, ready to do what must be done. And always, at the last moment, are battles won by those who remain devoted, whatever be the cause."

Zewlinski nodded his gray head gravely. "It was thus my own sons died in battle," said he. "It was as I would have had it. But you—you are a woman! These things are not for you."

"See," she interrupted, gently tapping his arm with her fan. "We must not be too much apart. Let us return."

As they turned back toward the head of the line, Josephine gave a half-exclamation. Two figures were approaching, each of which seemed to her familiar. An instant later she had recognized the young northern officer, Carlisle, whom she had met under such singular conditions. With him stalked the tall young German, Kammerer. Their eyes lighted suddenly, as they fell upon her, and both advanced eagerly. There was new dignity in her carriage now, but she greeted them warmly.

[Illustration: Two figures were approaching.]

"When we may, I shall hope to compare notes with you," she smiled. "You are still on parole to me."

"But you, Madam—you seem differently situated here. I am very glad to find it so." Carlisle was eager, flushed, frankly admiring.

"Yes, I scarce know which side the sea I belong. You know, I am half American, though my people lived abroad, in diplomatic work. By President Taylor I was chosen as one of the members of the Hungarian commission sent over by America to look into the cause of Hungary. In return, last year I had the honor of being asked to come to this country as one of the commission despatched to America in the interest of Hungary. I came over a certain time in advance, for reasons of my own. Meantime, I have had, it seems—well, call them adventures! I am not eager they should be known here. But if you like, you may call on me at my hotel—to-morrow?"

Both recognized a slight additional trace of hauteur in the deportment of the woman whom they now accosted. She herself saw a sort of hesitation on the part of Carlisle.

"I can't let you make any mistake about me," he began presently.

"How do you mean?"

"You are probably not advised about me. I'm a person of no consequence."

"An officer of his country's army can not say that of himself."

"But, I am no longer an officer of any army. I have been court-martialed—for my conduct there—you know—that fight at St. Genevieve. My abolitionist tendencies have always made me *persona non grata* in my own mess. There's been all sort of pressure brought on me to drop it. Now the government itself, not wishing these things to come to a focus, has ordered me to a court-martial. Very well, I've been sentenced. My parole is ended, for the law has acted on my conduct. Rather than go back many steps in rank, I have thrown up my commission. This morning I resigned. I am wearing my uniform, I don't doubt, for the last time."

"And that, although you fought in the cause of freedom! Although you have fought honorably in an earlier war! Is it not horrible!"

"I could not do otherwise," said he simply. "I have no regrets."

"But don't you see,"—she turned upon him suddenly—"it only leaves you all the more free!"

"I can not understand you."

"Will it not give you and your friend, Lieutenant Kammerer here, precisely the opportunity you've wished?"

"Still I do not follow you."

"My dear Countess," ventured the German, "I'll go anywhere under your orders. You may be sure of that."

She turned from them. "Come to my hotel, will you not, to-morrow? I may have something to say to you." Thus she passed back into the throng, and into the arms of fickle and repentant Washington, which marveled when she danced, flushed, excited, yet absorbed, with the gallant old general, himself intoxicated by the music and by all this warm talk of freedom, of equality, of democracy,—in Washington!

CHAPTER XXIV

In her apartments at the hotel the following morning Josephine St. Auban looked over the journals of the day. There were many columns of description of the only social event of the previous day thought worth extended mention. The visitors from Hungary were lauded to the skies. There did not lack many references to the similarity between the present struggles of the Hungarian people and those of our own earlier days. A vast amount of rampant Americanism was crowded into all these matters.

[Illustration: She looked over the journals of the day.]

Joined to this, there was considerable mention of the reappearance in Washington society of the beautiful Countess, Josephine St. Auban, now discovered to have been originally a member of this Hungarian commission, and recently journeying in the western states of the republic. This beautiful countess was now invested with a romantic history. She was a friend and protegee of the old General Zewlinski, a foreign noblewoman half American by birth, of rank, wealth and distinction, who had taken a leading part in the cause of Hungary in her struggle with the oppressing monarchies. Without any reference to earlier stories not unknown to them, and bolder as to Austria than those who then dwelt in the White House, the newspapers now openly and unanswerably welcomed this distinguished stranger to the heart of Washington. Unknowingly, when they gave her this publicity, they threw around her also protection, secrecy. As she read, the Countess St. Auban smiled. She knew that now there would be no second vehmgerichte. The government now would not dare!

What interested her more was the story at that time made current, of an unsuccessful attempt which had been made by a southern slave owner to reclaim his property in a northern state. The facts recounted that a planter of Maryland, with two relatives, had followed an escaped slave to the settlement of Christianville, Pennsylvania, where a little colony of fugitives had made common cause together. In this case, as was prescribed under the law, the slave owner had called to his aid a United States marshal, who in turn had summoned a large posse of his own. These had visited the home of the fugitive and called upon him to surrender himself to his owner. This the fugitive had refused to do, and he was backed in this refusal by a considerable party of men of his own race, some of them free men, and some fugitive slaves, who had assembled at his house.

"I'll have my property," asserted the slave owner, according to the report, "or I'll eat my breakfast in hell." One of the Marylanders had then fired upon the slave, and the fire was returned in general by the negroes. The old planter, a man of courage, was struck to the ground, killed by the blacks, his two relatives disabled, and several other men on both sides were wounded. The fugitive himself was not taken, and the arresting party was obliged to retire. Naturally, great exultation prevailed among the triumphant blacks; and this, so said numerous despatches, was fostered and encouraged by comment of all the northern abolitionist press.

Josephine St. Auban pondered over this barbarous recountal of an event which would seem to have been impossible in a civilized community. "It comes," said she, musing, "it comes! *Ca ira*! There will be war! Ah, I must hasten."

She turned to other papers, of private nature, in her desk. In a half hour more, she had gone over the last remittance reports of the agents of her estates in Europe. She smiled, nodded, as she tapped a pencil over the very handsome totals. In ten minutes more, she was ready and awaiting the call of Carlisle and Kammerer in her reception-room. In her mind was a plan already formulated.

At heart frank and impulsive, and now full of a definite zeal, she did not long keep them waiting to learn her mind.

"Are you still for the cause of freedom, and can you keep a secret, or aid in one?" she broke in suddenly, turning toward Carlisle. Looking at him at first for a time, inscrutably, as though half in amusement or in recollection, she now regarded him carefully for an instant, apparently weighing his make-up, estimating his sincerity, mentally investigating his character, looking at the flame of his hair, the fanatic fire of his deep set eye.

"I have sometimes done so," he smiled. "Is there anything in which I can be of service?"

"Time is short," was her answer. "Let us get at once to the point. I am planning to go into the work long carried on by that weak-minded Colonization Society; but on certain lines of my own."

"Explain, Countess!"

"It is my belief that we should deport the blacks from this country. Very well, I am willing to devote certain moneys and certain energies to that purpose. Granted I found it advisable and could obtain proper support, I might perhaps not return to Hungary for a time."

"Kammerer!" broke in Carlisle suddenly, "Listen! Do you hear? It's what we've said! It is precisely what you yourself have always said."

"That iss it!—that iss it!" exclaimed the young German. "The colonization—remoof them from this country to another, where they shall be by themselves. That only iss wise, yess. Elsewise must great war come—else must this Union be lost! Ah, Madam; ah, Madam! How great your heart, your mind. I kiss your hand."

"Listen!" she interrupted. "There are about three and one-third millions of them now. Say they are worth, old and young, large and little, one thousand dollars a head—monstrous thing, to put a price upon a human head, but suppose it. It would amount to but a few billions of dollars. What would a war cost between these two sections? Perhaps a million dollars a day! How much cheaper could these slaves be purchased and deported from these shores! Their owners regard them as property. The laws protect that belief. The Constitution establishes the laws. There is no peaceful way to end the turmoil, save by the purchase of these people. That is a solution. It will prevent a war. Let them be sent away to a place where they belong, rather than here."

"My dear Countess," said Carlisle, "you are, as usual, brilliant. Your imagination vaults—your daring is splendid. But as usual you are visionary and impractical. Buy them? To do this would require the credit of a nation! It would be subversive of all peace and all industry. You do not realize the sums required. You do not realize how vast are the complications."

She stepped closer to him in her eagerness.

"All it needs is money, and management. A start, and the country will follow. Mr. Fillmore himself was about to recommend it, in his last message. Let me furnish the money, and do you attend to the complications."

Carlisle rubbed his chin thoughtfully. "It's beautiful; it may be wise, but it's impossible. It would take a king's credit."

"At least we might begin with such funds as are already at hand," smiled the Countess St. Auban. "It might be difficult? I suppose the building of the pyramids was difficult. Yet they were begun. Yet they are finished. Yet they stand, complete, to-day."

"It is hardly for me to advise in a case so grave as that," said Carlisle. "I should not undertake it. Have you really considered?"

"I have often followed over the same old course of reasoning, South against North," she said, smiling at him. "Come now, a revolutionist and two abolitionists should do much. You still can fight, though they have taken away your sword."

"Some say that the courts will settle these mooted points," Carlisle went on; "others, that Congress must do so. Yet others are unwilling that even the courts should take it up, and insist that the Constitution is clear and explicit already. These Southerners say that Congress should make an end to it, by specifically declaring that men have a right to take into any new country what they lawfully own—that is to say, these slaves; because that territory was bought in common by North and South. The South is just as honest and sincere as the North is, and to be fair about it, I don't believe it's right to claim that the South wants the Union destroyed. A few hotheads talk of that in South Carolina, in Mississippi, but that is precisely what the sober judgment of the South doesn't desire. Let us match those secessionists against the abolitionists," he grinned. "The first think they have law back of them. The latter know they have none!"

"No," she said, "only the higher law, that of human democracy. No,—we've nothing concrete—except Lily!"

"Yes, but let me argue you out of this, Countess. Really, I can see no just reason why the proud and prosperous North should wish to destroy the proud and prosperous South. If the South remains in the Union it must be considered a part of the Union. New England did not believe in taxation without representation. Ought it to enforce that doctrine on the South?"

"You argue it very well, Sir, as well as any one can. The only trouble is that you are not convinced, and you do not convince. You are trying to protect me, that's all. I have no answer—except Lily! There are some things in the analysis from which you shrink. Isn't it true?"

"Yes, altogether true. We always come back to the bitter and brutal part of slavery. But what are we going to do for remedy? Anarchy doesn't suggest remedy. For my own part, sometimes I think that Millard Fillmore's idea was right—that the government should buy these slaves and deport them. That would be, as you say, far cheaper than a war. It was the North that originally sold most of the slaves. If they, the South, as half the country, are willing to pay back their half of the purchase price, ought not the North to be satisfied with that? That's putting principles to the hardest test—that of the pocket."

In his excitement he rose and strode about the room, his face frowning, his slender figure erect, martial even in its civilian dress. Presently he turned; "But it is noble of you, magnificent, to think of doing what a government hesitates to do! And a woman!"

"Could it be done?" she demanded. "It would require much money. But what a noble solution it would be!"

"Precisely. I rejoice to see that your mind is so singularly clear although your heart is so kind."

"You speak in the voice of New England."

"Yes, yes, I'm a New Englander. She's glorious in her principles, New England, but she carries her principles in her pocket! I admire your proposed solution, but that solution I fear you will never see. It is the fatal test, that of the pocket." But the idea had hold of him, and would not let him go. He walked up and down, excited, still arguing against it.

"The South, frankly, has always been juggled out of its rights, all along the line—through pocket politics—and I'm not sure how much more it can endure of the same sort of juggling. Why, John Quincy Adams himself, Northerner that he was, admitted that Missouri had the right to come in as a slave state, just as much as had Arkansas and Louisiana. Pocket-politics allowed Congress to trade all of the Louisiana Purchase south of thirty-six degrees, thirty minutes, excepting Arkansas, in exchange for the Floridas— and how much chance, how much lot and part had the Missourians in a country so far away as Florida? The South led us to war with Mexico in order to extend our territory, but what did the South get? The North gets all the great commercial and industrial rights. Just to be frank and fair about it, although I am a New Englander and don't believe in slavery, the truth is, the South has paid its share in blood and risk and money, but it didn't get its share when it came to the divide; and it never has."

"Precisely, my dear Captain. I delight to see you so broad-minded and fair. This plan of mine, to have any success, must be carried out on lines broad-minded and fair."

"But how adjust pocket interests on both sides? You'll see. You'll be left alone. It is easier to make a speech for liberty than it is to put the price of one slave in the hat passed for liberty. New England, all the North, will talk, will hold mass meetings, will pass resolutions commending resistance to the law —like this Christianville incident of which there's news this morning. You'll see the blacks commended for that. But you won't see much money raised to keep other blacks from being followed by their owners."

"Then leave it for those who see duty in more concrete form. Leave the cost to me. My only answer is—Lily."

And again and again her only answer to them both was—Lily. She told them her story, produced the girl herself and made her confirm it, offered her as concrete example to be presented in a platform campaign which might not end in talk alone—pleaded, argued, and won.

"Madam, I, too, kiss your hands," said Carlisle at last; and did so.

An hour after that, she had laid out a campaign for her two agents, and had arranged for the expenditure of an initial hundred thousand dollars.

CHAPTER XXV

It was dusk. Heavy shadows lay over the trees which lined the curving walks leading across a little park to the stately white house beyond. From that direction now appeared several gentlemen, advancing in scattering groups. They might almost have been made up of conspirators, so intent they seemed, so apprehensive lest even their thoughts might be read. Two of them drew apart,—one of these a slender bony man, the other a tall and dark man. The latter spoke almost moodily.

"I doubt your ability, my dear sir, to influence so shrewd a man in any such way as you suggest. Besides, he is not of our party."

"That's all the better. A man of our party might, could, would and should keep his mouth shut about such a ticklish matter; but outside our party, any who begins it has got to keep his mouth shut!"

"There is no other way," he added, smiling. "It must be done. The Countess St. Auban is here again! This band of Gipsy heathens from Hungary is also here. The country is wild over Kossuth. We'll have to accept this invitation to invite him! But Austria remains bitter against the countess. What we must do is to have her go back home with these commissioners from Hungary. There's ugly talk about the way she's been used. That fellow Carlisle—good riddance of him from the army—even confessed he engaged in a game of cards—" their heads bent together—"in short, the devil is to pay with the administration if this gets out. We can't banish her again. But how can we with dignity even it with her, so she will make no talk? If she likes, she can ruin us, because Carlisle can't be kept silent, now he's out of the army. And he's crazy over her, anyhow."

"So? I do not blame him."

"Yes. Therefore, since all of us have lacked wisdom in our own camp, we'd e'en do well to take wisdom where we can find it."

They parted, the last speaker presently to hail the nearest carriage. The driver a few moments later drew up at the front of a spacious and dignified brick building, whose reserved look might have pronounced it a private hotel or a club for gentlemen. The visitor seemed known, the door swinging open for him.

[Illustration: They parted, the last speaker hailing a carriage.]

156

"Louis," said he to the attendant, "is Mr. —— in?" He mentioned a name which even then was well known in Washington.

"I think you will find him in the reading-room, Sir," was the answer.

The inquirer passed to the right, entering a wide room with tables, books, heavy chairs, discreetly shaded lamps. At one table, drawn close to the light and poring over a printed page, sat a gentleman whose personality was not without distinction. The gray hair brushed back from a heightening forehead might have proclaimed him even beyond middle age, and his stature, of about medium height, acknowledged easy living in its generous habit. The stock and cravat of an earlier day gave a certain austerity to the shrewd face, lighted by a pair of keen gray eyes, which now turned to greet the new-comer. He rose, and both bowed formally before they advanced to take each other by the hand. They were acquaintances, if not intimate friends. Evidently this particular club no more enlisted its members from this or that political party than did either of the leading parties call upon any certain section for their membership.

"I am fortunate to find you here in Washington, my dear Sir," began the gentleman from Kentucky. "It is something of a surprise."

The wrinkles about the other's eyes deepened in an affable smile. "True," said he, "in the last twelve years I have three times sought to get back into Washington! Perhaps it would have been more seemly for me to remain in the decreed dignified retirement."

They joined in a laugh at this, as they both drew up chairs at the table side.

"You see," resumed the last speaker, "I am not indeed intruding here in national affairs, but only choose Washington for to-night. I have been thinking of a pleasure journey into the West, down the Ohio River—"

"Will you have snuff?" began his companion. "This is no import, I assure you, but is made by one of my old darkeys, on my plantation in Kentucky. He declares he puts nothing into it but straight leaf."

"My soul!" exclaimed the other, sneezing violently. "I suspect the veracity of your darkey. It is red pepper that he uses!"

"All the better, then, to clear our minds, my dear Sir. But let me first send for another product of my state, to assuage these pains." He beckoned to a servant, who presently, returned with tray and glasses.

"And now," he resumed, "what you say of your journey interests me immensely. No doubt you propose going down the river as far as Missouri?

The interest of the entire country is focused there to-day. Ah, yonder is the crux of all our compromise! Safe within the fold herself, that is to say above the fatal line of thirty-six degrees, thirty minutes, her case is simply irresistible in interest to-day, both for those who argue for and those who talk against the extension of slavery into our other territories."

"Yet your administration, to-day, my dear Sir, calls this 'finality.' Believe me, it is no more than a compromise with truth and justice! The entire North demands that slavery shall halt."

"The entire South refuses it!"

"Then let the South beware!"

"The North also may beware, my dear Sir!"

"We are aware, and we are prepared. Not another inch for slavery!"

"Hush!" said the other, raising a hand. "Not even you and I dare go into this. The old quarrel is lulled for a time. At last we have worked these measures through both the House and Senate. In the House the administration can put through at any time the Wilmot proviso prohibiting slavery, and although the Senate always has and always can defeat such a measure, both branches, and the executive as well, have agreed to put this dog to sleep when possible, and when found sleeping, to let him lie. My dear friend, it is not a question of principle, but of policy, to-day."

"Principles should rule policies!" exclaimed the other virtuously.

"Agreed! Agreed! We are perfectly at one as to that. But you know that Webster himself reiterates again and again that no man should set up his conscience above the law of his country. Your Free Soil party means not law, but anarchy,—and worse than that—it means disunion! Clay, Cass, Webster, Benton, even the hottest of the men from Mississippi and South Carolina, are agreed on that. My dear Sir, I say it with solemn conviction, the formation of a new party of discontent to-day, when everything is already strained to breaking, will split this country and plunge the divided sections into a bloody war!"

The other sat gravely for a time before he made reply. "Our people feel too sternly to be reconciled. We need some new party—"

Again the other raised a warning hand. "*Do not say that word*! Others have principles as much as you and I. Let us not speak with recklessness of consequences. But, privately, and without hot argument, my dear friend, the singular thing to me is that you, an old leader of the people, with a wide following in the North and South, should now be entertaining precisely the same principles— though not expressing them with the same reckless fervor —which are advanced by the latest and most dangerous abolitionist of the time."

"You do not mean Mr. Garrison? Any of my New York or Boston friends?"

"No, I mean a *woman*, here in Washington. You could perhaps guess her name."

The other drew his chair closer. "I presume you mean the lady reputed to have been connected with President Taylor's commission, of inquiry into affairs in Hungary—"

"Yes,—the 'most beautiful woman in Washington to-day.' So she is called by some—'the most dangerous,' by others."

"Has Kentucky forgotten its gallantry so fully as that? Rumor has reported the young woman to me as a charming young widow, of beauty, wealth and breeding."

"Yes, manners, and convictions, and courage—abolitionist tendencies and fighting proclivities. She is a firebrand—a revolutionist, fresh back from the Old World, and armed with weapons of whose use we old fogies are utterly ignorant. Having apparently nothing to lose whose loss she dreads, she is careless of all consequences. You, my dear Sir, speak of your moral adherence to some new party. You consider yourself one of the lamented Free Soil party, and hope a resurrection. This woman does not pause there—no. She comes here to Washington, at precisely the time of our final compromise, when all is peaceful, even slumberous,—and she preaches the crusade of fire and sword. My dear friend, if you seek a prophet, here is one; and if you want leadership in your dogma of no slavery north of thirty-six degrees, thirty minutes, here is prophet and leader in one!—And, believe me, one with arguments which make her dangerous to one man, two men, or any collection of men."

The other pondered. "I have never seen the lady," he remarked, at length. "Is she acquainted among the abolitionists of the North?"

"No. She trains in no one's camp. Indeed, socially she has been neglected in the North, for reasons said to have been urged in diplomatic circles."

"Something of an intrigante, eh?"

"At least enough to excite the anger and suspicion of Austria, the interest of England, the concern of France;—that's all!"

"Of what age is she?"

"Of about that age, my dear Sir, which our children or grandchildren might claim. I should say, twenty-three, twenty-four,—not over twenty-six, perhaps.

It is difficult to say. I have met her but rarely."

"You have me at disadvantage, even so," smiled the other. "It is, however, unnecessary for you to settle your cravat. It is quite straight; and besides, I think we are quite safe from intrusion of women here."

"You have never met this fair enthusiast? You are behind the times!" retorted the wily Kentuckian. "Perhaps you would like that honor? I think it could be arranged. Indeed," he added, after a moment spent in careful study of his companion's face, "I would even undertake to arrange it. My dear Sir, with your well known charm of manner with men, and women as well, you could in that case win the lasting plaudits of your country, if you but possessed the resolution!"

"In a cause so noble, I would do what I might! But what is the cause? And is it proper for one of my place to engage in it?"

"You could, I say, be hailed by the administration in power, not as the Father of your Country, perhaps, but as its savior. Take this woman out of our camp, and into your own. Flock your own fowl together, you Free Soilers! Take her out of Washington, get her back to Europe—where she belongs,—and, without jesting, my dear Sir, you shall have the backing next year, two years hence—in 1853,—any time you like—of the men who make this administration, and of the men behind this compromise. A majority of the House, an even division of the Senate—Listen, my dear friend, this is not idle talk, and these are no idle promises! I am serious. I speak to you in no wise ill-advised. To tell you the truth, we are frightened. She has stolen all our peace of mind, and stolen also some of our thunder—some of our cast-off and unthundered thunder."

"In what way?"

"Oh, nothing. It is of very little consequence. It is a bagatelle. All she proposes to do is to purchase all the slaves in the United States—out of her own funds—and ship them out of America."

"Great God!"

"Yes. We didn't dare it. She does. We didn't begin. She has begun. And since it has begun, who knows what army of the people—what *new party*—may fall in behind her? We want you to forestall all that. We don't want you to head that new party. We think you will do better to fall in with us, to accept the compliment of a European mission—and to take this fair firebrand with you. We are afraid to have her in Washington."

The other listened with a flicker of the eyelid, which showed his interest, but feigned lightness in his speech.

"In matters of gallantry, my dear friend, why does Kentucky need a substitute, or even an ally?"

"Kentucky, in the deference due to so great a man as yourself, yields to New York! Will you have snuff, Sir?"

"I thank you, I think not. But tell me, what is it that New York must do?"

"New York, my dear Sir, must transport, man-handle, murder, wheedle, bowstring, drown, and permanently lose Josephine, Countess St. Auban,— herself late back from Missouri, formerly of God knows where. I promise you, this country is only a tinder box, waiting for that sort of spark. To-morrow—but you remember, my dear Horatio!"

"But between now and to-morrow is rather a brief period. We have not yet invented means of traveling through the air. I could not well carry off this fair lady by main strength. My own plans unfortunately require some attention. And I think that, even were the trifling difficulty of the lady's consent overcome, I could not easily assume the role of savior of my country before the time of the departure of the next ship for Europe—even granted my enemies, the Whigs, will give a mission to an ex-Democrat and a Free Soiler like myself!"

"Not that I should not experience the most pleasureable emotions both in saving the country, my dear Sir," he saluted with his glass, "and of saving it in the company of so charming a person as this young lady is reported to be. The years have laid us under a certain handicap, my friend. Yet were this lady quite unattached, or her duena not wholly impossible, one might consider the distinguished role of disinterestedly saving one's country in the capacity at least of chaperon."

They looked at each other, and broke into laughter. Yet minds so keen as theirs long before them had read between lines on the printed page, under the outward mask of human countenances.

"Stranger things have happened!" said the gentleman from Kentucky.

"My soul and body' My dear Sir, you do not speak seriously?" His surprise was feigned, and the other knew it.

"I was never so serious in my life. My friend, it seems almost as though fate had guided me to your side to-night. At this time, when our diplomacy abroad is none too fortunate, and when our diplomacy at home is far more delicate and dangerous, you yourself, known the country over as a man of tact and delicacy, are the one man in the world to handle this very mission. It is the Old Fox of the North, after all, Free Soiler or not, who alone can smooth down matters for us. Our country had supreme confidence in you. This administration has such confidence still. It will give all that is seemly for one of your station to accept. It will not ask aught of party lines, this or that."

"Do you speak with authority other than your own?"

"It is not yet time for me to answer that."

"Yet you dare approach one who is in the opposing camp."

"But one whose camp we either hope to join, or whom we hope later to have in our own. Who can tell where party lines will fall in the next three years? All the bars may be down by then, and many a fence past mending."

"For the sake of harmony, much should be ventured."

"Excellent words, Sir."

"One owes a certain duty to one's country at any time."

"Still more excellent."

"And political success can be obtained best through union and not disunion of political forces."

"Most excellent of all! We rejoice to hear the voice of New York speaking in the old way."

"My faith, I believe you are serious in this! Have you really formulated any plans?" He was safe in the trap, and the other knew it.

"Sir, I will not discredit you by choosing methods. As to the results desired, I say no more."

"Yet we sit here and discuss this matter as though we contemplated a simple, proper and dignified act!"

"Murder is perhaps not legal, even for the sake of one's country. But suppose we halt this side of murder. Suppose that by means known only to yourself, and not even to myself, you gained this young woman's *free consent* to accompany you, say, to Europe—that would be legal, dignified, proper—and ah! so useful."

"And rather risky!"

"And altogether interesting."

"And quite impossible."

"Altogether impossible. Oh, utterly!"

"Quite utterly!"

They spoke with gravity. What the gentleman from New York really thought lay in his unvoiced question: "Could it by any possibility be true that the Fillmore administration would give me support for the next nomination if I agree to swing the Free Soil vote nearer to the compromise?" What the gentleman from Kentucky asked in his own mind, was this:

"Will he play fair with us, or will he simply make this an occasion to break into our ranks?" What they both did was to break out into laughter at least feignedly hearty. The Kentuckian resolved to put everything upon one hazard.

"I was just saying," he remarked, "that we have been told the adorable countess perhaps contemplates only a short visit in America after all. She might be easy to lead back to Europe, If necessary, you shall have a dignified errand made for you abroad—entirely what you yourself would call fitting. You must see to that. Your reward will come somewhere this side of Heaven."

"Again you have forgotten about—"

"I have forgotten nothing, and to show you that I speak with authority, I will tell you this: Within the hour the Countess St. Auban will leave her entertainment at the theater and return to her hotel. You see, we are advised of all her movements. We give you an hour to meet her at her hotel; an hour to persuade her. There the curtain drops.

"No one in Washington or in New York seeks to look beyond that curtain," he concluded slowly. "No one counsels you what to do, and indeed, no one can suggest. Only take this woman away, and lose her,—that is all! A few days or weeks will do, but for ever would be better. It is no light errand that is offered to you, and we are not fools or children to look at this altogether lightly. There is risk, and there is no security. Customarily the rewards of large risks and poor security are great—when there are any rewards."

[Illustration: "Only take this woman away and lose her."]

The gentleman from Kentucky rose as he spoke and, adroit in managing men, reached out his hand as though to take the other's and so to clench the matter. Yet his heart leaped in surprise—a surprise which did not leave him wholly clear as to the other's motives—when the latter met his hand with so hearty a grasp of affirmation.

"It should not be so difficult," he said. "It is only a case of logical argument. It is long since I have addressed the people, or addressed a lady, but I shall try my skill once more to-night! All that is necessary is to explain to this young lady that our political ambitions are quite the same, and that I might be of service did we share the same public means of travel in a Journey already planned by both. I was intending a visit to Europe this very summer."

"Sir, there is no other man owner both of the skill and courage to handle this matter. I hesitated to put it before you, but the method you suggest seems almost plausible. I trust you to make it appear wholly so to the fair lady herself."

"We might be younger and fare better at that sort of thing."

"Altogether to the contrary, my friend! Do not mistake this lady. Youth would be an absolute bar to success. Age, dignity, a public reputation such as yours, —these are the only things which by any possibility could gain success; and, frankly, even these may fail. At least, I honestly wish you success, and there has been no jest in what I said about the support of Mr. Fillmore's family and his party. You know that there is honesty even in politics, sometimes; and there is silence, I promise that. Take my advice. Put her in a sack, drop her overboard in mid-ocean. In return, all I ask of you is not to throw overboard the sack anywhere close to this country's shore! It was done once before, on the Ohio River, but the sack was not tied tightly enough. Here she is again! Wherefore, have a care with your sack strings, I beseech you.

"Louis, my hat; and get my carriage! Have a second carriage waiting here at once."

CHAPTER XXVI

THE DISTINGUISHED GENTLEMAN FROM NEW YORK

Meantime, the Countess St. Auban, innocent of these plans which had gone forward regarding her, completed her attendance at the entertainment which the evening was offering the elite of Washington, and in due time arrived at the entrance of her hotel. She found the private entrance to-night occupied by the usual throng, but hurried from the carriage step across the pavement and through the open door.

She made no ordinary picture now as she approached the brighter lights of the interior. Her garb, cut in that fashion which gave so scant aid to nature's outlines, was widely though not extremely hooped, the fabric of daintily flowered silk. As she pushed back the deep, double fronted dolman which served her for a wrap, her shoulders showed white and beautiful, as also the round column of her neck, shadowed only by one long drooping curl, and banded by a gleaming circlet of many colored gems. Her dark hair, though drawn low upon the temples in acknowledgment of the prevailing mode, was bound in fashion of her own by a gem-clasped, golden fillet, under which it broke into a riot of lesser curls which swept over ears and temples. Here and there a gleaming jewel confined some such truant lock, so that she glittered, half-barbaric, as she walked, surmounted by a thousand trembling points of light. Ease, confidence, carelessness seemed spoken alike by the young woman's half haughty carriage and her rich costuming. Midway in the twenties of her years, she was just above slightness, just above medium height. The roundness of shoulder and arm, thus revealed, bespoke soundness and wholesomeness beyond callowness, yet with no hint of years or bulk. Her hair certainly was dark and luxuriant, her eyes surely were large and dark, without doubt shaded by long and level brows. The nose was not too highly arched any more than it was pinched and meager—indeed, a triumph in noses, since not too strong, nor yet indicating a physique weak and ill nourished.

Vital, self-confident, a trifle foreign, certainly distinguished, at first there might have seemed a trace of defiance in the carriage, even in the glance of Josephine St. Auban. But a second look into the wide dark eyes would have found there rather a trace of pathos, bordering upon melancholy; and the lines of the mouth, strongly curved, would in all likelihood have gained that sympathy demanded by the eyes, betokening a nature warm and noble, not petty or mean, and certainly not insignificant.

Such was the woman of the hour in Washington, lately frowned on by the ladies as too beautiful, talked about by the gentlemen as too cold, discussed by some, adored by others, understood by none, dreaded by some high in power, plotted against by others yet more high in place.

She cast a hurried glance now at the clock which, tall and solemn, stood near by in the hall. It was upon the stroke of midnight only. Turning half questioningly to her maid, she heard a footfall. The manager of the hotel himself came to greet her, carrying a card in his hand, and with a bow, asking her attention.

"Well, then," began the young woman, in perfect English, glancing at the card. Her dark eyes rose to meet his. "It is impossible," she said. "You know my wishes very well."

"But, my dear Countess, have you noted this name?" began the manager.

"Of course, I know it. All the more reason there should be mistake."

"But I assure you, my dear Countess—"

A step sounded near by, and the curtains swung back, disclosing the entrance to one of the adjoining parlors of the hotel. The figure of a well-built and hale gentleman, past middle age, of dignified carriage and pleasant features, was revealed. Half hesitating, he advanced.

"My dear lady," he began, in a deep and melodious voice, "I come to you doubly handicapped, both as intruder and eavesdropper. I could not avoid hearing what you have said, and as listeners hear no good of themselves, I venture to interrupt. I am anxious that your first impression of me should be a good one, Madam!"

She dropped him a curtsy which was grace itself, her dark eyes looking straight into his face. Surprise brought a slightly heightened color to her cheek. Seeing her perturbation, the unbidden guest hastened to make what amends were possible.

[Illustration: She dropped him a curtsy.]

"You were saying it was a mistake, dear lady. But if so, the intrusion was on my part. I have wished to meet you quietly, if such may be your pleasure. I am alone. Opportunity has lacked for earlier announcement, for I have but reached town this evening."

She looked from one to the other still questioningly. The manager of the hotel, feeling discretion to be the best card to play, hurriedly bowed, and hastened away.

The Countess St. Auban hesitated for an instant, but guessed some errand here worth knowing. Having herself entered the inner room, with grace she signified that the elderly gentleman should first be placed; then, seating herself upon a divan somewhat nearer to the door and hence in shadow, she waited for him to go forward with the business which had brought him hither.

"Madam," he went on, "my dear Countess, I could but overhear you refer to my own name. If it has any reputation in your eyes, let that plead as my excuse for intruding in this manner. Believe me, nothing would induce me to take such a step except business of importance."

"It is, then, of business?" Her voice, as he noted once more, was clear and full, her enunciation without provincial slur, clean and highbred.

"I hope something not wholly outside your liking."

"Of course I do not understand." She sat still looking at him full, her hands, clasping her little fan, a trifle raised.

"Then let me hasten to make all plain. I am aware of a part of your history and of a part of your plans, Madam; I am not unaware of certain ambitions of your own—I am forced to be so frank in these conditions. You are interested in the cause of Hungary."

"Place it wider, Sir," she said. "In humanity!"

"Hence you have come to America to carry forward certain of your plans. Even now you have undertaken the greatest and most daring work of altruism this country ever knew."

She made no answer but to smile at him, a wide and half lazy smile, disclosing her white and even teeth. The jewels in her dark hair glistened as she nodded slightly. Emboldened, he went on:

"And you find all things at a deadlock in Washington to-day. Humanity is placed away in linen on the shelf in America, to-day. Dust must not filter through the protection of this mighty compromise which our two great parties have accomplished! We must not talk of principles, must not stir sedition, at this time. Whig and Democrat must tiptoe, both of them, nor wake this sleeping dog of slavery. Only a few, Madam, only a few, have the hardihood to assert their beliefs. Only a few venture to cast defiance even to the dictum of Webster himself. He says to us that conscience should not be above the law. I say to you, Madam, that conscience should be the only law."

"Are you for freedom, Sir?" she asked slowly. "Are you for humanity?"

"Madam, as I hope reward, I am! Those of us who dare say so much are few in numbers to-day. We are so few, my dear lady, that we belong together. All of us who have influence—and that I trust may be said of both of us, who now meet for the first time—we are so few that I, a stranger to you, though not, I trust, wholly unrecommended, dare come to you to-night."

"With what purpose, then. Sir?"

"With the immediate purpose of learning at first hand the truth of the revolutionary system in Europe. I have not been abroad of late, indeed not for some years. But I know that our diplomacy is all a-tangle. The reports are at variance, and we get them colored by partisan politics. This slavery agitation is simply a political game, at which both parties and all sides are merely playing. Party desirability, party safety—that is the cry in the South as much as in the North. Yet all the time I know, as you know, of the hundreds of thousands of men who are leaving Europe to come to this country. A wave of moral change is bound to sweep across the North. Madam, we dwell on the eve of revolution here in America as well as in Europe. Now do you see why I have come to you to-night? Have we not much in common?"

"I am glad," she said simply; "I am proud. Me you overrate, but my wishes and my hopes you do not overrate. Only,—" and she hesitated, "why to-night; why in this particular way?"

"I arrive at that. My own plans take me soon to Europe. I am determined to investigate upon the very ground itself this question of a national repression of the human conscience."

She sat a trifle more erect, a trifle more haughty. He seemed to read her thoughts.

"Let me hope that you also have planned an early return. We have much which we might discuss of common interest. There is much of interest in that country beyond, which we might see. I do not venture any suggestion for you, but only say that if it were within your own desires to travel in the company of a man whose former station at least ought to render your reputation safe, you and your servants will be welcome in my company. My party will have other gentlemen and ladies, not of mean station, I hope."

She looked at him, hesitating, studying. It was hardly a fair contest, this of youth and scant experience against suavity and shrewdness strengthened by years of public life.

"I am somewhat helpless, Sir," she said, at length. "To converse with one so able as yourself,—what woman of my ambitions would not be pleased with that? But I am a woman, and alone in the world. I am already denounced as careless. There already has been talk. Moreover, as you see, I am committed now fully to this great work of freeing and sending from America the negro slaves. Take them from this country. Replace them with three million men born closer to freedom and citizenship—"

"Yes. But you are here somewhat mysteriously; you come privately and secretly. What harm, then, if you return as privately and secretly as you have come to Washington? Let your agents carry on your work here. The mission on which I shall be engaged will have to do with Louis Kossuth."

"Ah!"

"Yes; and you know that noble patriot, I am told. Consider of what aid you might be to me. You speak his tongue, you know his history, you could supply me at once with information—Come, 'tis no idle errand. And, perhaps,—you will forgive me, since we both know how cruel is such gossip as this that has wronged you—the tongue of gossip wags the least when the eye of gossip has seen least. Tins is a most natural and proper—indeed, most convincing opportunity."

"That is precisely what I pondered, Sir." She nodded gravely.

"And let me add this," he continued: "every day you are here in Washington the tongue of rumor wags the more. Listen to me! Leave this place. Let gossip quiet down. It has been cruel with you; yet the public soon forgets. To remain and appear in public would freshen gossip anew. Come, it is an adventure! I swear it does not lack its appeal to me! Ah, would only that I were younger, and that it were less seemly and sedate! Dear lady, I offer you my apology for coming as I have, but large plans work rapidly at times, and there is little time to wait. Now there is but one word I can say; that you have courage and decision, I know."

He had risen, and unconsciously the young woman also had risen,—balancing, measuring, watching, warding, in this contest, all too unequal. Suddenly, with a swift and most charming smile she approached him a half step and held out her hand.

"You are a great man, Sir. Your country has found you great. I have always found the greatest men the simplest and most frank. Therefore I know you will tell me—you will satisfy any doubt I may feel—If I should ask a question, you would not condemn me as presuming?"

"Certainly not. Upon the contrary, my dear Countess, I should feel flattered."

She looked at him for an instant, then came up to the side of the table beyond which he had taken his seat. Leaning her chin upon her hand, her elbow upon the table, in a sudden posture of encounter, she asked him a question whose answer took him swiftly far back into his own past, into another and forgotten day.

"Did you ever hear of Mr. John Parish, Sir?" she demanded.

The suave countenance before her was at first blank, then curious, then intent. His mind was striving to summon up, from all its many images, this one which was required. It was a brain which rarely forgot, even though years had passed; and had it been able to forget, so much had been the better for the plans of the gentleman from Kentucky, and for the success of his proposed European mission.

At last, slowly, a faint flush passed over the face she was regarding so intently. "Yes, I remember him very well," he replied. "He has not for very many years, been in this country. He died abroad, some years since. I presume you mean Mr. Parish of New York—he is the only one I recall of that name at least. Yes; I knew such a man."

"That was very long ago?"

"It was when I was much younger, my dear Countess."

"You knew him very well, then?"

"I may say that I did, Madam."

"And you'll tell me; then—tell me, was it true that once, as a wild rumor had it, a rumor that I have heard—that once you two played at cards—"

"Was that a crime?" he smiled.

"But with him, at cards with him, Mr. John Parish, a certain game of cards with him—one day,—a certain winter day years ago, when you both were younger—when the train was snowbound in the North? And you played then, for what? What were the stakes then, in that particular game with Mr. John Parish? Do you chance to recall?"

"Madam, you credit me with frankness. I will not claim even so much. But since you have heard a rumor that died out long years ago—which was denied —which even now I might better deny—since, in fact you know the truth— why should I deny the truth?"

"Then you two played a game, at cards,—for a woman? And Mr. Parish won? Was it not true?"

A new and different expression passed over the face of the gentleman before her. Her chin still rested in her hand, her other arm, long, round, white, lay out upon the table before him. He could see straight into her wide eyes, see the heave of her throat now under its shining circlet, see the color of her cheek, feel the tenseness of all her mind and body as she questioned him about his long forgotten past.

"Why do you ask me this?" he demanded at last. "What has that to do with us? That was long ago. It is dead, it is forgotten. Why rake up the folly of a deed of youth and recklessness, long years dead and gone? Why, the other man, and the woman herself, are dead and gone now, both of them. Then, why?"

"I will tell you why. That happened once in my own experience."

"Impossible!"

"Yes, impossible. It should have been impossible among men at this day of the world. But it happened. I also had the distinguished honor to be the stake in some such game, and that because—indirectly because—I had won the enmity, the suspicions at least—well, we will say, of persons high in authority in this land."

"But, my dear young lady, the conditions can not have been the same. Assuredly the result was not the same!"

"By whose credit, then? Who thinks of a woman? Who is there whose hand is not raised against her? Each member of her own sex is her enemy. Each member of the opposite sex is her foe. One breath, one suspicion, and she becomes fair game, even under the strictest code among men; and then, the man who did not dare would be despised because he would not dare. Her life is one long war against suspicion. It is one long war against selfishness, a continued defense against desire, gratification. She is, even to-day, valued as chattel—under all the laws and conventions built about her runs the chattel idea. She is a convenience. Is that all?"

"My dear lady, it is not for me to enter into discussion of subjects so abstruse, so far removed at least from my proper trend of thought—our proper trend of thought, if you please. I must admit that act of folly, yes. But I must also end the matter there."

"Then why should not I end our matter there, Sir? It seems to me that if in any usual way of life, going about her business honestly, paying her obligations of all sort—even that to her crucifix at night—a woman who is clean wishes to remain clean, to be herself,—why, I say, if that may not be, among men great or small, distinguished or unknown, then most fortunate is she who remains aloof from all chance of that sort of thing. Sir, I should not like to think that, while I was in my room, for the time removed from the society of the gentlemen who should be my protectors, there was going on, let us say, somewhere in the gentlemen's saloon, a little enterprise at chance in which —"

"But, my dear lady, you are mad to speak in this way! Lightning, even lightning of folly, does not strike twice in the same place."

"Ah, does it not? But it has!"

"What can you mean? Surely you do not mean actually to say that you yourself ever have figured in such an incident?"

She made no answer to him, save to look straight into his eyes, chin in hand still, her long white arm lying out, motionless, her posture free of nervous strain or unrest. Slowly her lips parted, showing her fine white teeth in a half smile. Her eyes smiled also, with wisdom in their look.

The venerable statesman opposed to her all at once felt his resources going. He knew that his quest was over, that this young woman was after all able to fend for herself.

"What would you do?" she demanded of him. "If you were a woman and knew you were merely coveted in general, as a woman, and that you had been just cheaply played for in a game of cards, in a public place—what would you do, if you could, to the man who lost—or the man who won? Would you be delivered over? That woman, was she—but she could not help herself; she had no place to turn, poor girl? And she paid all her life, then, for some act earlier, which left her fair game? Was that it?"

"But you, my dear girl! It is impossible!"

"I was more fortunate, that is all. Would you blame me if I dreaded the memory of such an incident; if I felt a certain shrinking from one who ever figured in such an incident? If I could trust—but then, but then—Are you very sure that Mr. Parish loved that woman?"

"I am sure of it," answered the old man soberly. "Did he use her well?"

"All her life. He gave her everything—"

"Oh, that is nothing! Did he give her—after he had learned, maybe, that she was not what he had thought—did he give her then—love—belief, trust? Did he—are you very sure that any man in such case, after such an incident, *could* have loved, really loved, the woman whom he held in that way—"

"I not only believe he might, my dear girl, but I know that in this one case— the only one of my experience"—he smiled—"such was the truth. There was some untold reason why they two did not, or could not, marry. I do not go into that.

"Consider, my dear girl," he resumed; "you are young, and I am so old that it is as though I too were young now and had no experience—so we may talk. Our life is a contest among men for money and for love; that is all success can bring us. In older days men fought for that. To-day we have modified life a little, and have other ways; but I fancy the game in which that certain lady figured was only one form of contest—it was a fight, the spoils to go to the victor."

"Horrible! But you might have been the victor? In that case, would you have loved her, would you have used her well, all your life, and hers?"

He drew back now with dignity. "Madam, my position in later years defends me from necessity of answering you. You are young, impulsive, but you should not forget the proprieties even now—" His face was now hotly flushed.

"I ask your pardon! But *would* you?"

He smiled in spite of himself, something of the old fire of gallantry still burning in his withered veins. "My dear girl, if it were yourself, I would! And by the Lord! I'd play again with Parish, or any other man, if my chance otherwise, merely by cruel circumstances, had been left hopeless. Some one must win."

"But how could the winner be sure? How could the—how did she—I would say—"

"Dear girl, let us not be too cold in our philosophy, nor too wise. I can not say how or why these things go as they do. All I know is that the right man won in that case, and that he proved it later, by each act of kindness he gave her, all her life. This, my dear, is an odd world, when it comes to all that."

"Was he—did he have anybody else in the world who—"

"Oh, only a wife, I believe, that was all!"

"Did she die, soon? Was there ever—"

"How you question! What do you plan for *yourself*? My word! You are putting me through a strange initiation on our first acquaintance, my dear Countess! Let us not pursue such matters further, or I shall begin to think your own interest in these questions is that of the original Eve!"

"To the victor does not always belong the spoils," she said slowly. "Not till he has won—earned them—in war, in conquest! Perhaps conquest of himself."

[Illustration: "To the victor does not always belong the spoils."]

"You speak in enigmas for me, my dear Countess."

She shook her head slowly, from side to side. "That poor girl! Did she ever feel she had been won in the real game, I wonder? To whom would belong herself—if she felt that she had something in her own life to forget, some great thing to be done, in penance perhaps, in eagerness perhaps, some step to take, up—something to put her into a higher plane in the scheme of life? To do something, for some one else—not just to be selfish—suppose that was in her heart; after that game?"

"Why, you read her story as though you saw it! That was her life, absolutely. Never lived a woman more respected there, more loved. She disarmed even the women, old and young—yes, even the single ones!"

"It is an odd world," she said slowly. "But"—drawing back—"I do not think I will go back to Europe. It would delight me to meet again my friend, the patriot Kossuth. But here I have many ideas which I must work out."

"My dear Countess, you oppress me with a sense of failure! I had so much hoped that you would lend your aid in this mission of my own abroad. You would be valuable. You are so much prized in the opinions of the administration, I am sure, that—"

"What do you mean? Does the administration know of me? *Why* should it know? What have I done?"

But the old statesman before her was no such fool as to waste time in a lost cause. This one was lost, he knew, and it booted little for him to become involved where, even at the best issue, there was risk enough for him. He reflected that risk must have existed even had this young lady been a shade more dull of mind, of less brilliant faculty in leaping to conclusions and resolutions. She *was* a firebrand, that was sure. Let others handle such, but not that task for him!

"Now you ask questions whose answers lie entirely beyond my power," he replied easily. "You must remember that I am not of this party, let alone this administration. My own day in politics has past, and I must seek seclusion, modestly. I own that the mission to Europe, to examine in a wholly non-partisan way, the working out there of this revolutionary idea—the testing on the soil of monarchies of the principle of democratic government—has a great appeal to me; and I fancied it would offer appeal also to yourself. But if—"

"All life is chance, is it not? But in your belief, does the right man always win?"

He rose, smiling, inscrutable once more, astute and suave politician again, and passing about the table he bowed over her hand to kiss it.

"My dear Countess," he said, "my dear girl, all I can say is that in the very limited experience I can claim in such matters, the victor usually is the right man. But I find you here, alone, intent on visionary plans which never can be carried out, undertaking a labor naturally foreign to a woman's methods of life, alien to her usual ideas of happiness. So, my dear, my dear, I fear you yourself have not played out the game—you have not fulfilled its issue! The stakes are not yet given over! I can not say as to the right man, but I can say with all my heart that he who wins such prize is fortunate indeed, and should cherish it for ever. See, I am not after all devoid of wit or courage, my dear young girl! Because, I know, though you do not tell me, that there is some game at which you play, yourself, and that you will not stop that game to participate in my smaller enterprise of visiting Kossuth and the lands of Europe! I accept defeat myself, once more, in a game where a woman is at stake. Again, I lose!"

There was more truth than she knew in his words, for what was in his mind and in the minds of others there in Washington, regarding her, were matters not then within her knowledge. But she was guided once more, as many a woman has been, by her unerring instinct, her sixth sense of womanhood, her scent for things of danger. Now, though she stood with face grave, pensive, almost melancholy, to give him curtsy as he passed, there was not weakness nor faltering in her mien or speech.

"But he would have to *win!*" she said, as though following out some train of thought. "He would first need to win in the larger game. Ah! What woman would be taken, except by the man who really had won in the real game of life."

"You would demand that, my dear?" smiled the pleasant gentleman who now was bowing himself toward the door.

"I would demand it!"

By the time he had opportunity to rally his senses, assailed as they were by the sight of her, by the splendor of her apparel, by the music of her voice, the fragrance which clung about her, the charm of her smiles,—by the time, in short, which he required to turn half about, she was gone. He heard her light step at the stair.

"My soul!" he exclaimed, wiping his brow with a silken kerchief. "So much for attempting to sacrifice principle—for expecting to mix Free Soil and Whig! Damn that Kentuckian!"

CHAPTER XXVII

A SPLENDID FAILURE

If it is easy to discover why there was no special embassy sent by this government to Turkey for the purpose of inviting the distinguished patriot Kossuth to visit America, (that matter being concluded in rather less formal fashion after the return home of the Hungarian committee of inquiry—a ship of our navy being despatched to carry him to our shores) it with equal ease may be understood why the Countess St. Auban after this remained unmolested. A quaking administration, bent only on keeping political matters in perfect balance, and on quenching promptly, as best it might, any incipient blaze of anti-slavery zeal which might break out from its smoldering, dared make no further move against her. She was now too much in the public eye to be safe even in suppression, and so was left to pursue her own way for a time; this the more readily, of course, because she was doing nothing either illegal or reprehensible. Indeed, as has been said, she was only carrying out in private way a pet measure of Mr. Fillmore himself, one which he had only with difficulty been persuaded to eliminate from his first presidential message —that of purchasing the slaves and deporting them from our shores. The government at Washington perforce looked on, shivering, dreading lest this thing might fail, dreading also lest it might not fail. It was a day of compromise, of cowardice, of politics played as politics; a day of that political unwisdom which always is dangerous—the fear of riding straight, the ignorance of the saving quality of honest courage. Wherefore, matters went on thus, fit foundation now building for that divided and ill-ordered house of this republic, whose purification could only be found in the cleansing catastrophe of fire so soon to come.

As to the unfortunate work in which this warm-hearted enthusiast thus impulsively engaged, small comment need be made, since its failure so soon was to become apparent to the popular mind. The Countess St. Auban was not the first to look to colonization and deportation as the solution of the negro problem in America. But as the Colonization Society for more than a decade had failed to accomplish results, so did she in her turn fail. In a work which continued through all that spring and summer, she drew again and again upon her own private fortune. Carlisle and Kammerer had charge of the details, but she herself was the driving force of the enterprise. While they were abroad lecturing and asking contributions to their cause—taking with them the slave girl Lily as an example of what slavery had done—she remained at Washington. They actually did arrange for the deportation of a ship-load of blacks to Hayti, another ship-load to Liberia. A colony of blacks whose freedom had been purchased was established in Tennessee, others were planned for yet other localities. It was part of her intent to establish nuclei of freed blacks in different portions of the southern section.

In all this work Lily, late servant of Josephine St. Auban, assumed a certain prominence, this being given to her not wholly with wisdom. Although but little negro blood remained in her veins, this former slave had not risen above the life that had surrounded her. Ignorant, emotional, at times working herself into a frenzy of religious zeal, she was farthest of all from being a sober judge or a fair-minded agent for the views of others. Yet in time her two guardians, Carlisle and Kammerer, unwisely allowed her more and more liberty. She was even, in times of great hurry, furnished funds to go upon trips of investigation for herself, as one best fitted to judge of the conditions of her people. As to these details, Josephine St. Auban knew little. There was enough to occupy her mind at the center of these affairs, where labors grew rapidly and quite beyond her original plan.

As is always the case in such hopeless enterprises, the expenses multiplied beyond belief. True, contributions came meagerly from the North, here and there some abolitionist appearing who would do something besides write and preach. In all, more than a half million dollars was spent before the end of the year 1851. Then, swiftly and without warning, there came the end.

One morning, almost a year after her return to Washington, Josephine St. Auban sat in her apartments, looking at a long document inscribed in a fine, foreign hand. It was the report of the agent of her estates in Prance and Hungary. As she read it the lines blurred before her eyes. It demanded an effort even of her superb courage fairly to face and meet the meaning. In fact, it was this: The revolution of Louis Napoleon of 1851 had resulted in the confiscation of many estates in France, all her own included. As though by concert among the monarchies of Europe, the heavy hand of confiscation fell, in this nation and in that. The thrones of the Old World are not supported by revolutionists; nor are revolutionists supported by the occupants of thrones. Her Hungarian lands had followed those which she had owned in France. The rents of her estates no longer could be collected. Her revenues were absolutely gone. Moreover, she herself was an exile.

[Illustration: She herself was an exile.]

Thus, then, had her high-blown hopes come to an end. It was proof of the splendid courage of the woman that she shed not a tear. Not a lash trembled as presently she turned to despatch a message for her lieutenant, Carlisle, to come to her. The latter was absent at some western point, but within two days he appeared in Washington and presently made his call, as yet ignorant of what were his employer's wishes.

He himself began eagerly, the fanatic fire still in his eye, on details of the work so near to his soul. "My dear Countess," he exclaimed, even as he grasped her hands, "we're doing splendidly. We'll have the whole Mississippi Valley in an uproar before long. All the lower Ohio is unsettled. Missouri, Illinois, Indiana are muttering as loudly as New England. I hear that Lily has led away a whole neighborhood over in Missouri. A few months more like this, and we'll have this whole country in a turmoil. It's bound to win—the country's bound to come to its senses—if we keep on."

"But we can not keep on, my dear Sir," she said to him slowly. "That is why I have sent for you."

"How do you mean? What's wrong? Can not keep on—end our work? You're jesting!"

"No, it is the truth. Kossuth is in Turkey. Shall I join him there? Where shall I go? I'm an exile from France. I dare not return to Hungary."

"You—I'll—I'll not believe it! What do you mean?"

"I am ruined financially, that's all. My funds are at an end. My estates are gone! My agent tells me he can send me no more money. How much do you think," she said, with a little *moue*, "we can do in the way of deporting blacks out of my earnings—well, say as teacher of music, or of French?"

"I'll not believe it—you—why, you've been used to riches, luxuries, all your life! And I—why, I've helped impoverish you! I've been spending your money. A ship-load of blacks, against you? My God! I'd have cut my hand off rather."

She showed him the correspondence, proof of all that she had said, and he read with a face haggard in unhappiness.'

"There' There!" she said. "You've not heard me make any outcry yet, have you? Why should you, then? I have seen men lay down their lives for a principle, a belief. You will see that again. Should not a woman lay down her money?

"But as to that," she went on lightly, "why, there are many things one might do. I might make a rich alliance, don't you think?"

He suddenly stiffened and straightened, and looked her full in the eye, a slow flush coming across his face.

"I couldn't have said it any time before this," said he. "It has been in my heart all along, but I didn't dare—not then. Yes, a rich alliance if you liked, I do not doubt. There's a poor one waiting for you, any time you like. You know that.

You must have seen it, a thousand times—"

She advanced to him easily and held out both her hands. "Now, now!" she said. "Don't begin that. You'll only hurt us both. My lieutenant, visionary as myself! Ah, we've failed."

"But everybody will blame you—you will have no place to go—it will be horrible—you don't begin to know what it means. Of course, we have made mistakes."

"Then let's not make the worst mistake of all," she said.

"But we could do so much—"

She turned upon him suddenly, pale, excited. "Do not!" she cried. "Do not use those words! It seems to me that that is what all men think and say. 'How much we could do—together!' Do not say that to me."

At this he sobered. "Then there is some one else?" he said slowly. "You've heard some one else use those words? I couldn't blame him. Well, I wish him happiness. And I wish you happiness, too. I had no right to presume."

"Happiness!—what is that?" she said slowly. "I've been trying to find it all my life. My God! How crooked were all the mismated planets at my birth! I haven't been happy myself. I do not think that I've added one iota to the happiness of any one else, I've just failed, that's all. And I've tried so hard— to do something, something for the world! Oh, can a woman—can she, ever?" For once shaken, she dropped her face an instant in her hands, he standing by, mute, and suffering much as herself at seeing her thus suffer.

"But now," she continued after a time, "—I want to ask you whether I've been ungenerous or vindictive with you—"

"Vindictive? You? Never! But why should you be?"

"Captain," she said easily, "my lieutenant, my friend, let me say—I will not be specific—I will not mention names or dates; but do you think, if you were a woman, you could ever marry a man who once, behind your back, with not even eagerness to incite him, but coolly, deliberately—had played a game of cards for—you?"

He stiffened as though shot. "I know. But you misunderstand. I did not play for you. I played to relieve a situation—because I thought you wished— because it seemed the solution of a situation hard for both of us. I thought—"

"Solution!" She blazed up now, tigerlike, and her words came through set lips. "I'd never have told you I knew, if you hadn't said what you have. But— a solution—a plan—a compromise! You ought to have played for me! You ought to have played for me; and you ought to have won—have won!"

[Illustration: You ought to have played for me!]

He stood before a woman new to him, one so different from the grateful and gracious enthusiast he had met all these months that he could not comprehend the change, could not at once adjust his confused senses. So miserable was he that suddenly, with one of her swift changes, she smiled at him, even through her sudden tears. "No! No!" she exclaimed. "See! Look here!"

She handed him a little sheet of crumpled note paper, inscribed in a cramped hand, showed him the inscription—"Jeanne Fournier."

"You don't know who that is?" she asked him.

"No, I don't know."

"Why, yes, you do. My maid—my French maid—don't you remember? She married Hector, the cooper, at St. Genevieve. Now, see, Jeanne is writing to me again. Don't you see, there's a baby, and it is named for me—who has none. Good-by, that money!"—she kissed hand to the air—"Good-by, that idea, that dream of mine! That's of no consequence. In fact, nothing is of consequence. See, this is the baby of Jeanne! She has asked me to come. Why, then, should I delay?"

Whether it were tears or smiles which he saw upon her face Carlisle never could determine. Whether it were physical unrest or mental emotion, he did not know, but certainly it was that the letter of the agent remained upon the table untouched between them while Josephine St. Auban pressed to her lips the letter from Jeanne, her maid.

"Why, I have not failed at all!" said she. "Have I not cared for and brought up this Jeanne, and is there not a baby of Jeanne, a baby whom she has named for me?"

Carlisle, mute and unnoticed, indeed, as he felt almost forgotten, was relieved when there came a knock at the door. A messenger bearing a card entered. She turned toward him gravely, and he could only read dismissal now. Mute and unhappy, he hurried from the room. He did not, however, pass from the stage of activity he had chosen. He later fought for his convictions, and saw accomplished, before, with so many other brave men, he fell upon the field of battle—accomplished at vast cost of blood and tears—that work which he had been inspired to undertake in a more futile form.

"You may say to this gentleman that I shall join him presently, in the parlor at the right of the stair," said Josephine St. Auban after a moment to the messenger.

CHAPTER XXVIII

As she entered the room, there rose to meet her a tall gentleman, who stood gravely regarding her. At sight of him she paused, embarrassed. No figure was more familiar in Washington, yet none was less to be expected here. There was no mistaking the large frame, the high brow, the dark and piercing eye, the costume—that of another day. Involuntarily, although her first impression (based upon other meetings with distinguished men) was one more of apprehension than of pleasure, she swept him a deep curtsy. With the grace of a courtier he extended a hand and led her to a chair.

"You know me, Madam?" he demanded, in a deep and bell-like voice. "I know you, as well. I am delighted, I am honored, to announce that I come to you as a messenger."

"It is an honor that you come in any capacity, Sir. To what may I attribute so kind a visit, to one so unimportant?"

"No, no, my dear Countess. We rate you very high. It is the wish of a certain gentleman to have you attend a little meeting which will not welcome many out of all this city. It is informal and unofficial, my dear lady, but all those who will be there will be glad to have your attendance. It was thought well for me to drop in to interrogate your pleasure in the matter."

"It is a command, Sir! Very well, at what time, then?"

"If it should please you, it would delight me to accompany you at once, my dear lady! My carriage is waiting now."

Josephine St. Auban did not lack decision upon her own part. Something told her that no danger this time lurked for her.

"Pardon me for just one moment then, Sir," she answered. A few moments later she returned, better prepared for the occasion with just a touch to her toilet; and with a paper or two which with some instinct she hastily snatched up from her desk. These latter she hurriedly crowded into her little reticule. They took the carriage and soon were passing through the streets toward the most public portion of the city of Washington.

They entered wide grounds, and drew up before a stately building which lay well back from the street. Entering, they passed through a narrow hall, thence into a greater room, fitted with wide panels decorated with many portraits of men great in the history of this country. There was a long table in this room,

181

and about it—some of them not wholly visible in the rather dim light—there were several gentlemen. As her tall escort entered with a word of announcement, all of these rose, grave and silent, and courteously bowed to her. There approached from the head of the room a tall, handsome and urbane gentleman, who came and took her hand. He, some of these others, she could not fail to know. She had come hither without query or comment, and she stood silent and waiting now, but her heart was racing, her color faintly rising in spite of all her efforts to be calm.

[Illustration: They entered wide grounds.]

"My dear lady," he began, in a voice whose low, modulated tones scarce could fail to please any ear, "I thank you for your presence here. Will you not be seated? It is a very great honor that you give us, and all of these gentlemen appreciate it."

Josephine St. Auban curtsied and, remaining silent and wondering, assumed the seat assigned her, at the right hand of the tall and grave gentleman who had escorted her hither, and who now courteously handed her to her place.

"We meet absolutely without formality, my dear Madam," went on the tall and kindly man who had greeted her. "What goes on here is entirely unofficial and, as I need not say, it is altogether private; as you will remember."

"You will perhaps pardon my diffidence at such a time and place, Sir," she began, at last. "It is difficult for me to understand what small merit, or large error, of mine should bring me here."

"Madam, we wish that your abilities were smaller," smiled the tall gentleman. "That is the very thing of which we wish to speak. It is your activities which have seemed to us matters of concern—indeed, of kindly inquiry, if you do not mind. These gentlemen, I think, I do not need to introduce. We are all of us interested in the peace and dignity of this country."

"Have I done anything against either?" asked she.

"Ah, you have courage to be direct! In answer, I must say that we would like to ask regarding a few things which seem to be within your own knowledge. You, of course, are not unaware of the popular discontent which exists on this or the other side of the great political question in America to-day. We are advised that you yourself have been a traveler in our western districts; and it seemed to us likely that you might be possessed of information regarding matters there of which we get only more interested, more purely partisan, reports."

"That is not impossible," was her guarded reply. "It is true, I have talked with some in that part of the country."

"You were witness of the anxiety of our attempt to keep war and the talk of it far in the background,—our desire to preserve the present state of peace."

"Assuredly. But, Sirs, you will forgive me,—I do not believe peace will last. I thought so, until this very day. In my belief, now, there will be war. It can not be averted."

"We are glad to hear the belief of all, on all sides," was the courteous rejoinder. "We ourselves hope the compromise to be more nearly final. Perhaps you as well as others hold to the so-called doctrine of the 'higher law'? Perhaps you found your politics in Rousseau's *Nouvelle Heloise*, rather than in the more sober words of our own Constitution?" His eyes were quizzical, yet not unkind.

"Certain doctrines seem to endure," was her stout answer, kindling. "I am but a woman, yet I take it that anything that I can say will have no value unless it shall be sincere. To me, this calm is something which can not endure."

"There at least do not lack others who are of that belief. But why?"

"They told me in the West that the South has over three million slaves. They told me that the labor of more than seven million persons, black and white, is controlled by less than a third of a million men; and of all that third of a million, less than eight thousand practically represent the owners of these blacks, who do not vote. Gentlemen, I have been interested in the cause of democracy in Europe—I do not deny it—yet it seems to me an oligarchy and not a democracy which exists in the American South. The conflict between an oligarchy and a natural democracy is ages old. It does not die. It seems to me that there is the end of all compromise—in the renewed struggle of men, all over the world, to set up an actual government of their own,—not an oligarchy, not a monarchy, not of property and wealth, but of actual democracy. It must come, here, some day."

"It is unusual, my dear lady, to find one of your sex disposed to philosophy so deep and clear as your own. You please us. Will you go on?"

"Sir, your courtesy gives me additional courage,". was her answer. "You have asked me for my beliefs—and I do not deny that I have some of my own, some I have sought to put in practice. To me, another phase of this question lies in something which the South itself seems not to have remembered. The South figures that the cost of a laboring man, a slave, is perhaps a thousand or fifteen hundred dollars. The South pays the cost of rearing that man. Any nation pays the cost of bringing up a human being. Yet, within this very year, Europe has sent into the North and into the West a third of a million of men *already* reared, already *paid* for. Sir, you ask me what will be the result of this discontent, the result of this compromise. It seems to me plainly written in those two facts—industrial, not political facts. The 'finality' of this compromise, its final issue, will be established by conditions with which laws or their enforcement have little to do. Yet statesmen try to solve such a question by politics. I myself at one time thought it could endure—but only if all the blacks were bought, paid for and deported, to make room for those who come at no cost to us. I thought for a time it could be done. I have tried to do it. I have failed. I do not think others will follow in my attempt."

"We have not undervalued, Madam, either the brilliance or the profundity of your own active intellect! What you say is of interest. We already have followed with profound interest your efforts. Your words here justify our concern in meeting you. This is perhaps the first time in our history when a woman has been asked to meet those most concerned in even so informal an assemblage as this, at precisely this place."

There were gravity and dignity in his words. The majesty of a government, the dignity of even the simplest and most democratic form of government, the unified needs, the concentrated wish of many millions expressed in the persons of a few,—these are the things which can not fail to impress even the most ignorant and insensitive as deeply as the most extravagant pageantry of the proudest monarchy. They did not fail to impress Josephine St. Auban, brilliant and audacious thinker though she was, and used to the pomp of Old World courts. At once she felt almost a sense of fright, of terror. The silence of these other gentlemen, so able to hold their peace, came to her mind with the impress of some mighty power. She half shrank back into her chair.

"Madam, you have no need of fear," broke in the deep voice of the gentleman who had escorted her thither, and who now observed her perturbation. "We shall not harm you—I think not even criticize you seriously. Our wish is wholly for your own good."

"Assuredly," resumed the first speaker. "That is the wish of all my friends here. But let us come now to the point. Madam, to be frank with you, you have, as we just have said, been much concerned of late with attempts at the colonization and deportation of negroes from this country. You at least have not hesitated to undertake a work which has daunted the imagination of our ablest minds. Precisely such was once my own plan. My counselors dissuaded me. I lacked your courage."

"There seemed no other way," she broke in hurriedly, her convictions conquering her timidity. "I wanted so much to do something—not alone for these blacks—but something for the good of America, the good of the world. And I failed, to-day."

"The work of the Colonization Society has gone on for many years," gently

184

insisted the first speaker, raising a hand, "and made it no serious complications. Your own work has been much bolder, and, to be frank, there *have* been complications. Oh, we do not criticize you. On the contrary, we have asked your presence here that we might understandingly converse on these things to which you have given so much attention."

"If I have erred," she ventured, "it has been done within the limitations of human wisdom; yet my convictions were absolutely sincere—at least I may assure you of so much. I have not wished to break any law, to violate convictions on either side. I only wanted to do some good in the world."

"We are quite sure, my dear lady, that the sentiments of your mind are precisely those of our own. But perhaps you may be less aware than ourselves of complications which may rise. Our friend who sits by you has found occasion to write again in unmeasured terms to the representatives of Austria. We are advised of your affiliations with the Hungarian movement—in short, we are perhaps better advised of your movements than you yourself are aware. We know of these blacks which have been purchased and deported by your agents, but we also know that large numbers of slaves have been enticed away from their owners, that whole plantations have been robbed of their labor, and this under the protection—indeed, under the very *name*—of this attempt which you have set on foot. Has this been done by your knowledge, Madam? I anticipate your answer. I am sure that it has not."

"No! No!" she rejoined. "Assuredly, no! That is a matter entirely without my knowledge. You shock me unspeakably by this news. I have not heard of it. I should be loath to believe it! I have spent my own funds in this matter, and I have told my own agents to do nothing in the slightest contravention of the laws."

"None the less, these things have been done, my dear lady. They have awakened the greatest feeling in the South—a feeling of animosity which extends even to the free colonies of blacks which have been established. The relations between the two great sections of this country are already strained sufficiently. We deprecate, indeed we fear, anything which may cause a conflict, an outbreak of sectional feeling."

"Gentlemen, you must believe me," she replied, firmly and with dignity, "I have been as ignorant as I am innocent of any such deeds on the part of my agents. While I do not agree that any human being can be the property of another, I will waive that point; and I have given no aid to any undertaking which contemplated taking from any man what he *himself* considered to be his property, and what the laws of the land accorded him as his property. My undertaking was simply intended as a solution of *all* those difficulties—for both sides, and justly—"

"Madam, I rejoice to hear those words,—rejoice beyond measure! They accord entirely with the opinion we have formed of you."

"Then you have watched me!—I have been—"

"This is a simple and democratic country, Madam," was the quiet answer, although perhaps there might have been the trace of a smile on the close-set mouth of the speaker. "We do not spy on any one. Your acts have been quite within public knowledge. You yourself have not sought to leave them secret. Should these facts surprise you?"

"They almost terrify me. What have I done!"

"There is no need of apprehension on your part. Let us assure you of that at once. We are glad that you, whom we recognize as the moving spirit in this deportation enterprise, have not sanctioned certain of the acts of your agents. There was one—a former army officer—with whom there labored a revolutionist, a German, recently from Europe. Is it not so?"

"It is true," she assented. "They were my chief agents. But as for that officer, this country has none more eager to offer his sword to the flag when the time shall come. I am sure it is but his zeal which has caused offense. I would plead for his reinstatement. He may have been indiscreet."

"We shall listen to what you say. But in addition to these, there was a former slave girl, who has been somewhat prominent in meetings which these two have carried on in different parts of the country. In the words of the southern press, this girl has been used as a decoy."

"Lily!" exclaimed Josephine. "It must have been she! Yes, I had such a person in my employ—in very humble capacity. But, Sir, I assure you I have not seen her for more than two months. I had supposed her busy with these others on the lecture platform."

"She is not now so engaged," interrupted a voice from the shadows on the other side of the table.

"Then she has been arrested?" demanded Josephine.

"That is not the term; yet it is true that she sailed on one of your own colonization ships last week. Her fortune will lie elsewhere hereafter. It was her own wish."

A sudden sense of helplessness smote upon Josephine St. Auban. Here, even in this republic, were great and silent powers with which the individual needed to contend. Absorbed for the time in that which was nearest her heart, she had forgotten her own fortunes. Now she suddenly half rose for the first time.

"But, gentlemen," said she, as she held out in her hand some papers which crackled in her trembling grasp,—"after all, we are at cross purposes. This is not necessary. My own work is at an end, already! This very morning it came to an end, and for ever. Will you not look at these?"

[Illustration: "My own work is at an end."]

"How do you mean, Madam?" The tall grave man near by turned upon her his beetling brows, his piercing dark eyes. "Your work was worthy of approval in many ways. What has happened that it should cease?"

"This!" she said, handing to him the papers which she held. "I have a report to-day from my agents in Europe. Gentlemen, since I must mention these things,—I have been possessor of a fortune in my own name which might have been called considerable. I had estates in France and in Austria. This advises me that my estates have been confiscated by the governments in both countries—they got word there, in some way—"

"It was Hulsemann!" ejaculated the dark man, as to himself. "Austria's man here!"

She went on: "If I am not welcome in this country, whither shall I go? I am an exile as I stand before you. I am a widow. I have no living kin. Moreover, I am an exile, impoverished, as I stand. My fortune has been dissipated— honestly so, gentlemen; but since it is gone, my powers are at an end. If I have displeased you, I shall do so no longer. Here are my proofs."

She placed her papers in the hand of her escort, the nearest of these grave and silent men. A nod from the leader at the head of the table caused this tall and dark gentleman to rise and seek a place closer to the window in order that he might find better light for reading. His glasses upon his nose, he scanned the papers gravely. A sudden smile broke out upon his face, so that he passed a hand across his face to force it back into its usual lines of gravity.

"Gentlemen," said he, at length, solemnly, "this lady has been kind to come to meet us, and you all are witness that her dealings have been perfectly frank and sincere. I confess, however, I am somewhat puzzled over this document which she has given me. I presume we may well mark it 'Exhibit A.' If you do not mind, I will read it to you."

Slowly, deliberately, employing all the tones of his deep and sonorous voice, which before then had thrilled audiences of thousands in every portion of his country, he read; his face studiously turned away that he might not see the dismayed gestures of the woman who had handed him these papers:

"MY DEAR MADAME:

"I take in hand my pen to tell you how life goes with us in this locality. The business of Hector is improved one half this year. We have green blinds on all sides of the house, and a vine that grows also. The mother of Hector is kind to me. We have abundance and peace at this place. But, Madame, that which it is which I write you, there is come but now the baby of Hector and myself Jeanne. In all this locality there is no baby like this. Madame, we have said to name it for yourself, Josephine St. Auban Jeanne Marie Fournier. Moreover, Madame, it is advise that for a baby so remarkable a godmother is necessary. I take my pen in hand to inquire of madame whether in the kindness of her heart madame could come to see us and be present at this christening of this child most extraordinary. I have the assurance also of Hector that the remarkable qualities of this baby will warrant the presence of madame. A reply *poste restante*, address on St. Genevieve in Missouri, will arrive to your faithful and obedient servant,

"JEANNE."

Before this singular document had been half concluded there were sounds of shifting chairs, bursts of stifled laughter. The tall grave man nevertheless went on, solemnly finishing this communication. As for Josephine, she had shrunk back in her chair, knowing not which way to turn.

"Sirs," concluded the gentleman who now occupied the floor, "while I do not find full confirmation herein of all the statements this lady has made to us, I do discover this document to be not without interest. At its close, I find in a different handwriting—Madam, may I guess it to be your own?—the addendum—let me see,—Ah, yes, it says merely two words: '*The darling!*'"

He approached, and laid just the lightest, gentlest hand upon the shoulder of the disturbed woman, who sat speechless, her face suffused. "Your documents are regular, Madam," he said kindly. "As for this other, which perhaps was the one you intended me to read, that is private matter. It is not necessary even for myself to read it. There will be no further exhibits in this case. I am sure that I voice the feeling of every gentleman present here however, Madam, if I say that although we have not curiosity as to the terms of this communication, we have deep regret over its advices to you. If your fortunes have been ruined, they have been ruined in a cause in which a kind heart and an active brain were deeply enlisted. You have our regrets."

"Sir!" He turned now toward the tall gentleman who sat silent at the head of the table. "I am sure there is no further need for this lady's attendance here. For my own part, I thank her. She has offered us no remedy, I fear. In turn, there seems none we can extend to her."

"Wait a moment!" interrupted a voice from the opposite side of the table.

The leader shifted in his seat as he turned toward Josephine St. Auban. "This is the gentleman from Kentucky," he said. "We usually find his words of interest. Tarry, then, for just a moment longer."

A tall figure was visible in the half light, as the clear voice of the gentleman so described went on.

"Sir, and gentlemen, there is no Kentuckian,—no, nor any man from any other state here present—who could suffer this matter to conclude just as it is now. This is not all. This matter but begins. We have invited to attend us a lady whose activities we considered dangerous,—that is the plain truth of it, and we all know it, and she may know it. Instead of that, we find here with us now a woman in distress. Which of us would have the courage to endure with equal equanimity that which she faces now? It has already been said here that we have been not unmindful of the plans of this lady, not wholly unacquainted with her history. We know that although a revolutionist at heart, an alien on our shores, her purposes have been clean, have been noble. Would to God we had more such in our own country! But now, in a plan which has proved wholly futile before her time, which would prove futile after it, even though backed by the wealth of a nation,—she has failed, not to our ruin, but to her own.

"It is not without my knowledge that this lady at one time, according to popular report, was asked to undertake a journey which later resulted, in considerable personal inconvenience, not to say indignity, to herself. Is there no way, gentlemen, in which, especially in consideration of her present material circumstances, this government—I mean to say this country—can make some amends for that?"

"Madam," began the leader at the head of the table, "I did not predict wrongly regarding our friend from Kentucky; but in reply to him, I myself must say, as I have already said, we are but a simple republic,—all our acts must be open and known. What special fund, my dear sir,"—this to the speaker, who still retained his position,—"in what manner, indeed, could this be arranged?"

"In the easiest way in the world," rejoined the Kentuckian. "This lady, whatever be her nationality, is at heart much identified with the cause of Hungary, which she has been so good as to confuse with our own cause here in America. Her idea is to advance democracy—and to advance pure nationalism. Very well. We have already invited Louis Kossuth to come to America as the guest of this country. Even now one of the vessels of our navy is approaching his port of exile in Turkey to carry him hither. In the entertainment of Louis Kossuth large sums of money will be—and it is proper that they should be—expended. The people demand it. The dignity of this nation must be maintained. Popular approval will meet the proper expenditures for any such entertainment.

"Now then, gentlemen,"—and he raised an argumentative forefinger,—"there must be committees of entertainment; there must be those able to interpret, those competent to arrange large plans, and to do so courteously, with dignity." He bowed toward the somewhat dejected figure of the only woman present, who scarce ventured to raise her eyes to his, startled as she was by the sudden turn of events,

"Now, Sir, we all understand this is wholly unofficial and informal; we understand that there is no special fund which could be devoted to any such purpose as I have suggested—unless it were precisely this fund for the Kossuth entertainment! Gentlemen, it is not the part of a host to set a limit upon the visit of a guest. It is my belief that Kossuth will remain on these shores for at least *ten years*, and that he will need entertainment for each of those ten years at least!" A gentle applause met this speech. The speaker himself smiled as he went on.

"For a competent committee head, charged with the duty of making that entertainment gracious and dignified and worthy alike of the Old World and the New, I should think that an annual expenditure of, say, eight thousand or ten thousand dollars, would not be inadequate! If this lady, whose kind heart and brilliant mind, as our honored friend has said, both have been shown before us to-day,—if she would agree,—if she would *accept*,—some such provision as this from this fund, I am entirely clear in my own mind as to both the wisdom and the absolute propriety of extending this offer to her!"

He sat down. Laughter and applause met his remarks. Thus, and gallantly, did Kentucky make amends.

"Madam," at length interrogated the tall man at the head of the table, bending upon her his gaze, as did all these other grave figures present,—"provided this matter might be arranged, would it be within your pleasure to accept some such remuneration as that, for services which should be given quite within your wishes? I need not say," he added, turning his gaze along each side of the long table, "that this is something which, *in view of all circumstances*, to me also seems quite within dignity, decency and absolute public propriety."

But Josephine St. Auban could make no reply. Her face was hidden in her hands, and only her heaving shoulders showed the sudden emotion which had swept upon her overstrained soul. At last she felt a gentle hand touch hers. She raised her head as, one after another, these men approached, each extending his hand to her and bowing in salutation. Presently the room was deserted.

In the hall the gentleman from Kentucky passed his arm within that of a tall man, obviously from the North.

"I have just got word within the week of the arrival of a daughter at my own home out in Kentucky," said he. "I am in a position to understand all and several the statements in Exhibit A, my dear Sir! 'The darling!'

"But what a woman,—what a woman!" he went on meditatively. "Sir, if I were a single man, as I am a married man, I should offer to her, upon the spot, a union, now and for ever, one and inseparable!"

CHAPTER XXIX

It was the daily custom of Hector to be upon hand at the dock for the landing of each and every steamer which touched at St. Genevieve, bound either up or down the Mississippi, and his business of cooperage never was allowed to infringe upon these more important duties. Accordingly, on a certain day late in the winter, although he had no special reason to be present, Hector was among those who waited for the boat to land, with no purpose more definite than that of giving a hand with her line at a snubbing post. He was much surprised when he saw coming from the gang-plank, and beckoning to him, a distinguished and handsomely clad lady. For an instant, abashed, he could find no speech; then suddenly he jerked off his cap, and stood smiling.

"It is Madame!" he exclaimed. "*Ah, bon jour! Bon jour! Ah, c'est Madame!*"

"Yes," rejoined Josephine St. Auban, "it is I. And I am glad to see St. Genevieve again, and you, Monsieur Hector. Tell me,—ah, about that infant, that baby of ours!!

"Madame, believe me, there is none such in all the valley! Come!"

It was a proud and happy Jeanne who greeted her former mistress at the little cottage with the green blinds, and the ivy, which lay close upon the street of St. Genevieve,—Jeanne, perhaps a trifle more fleshy, a shade more French and a touch less Parisian in look, more mature and maternal, yet after all, Jeanne, her former maid. Woman fashion, these two now met, not without feminine tears, and forgetful of late difference in station, although Jeanne dutifully kissed the hand held out to her. The first coherent speech, as in the case of Hector, was regarding this most extraordinary infant, whose arrival seemed to be thus far regarded as a matter of national importance. In this view also shared Madame Fournier the elder, mother of Hector, who also presently welcomed the new-comer to the home.

[Illustration: Woman fashion, these two now met.]

A strange feeling of relief, of rest and calm, came over Josephine St. Auban, a lady of rank in another world, where an incident such as this could not have been conceived. Here it seemed not only possible but covetable. The first babble of congratulations and greetings over, she settled down to the quiet of the room assigned to her, and gave a sigh as of one who at last finds harborage. If only this might go on for ever! If only the street might always be thus silent, the roof thus sheltering, the greetings of simple friends thus comforting! She made no plans for herself, no announcement to others of possible plans. It was enough to remain thus, for a night at least. She was very weary, body and soul. The pathetic droop at the corners of her brave gay mouth must have brought sympathy to any who had known her earlier.

"We are not rich, Madame Countess," said Hector the next morning at the breakfast table, "but, my faith, it is not so bad here. We have not much to offer Madame, but such as it is, it is quite hers. With what riches could she produce a hen to lay eggs more perfect than those which madame beholds this morning? They are the eggs of Mildred, our most special hen. And this cream, it is from our cow Suzanne, whose like one does not find in any land for docility and amiability of disposition. Our roof is small, but it is ours. We have a yard so large as forty feet to the street yonder. What more does one demand for flowers or for the onion with green top in the spring? The couch of madame, was it not soft? Yes? It is from fowls of this very valley. That scene from the window there, is it not beautiful? Oh, very well! Others may possess in greater abundance than we, but as for myself, my business of the cooperage prospers,—behold my excellent wife Jeanne, yonder,—and this daughter of ours! What more could human being ask?"

Time and again, Josephine found herself repeating this same question,—What more could be asked than this? What more did the great world offer? It had not offered her, long used to luxury, so much as this. To Hector at this moment she made evasive answer. "I could willingly tarry with you always, Hector," said she, "if that were right."

"Right?" demanded Hector, swelling out his chest, "Why is it not right?" He doubled up a mighty arm to show where the muscles rose upon it. "See, I am strong! What is one more mouth to feed—could it even come to that for one of madame's wealth? Madame but jests. Did not madame bring me that Jeanne there? Ah, if only it were right for her to linger with us, how happy we should be! Madame is a noblewoman, we are but poor; yet she has honored us. Very well, then, what good to wonder about the future? Madame is rich, that is true. Suppose even she were poor, would it not be possible for madame to settle down here in St. Genevieve, and to teach the language of France—far better, to teach the English to these ignorant French?"

The sturdy speech of the fresh-looking, good-hearted fellow, touched the heart of a woman so world weary. For a time she said nothing of plans, even to herself. It was not long before the baby of Jeanne found a place upon her knee, and Jeanne herself, though jealous, was willing to surrender her dearest rights, at least for a time.

But always the eyes of this world weary woman were lifted up to the hills. She found herself gazing out beyond the street of St. Genevieve, toward the

Ozarks, where once she had traveled—true, against her will, but yet through scenes which she now remembered. And always there came up in her mind a question which she found no way to ask. It was Jeanne herself who, either by divination or by blunder, brought up the matter.

"Madame remembers that man yonder, that savage, Dunwodee?" she began, apropos of nothing. "That savage most execrable, who was so unkind to madame and myself—but who made love so fiercely? I declare, Madame, I believe it was Monsieur Dunwodee set me listening to Hector! *Eh, bien!*"

They were sitting near the window, looking out upon the bleak prospect of the winter woods. For the time Josephine made no comment, and Jeanne went on.

"He has at last, thank heavens, come to justice. Is it not true that human beings find ever their deserts?"

"What do you mean, Jeanne?"

"Of the Congress of this state, where he is so long a member, he is now not a member. He has fail', he has been defeat'."

"I thought he was sure of reelection so long as he chose," commented Josephine, with feigned indifference.

"There is talk—I do not understand these matters—that he has change' his coat, as one says, and gone over to the side of that man Benton. Yet one says that Benton was always his enemy! Me, I do not understand. I have the baby."

"What is that you tell me?" suddenly demanded Josephine. "That Mr. Dunwody has *changed* his political beliefs—that he has become Free Soiler?"

Jeanne nodded. "I think it is so name'. I know little of such matters, naturally. To me, my infant here is of much more importance than any question of free soil. It is possible in this country that one day this infant—were it of opposite sex—might arrive to be governor of this state—who knows? It is possible, in the belief of Hector, that this infant, were it a boy, might even become president of this great republic. Ah, well, there are hopes. Who shall set bounds to the achievement of a child well born in this country of America? Is it established that Hector and I may not, at a later time, be blessed with a son? Is it established that that son shall not be president? Is it not necessary that *some* boy shall grow up to be a president? Very well! Then who shall say that a child of ours, if of a proper sex, Madame, should not one day be president of this republic?"

"Yes, yes, Jeanne! I do not doubt that. But now you were speaking of Mr. Dunwody—"

"Yes, that is true. I was rejoicing that at last he has been defeat', that he has fail', that he has met with that fate which should be his. Now he has few friends. It is charge' against him—well, Madame, perhaps it were as well not to repeat all of that."

"I can understand," said Josephine slowly. "I can guess. Yes, I know."

Jeanne nodded. "Yes, they bring up stories that at one time you and I—well, that we were there at Tallwoods. But these wild people here, who shoot, and fight with knives, they are of all peoples in the world the most strict and the most moral, the most abhorrent of what is not their own custom of life. Behold, that droll Mr. Bill Jones, in jest perhaps, expressed to others his belief that at one time there was a woman conceal' about this place of Tallwoods! Yes! Madame knows with what ground of justice this was said. Very well! The people took it up. There was comment. There was criticism. These charges became public. It was rumored thus and so in all the district of Mr. Dunwodee. He has fought the duel—oh, la, la!

"Ah, well, as for madame, by this time she was far away. None knew her name. None doubted regarding her. But as for Mr. Dunwodee, he was here,— he was discover'! Behold it all! At the election he was defeat'. Most easily did this happen, because, as I have said, he no longer was of the same political party which formerly had chosen him. There you have him. That has come to him which he has deserve'!"

The eyes of Josephine St. Auban flashed with interest over this intelligence. "He has changed his belief, his party! But no, it is not possible that he should come out for *our* party, *our* cause, Jeanne,—*our* cause, for the people of the world—for liberty! I wish I might believe it. No. It can not be true."

"Yet it is true, Madame. A turncoat! Bah!"

"No, Jeanne! Not in the least should you feel contempt tempt for a man who honestly changes a belief. To turn from error, is not that always wisdom?"

But Jeanne only shrugged her shoulders, and held out her hands for the baby. "It is naught to me," said she. "We are happy here under this roof, are we not?"

"Precisely. We are safe here. That child yonder is safe here. But how long shall we be safe if there are not those to keep this roof protected? The law, Jeanne,—the Justice, back of the law,—are these things of no interest to you?"

"At least, when it comes to roofs," reiterated Jeanne. "Monsieur Dunwodee has pulled down his roof about his ear."

"Yes! Yes! Thank God! And so did Samson pull down the pillars about him when he had back his strength!"

"Madame has given me occasion to disappear," rejoined Jeanne, with a resigned shrug. "I do not always find myself able to follow the lofty thought of madame. But, at least, for these people of St. Genevieve there is no doubt. They have argue' among theirself. The vote here is against Monsieur Dunwodee. He is what one calls depose'.

"But then, Madame," she added presently, as she turned at the door, with the baby on her arm, "if madame should wish to explore the matter for herself, that is quite possible. This night, perhaps to-morrow, Monsieur Dunwodee himself comes to St. Genevieve. He is to meet the voters of this place. He wishes to speak, to explain. I may say that, even, he will have the audacity to come here to advocate the cause of freedom, and the restriction of those slavery for which hitherto he has labor' so valiant. Perhaps there will be those who care to listen to the address of a man of no more principle. For me and for my husband Hector—we do not argue. Hector, he is for Monsieur Dunwodee. Save as a maker of love, Madame, I am not!"

Josephine made no immediate reply. A tall mirror with pretentious golden frame hung opposite to her across the room. A few moments later, with a start, she suddenly pulled herself together, discovering that she had been gazing steadfastly into the glass.

[Illustration: Gazing steadfastly into the glass.]

CHAPTER XXX

THE TURNCOAT

It was late in the sunlit afternoon when there rode into the head of the street of old St. Genevieve a weary and mud-stained horseman, who presently dismounted at the hitching rail in front of the little inn which he favored with his company. He was a tall man who, as he turned down the street, walked with just the slightest trace of a limp.

This traveler did not turn into the inn, did not pause, indeed, at any of the points of greater interest, but sought out the little cooper shop of Hector Fournier. That worthy greeted him, wiping his hands upon his leathern apron.

"Eh, bien, then, it is Monsieur Dunwodee! Come in! Come in! I'll been glad for see you. There was those talk you'll would not came."

"Yes, I have come, Hector," said Dunwody, "and naturally, I have come to see you first. You are one of the few political allies that I have left. At least, if you don't believe the way I do, you are generous enough to listen!"

"But, Monsieur, believe me, the situation here is difficult. I had a list here of twelve citizen of St. Genevieve who were willing for listen to Monsieur Dunwodee to-night in a grand mass meeting; but now talk has gone out. There is much indignation. In fact, it is plan'—"

"What do you mean? What is going on?" demanded Dunwody.

"Alas! Monsieur, it is with regret I announce that the majority of our citizen, who so dislike Monsieur Benton and his views, are much in favor of riding upon a rail, after due treatment of the tar and the feather, him who lately was their idol; that is to say, yourself, Monsieur!"

Dunwody, his face grim, leaned against the door of the little shop. "So that is the news?" said he. "It seems hardly generous, this reception of St. Genevieve to myself! It is too bad that my friend, Mr. Benton, is not here to share this hospitality of yours!"

"As I have said, alas! Monsieur!"

"But, now, as to that, Hector, listen!" said Dunwody sharply. "We will hold the meeting here just the same. We do not run away! To-night, in front of the hall there.

"But why trouble about that?" he added, almost lightly. "What comes, comes. Now, as to yourself and your mother—and your wife?"

"And those baby!" exclaimed Hector. "Assuredly monsieur does not forget the finest baby of St. Genevieve? Come, you shall see Josephine St. Auban Jeanne Marie Fournier—at once, *tout de suite. Voila!*" Hector was rolling down his sleeves and loosening the string of his leathern apron. Suddenly he turned.

"But, Monsieur," he said, "come, I have news! It is a situation *un peu difficile*; but it can not be concealed, and what can not be concealed may best be revealed."

"What news?" asked Dunwody. "More bad news?"

"Not in the least, as we of my household regard it. With monsieur, I am not so certain. It is *quelque chose un peu difficile, mais oui.* But then—Monsieur remembers that lady, the Countess—?"

"Countess? Whom do you mean?"

"Who but our madame, the Countess St. Auban in her own right? She who gave me my Jeanne—*at Tallwoods*, Monsieur! Have you not known? She is, here. She is *chez nous.* Of wealth and distinction, yes, she has traveled in this country merely for divertisement—but the Countess St. Auban, yes, she pauses now with the cooper, Hector Fournier! Does one find such beauty, such distinction, such gentleness, such kindness, such courteousness elsewhere than among the nobility?"

"When did she come?" demanded Dunwody quietly.

"But yesterday, upon the boat; without announcement. She is at this very moment at my house yonder, busy with that baby, Josephine St. Auban Jeanne Marie Fournier, named for a countess! But do not turn back! Monsieur himself has not yet seen the baby. Come!" For one moment Dunwody paused; then, quietly, he accompanied Hector, making no comment. He limped just slightly. He was older—yes, and graver.

The mother of Hector met them even before the gate was opened. Her voice called to the door her daughter Jeanne, who was shaking hands with Dunwody before he was half way up the walk. The ejaculations of Jeanne attracted yet another ear farther within the house. A moment later Dunwody saw pass before the door a figure which he recognized, a face which called the blood to his own face. An instant later, forgetting everything, he was at the door, had her hands in his own.

"It is you!" he exclaimed. "How does it happen? It is impossible!"

Her face had more color than for days. "Yes, it is unexpected," she said simply, at last. "Everything is unexpected. But of all things possible, this it seems to me is best—to come here—to rest for a time."

"You are passing through to St. Louis?"

"Perhaps," she said. "My plans for the moment are somewhat unsettled. I stopped off here, as no doubt you know, to serve as godmother to this baby of Jeanne's! It is an important errand."

"But monsieur has not perfectly examined this infant as yet," interrupted Hector. "See, it has the eyes of Jeanne,—it has—"

"It is a darling!" said Josephine gently, and stroked the somewhat scanty hair of the heiress of the Fournier estates.

In some way, a moment later, they were apart from the protestations of the fond parents. They found themselves alone, in the special apartment reserved for guests of distinction. An awkward moment ensued. Josephine was first to break the silence. Dunwody could only sit and look at her, devouring each line, each little remembered gesture of her. Yes, it was she—a little older and graver and thinner, yes. But it was she.

"I was talking with Jeanne this very morning," she said. "She was telling me some story that you have been unfortunate—that there have been—that is to say—political changes—"

He nodded, "Yes. Perhaps you know I have lost my place with my people here? I am done for, politically."

He continued, smiling; "Just to show you the extent of my downfall, I have heard that they are intending to tar and feather me to-night,—perhaps to give me a ride upon a rail! That is the form of entertainment which in the West hitherto has generally been reserved for horse-thieves, unwelcome revivalists, and that sort of thing. Not that it terrifies me. The meeting is going to be held!"

"Then it is true that you are to speak here to-night—and to uphold doctrines precisely the reverse of what—"

"Yes, that is true." He spoke very quietly.

"I had not thought that possible," she said gently.

"Of course," she added, "I have been in entire ignorance of alt matters out here for a year past. I have been busy."

"Why should you follow the political fortunes of an obscure Missourian?" he asked. "On the contrary, there is at least one obscure Missourian who has followed yours. I have known pretty much all you have been doing of late. Yes, you at least have been busy!"

As usual, she hung on the main point. "But tell me!" she demanded of him presently, a little added color coming into her cheeks. "Do you mean to say to me that you really remember what we talked about—that you really—"

He nodded, smiling. "Don't you remember we talked about faith, and how to get hold of it? And I said I couldn't find it? Well, I have no apologies and no explanations. All I have to say is that I fought it out, threshed it all over, and then somehow, I don't know how,—well, faith *came* to me,—that is all. I waked up one night, and I—well, I just knew. That is all. Then I knew I had been wrong."

"And it cost you everything."

"Just about everything in the world, I reckon, so far as worldly goods go. I suppose you know what you and your little colonization scheme have done to me?"

"But you—what do you mean?"

"Why, didn't you know that? Weren't Carlisle and Kammerer your agents; and didn't Lily, our late disappearing slave and also late lecturing fugitive yonder, represent them? Don't you really know about that?"

"No, I had nothing to do with their operations."

"Do you mean to tell me that it was—Oh, I am glad you do not know about it," he said soberly, "although I don't understand that part of it."

"Won't you explain?" she besought him.

"Now, the truth is—and that is the main reason of all this popular feeling against me here—that Lily, or these men, or people like them, took away every solitary negro from my plantation, as well as from two or three others neighboring me! They didn't stop to *buy* my property—they just *took* it! You see, Madam,"—he smiled rather grimly,—"these northern abolitionists remain in the belief that they have all the virtue and all the fair dealing in the world. It has been a little hard on my cotton crop. I will not have any crop this fall. I had no labor. I will not have any crop next summer. With money at twelve per cent. and no munificent state salary coming in,—that means rather more than I care to talk about."

"And it was I—*I* who did that for you! Believe, believe me, I was wholly innocent of it! I did not know!—I did not! I did not! I would not have done that to my worst enemy!"

"No, I suppose not; but here is where we come again to the real heart of all of these questions which so many of us feel able to solve offhand. What difference should you make between me and another? If it is right for the

North to free all these slaves without paying for them, why should there be anything in my favor, over any one of my neighbors? And, most of all, why should you not be overjoyed at punishing me? Why am I not your worst enemy? I differed from you,—I wronged you,—I harmed you,—I did everything in the world I could to injure you. At least you have played even with me. I got you Lily to take along. And I even once went so far as to tell you my own notion, that the blacks ought to be deported. Well, you got mine!"

"I never meant it! I never intended it! It was done wholly without my knowledge! I am sorry! I am sorry!"

"You need not be sorry. It is only one of the consequences of following one's faith. Anyhow, I'm just a little less inconsistent than Mr. Benton, who had always been opposed to slavery, although he still owns slaves. The same is true of Mr. Clay. They both have been prominent politically. Well, set them free of their slaves, and they and I would be about even, wouldn't we? It comes to being pretty much on foot, I must confess."

"I can understand that," said she. "For that matter, we are both ruined; and for the same reason."

"What do you mean? And, tell me, once more, who are you? You certainly have stirred things up!"

"As to the latter, it makes little difference," said she. "I will confess to being a revolutionist and a visionary reformer; and an absolute failure. I will confess that I have undertaken things which I thought were within my power, but which were entirely beyond me. Well, it has ruined me also in a material way."

"How, do you mean?"

"This colonization work was carried on by my own funds. It is not long ago that I got a letter, saying that my funds were at an end. I had some small estates in the old country. They are gone,—confiscated. My last rents were not collected."

She, in turn, smiled, spreading out her hands. "You see me here in St. Genevieve, perhaps on my way to St. Louis. Tell me, is there demand for persons of foreign experience, who understand a little French, a little English, perhaps a little music? Or could there perhaps be a place for an interpreter in Hungarian, French or English?"

[Illustration: She turned, spreading out her hands.]

It was his turn to show consternation. "Is it indeed true?" he said. "Now it is time for me to say I am sorry. I do not understand all about it. Of course I could see all along that an immense amount of money was being paid into this colonization folly. And it was your money, and you are ruined,—for the same hopeless cause! I am sorry, sorry! It's a shame, a shame!"

"I am not sorry," said she. "I am glad! It is victory!"

"I will not say that!" he burst out. "I will not admit it, not confess it. It is all right for me, because I'm a man. I can stand it. But you—you ought to have ease, luxury, all your life. Now look what you have done!"

There came a sudden knock at the door, and without much pause. Hector entered, somewhat excited.

"Monsieur,—Madame!" he exclaimed. "One comes!"

"Who is it?" demanded Dunwody, frowning.

"*Mon pere*! He is come but now from Tallwoods, Monsieur."

"What is wrong out there? Tell him to come in."

"I go."

A moment later, Dunwody left the room, to meet old Eleazar, who made such response as he could to the hurried queries. "Monsieur," said he, "I have ridden down from the hills. There is trouble. In the neighborhood are some who are angry because their negroes have disappear'. They accuse Monsieur Dunwodee of being the cause, and say that he is traitor, a turncoat. This very night a band are said to plan an attack upon the house of monsieur! I have met above there Monsieur Clayton, Monsieur Bill Jones, Monsieur le Docteur Jamieson, and others, who ride to the assistance of Monsieur Dunwodee. It is this very night, and I—there being no other to come—have come to advise. Believing that monsieur might desire to carry with him certain friends, I have brought the large carriage. It is here!"

"Thank God!" said Dunwody, "they don't vote with me, but they ride with me still—they're my neighbors, my friends, even yet!

"Hector," he exclaimed suddenly,—"come here!" Then, as they both listened, he went on: "Tell the people there can not be a meeting, after all. I am going back to my house, to see what is on up yonder. Hector, can you get a fresh horse? And are there any friends who would go with you?"

The sturdy young cooper did not lack in courage, and his response was instant. "Assuredly I have a horse, Monsieur," was his reply. "Assuredly we have friends. Six, ten, seven, h'eight person shall go with us within the hour! But I must tell—"

Jeanne was at his elbow, catching scent of something of this, guessing at possible danger. She broke out now into loud expostulations at this rashness of her spouse, parent of this progeny of theirs, thus undertaking to expose himself to midnight dangers. Hector, none the less, shook his head.

"It is necessary that one go armed," commented Eleazar calmly. He patted with affection the long barreled piece which lay over his own arm.

Much of this conversation, loud and excited as it was, could not fail to reach the ears of Josephine, who presently had joined them, and who now heard the story of the old man, so fully confirming all Dunwody said.

"There is trouble! There is trouble!" she said, with her usual prompt decision. "There is room for me in the coach. I am going along."

"You—what in the world do you mean? You'll do nothing of the sort!" rejoined Dunwody. "It's going to be no place for women, up there. It's a *fight*, this time!"

"Perhaps not for Jeanne or Hector's mother, or for many women; but for me it is the very place where I belong! *I* made that trouble yonder. It was I, not you, who caused that disaffection among the blacks. Your neighbors ought to blame me, not you—I will explain it all to them in a moment, in an instant. Surely, they will listen to me. Yes, I am going."

Dunwody looked at her in grave contemplation for an instant.

"In God's name, my dear girl, how can you find it in your heart to see that place again? But do you find it? Will you go? If you insist, we'll take care of you."

"Of course! Of course!" she replied, and even then was busy hunting for her wraps. "Get ready! Let us start."

"Have cushions and blankets for the carriage, Eleazar," said Dunwody quietly. "Better get a little lunch of some sort to take along. Go down to the barn yonder and get fresh horses. I don't think this team could stand it all the way back."

CHAPTER XXXI

The travel-stained figures of Doctor Jamieson, Judge Clayton and the Honorable William Jones met the Dunwody coach just as it was leaving at the upper end of St. Genevieve's main street. They also had found fresh horses, and in the belief of Dunwody it was quite as well that they rode horseback, in common with the followers of Hector, who presently came trooping after him. The interior of the coach seemed to him more fittingly reserved for this lady and himself. None the less, the Honorable William had abated none of his native curiosity. It was his head which presently intruded at the coach window.

"Ah, ha!" exclaimed he. "What? Again? This time there is no concealment, Dunwody! Come, confess!"

"I will confess now as much as I ever had to confess," retorted Dunwody angrily. "If you do not know yet of this lady, I will introduce you once more. She is the Countess St. Auban, formerly of Europe, and now of any place that suits her. It is no business of yours or of mine why she was once there, or cares to go there again; but she is going along with us out to Tallwoods."

Judge Clayton made salutation .more in keeping with good courtesy than had his inquisitive friend. "I have been following the fortunes of this lady somewhat attentively of late," he said, at length. "At least, she has not been idle!"

"Precisely!" ventured Josephine, leaning out the window. "That is why I am coming to-night. I understand there has been trouble down here,—that it came out of the work of our Colonization Society—"

"Rather!" said Clayton grimly.

"I was back of that. But, believe me, as I told Mr. Dunwody, I was not in the least responsible for the running off of negroes in this neighborhood. I thought, if I should go out there and tell these other gentlemen, that they would understand."

"That's mighty nice of you," ventured the Honorable William Jones. "But if we don't git there before midnight, they'll be so full of whisky and devilment that *I* don't think they'll listen even to you, Ma'am."

"It is pretty bad, I'm afraid," said Judge Clayton. "What with one thing and another, this country of ours has been in a literal state of anarchy for the last year or two. What the end is going to be, I'm sure I don't see.

"And the immediate cause of all this sort of thing, my dear Madam," he continued, as he rode alongside, "why, it seems to be just that girl Lily, that we had all the trouble about last year. By the way, what's become of that girl? Too bad—she was more than half white!"

[Illustration: By the way, what's become of that girl?]

"Yes, it is all about that girl Lily," said Josephine slowly, restraining in her own soul the impulse to cry out the truth to him, to tell him why this girl was almost white, why she had features like his own. "That is the trouble, I am afraid,—that girl Lily, and her problem! If we could understand all of that, perhaps we could see the reason for this anarchy!"

The group broke apart, as the exigencies of the road traveled required. Now and again some conversation passed between the occupants of the carriage and the horsemen who loosely grouped about it as they advanced. The great coach swayed its way on up through the woods into the hills, over a road never too good and now worse than usual. They had thirty miles or more to drive, most of it after dark. Could they make that distance in time?

Dunwody, moody, silent, yet tense, keyed to the highest point, now made little comment. Even when left alone, he ventured upon no intimate theme with his companion in the coach; nor did she in turn speak upon any subject which admitted argument. Once she congratulated him upon his recovery from what had seemed so dangerous a hurt.

"But that is nothing now," he said. "I got off better than I had any right,— limp a little, maybe, but they say that even that is mostly a matter of habit now. Jamieson says his fiddle string may have slipped a little! And you?"

"Oh, perfectly well," she answered. "I even think I may be happy—you know, I must start my French and English classes before long."

Silent now in part as to matters present, wholly silent as to matters past, these two went on into the night, neither loosing the tight rein on self. Swaying and jolting its way upward and outward into the wilder country, the coach at last had so far plunged into the night that they were almost within touch of the valley in which lay the Dunwody lands. Eleazar, the trapper, rode on the box with the negro driver who had been impressed into service. It was the old trapper who at length called for a halt.

"Listen!" said he. "What is that?"

Dunwody heard him, and as the coach pulled up, thrust his head out of the window. The sound was repeated.

"I hear it!" cried he. "Rifle firing! I'm afraid we're going to be too late. Drive on, there, fast!"

Finally they reached the point in the road just below the shut-in, where the hills fell back in the approach to the little circular valley. Dunwody's gaze was bent eagerly out and ahead. "My God!" he exclaimed, at length. "We are too late! Look!"

At the same moment there came excited cries from the horsemen who followed. Easily visible now against the black background of the night, there showed a flower of light, rising and falling, strengthening.

"Drive!" cried Dunwody; and now the sting of the lash urged on the weary team. They swung around the turn of the shut-in, and came at full speed into the approach across the valley. Before them lay the great Tallwoods mansion house. It stood before them a pillar of fire, prophetic, it might be repeated, of a vast and cleansing catastrophe soon to come to that state and this nation; a catastrophe which alone could lay the specter in our nation's house.

They were in time to see the last of the disaster, but too late to offer remedy. By the time the coach had pulled up at the head of the gravel way, before the yet more rapid horsemen had flung themselves from their saddles, the end easily was to be guessed. The house had been fired in a half score places. At the rear, even now, the long streaks of flame were reaching up to the cornice, casting all the front portion of the house, and the lawn which lay before it, into deep shadow. The shrubbery and trees thus outlined showed black and grim.

The men of the Tallwoods party dashed here and there among the covering of trees back of the house. There were shots, hastily exchanged, glimpses of forms slinking away across the fields. But the attacking party had done their work; and now, alarmed by the sudden appearance of a resistance stronger than they had expected, were making their escape. Once in a while there was heard a loud derisive shout, now and again the crack of a spiteful rifle, resounding in echoes against the hillsides.

Dunwody was among the first to disappear, in search of these besiegers. For an instant Josephine was left alone, undecided, alarmed, in front of the great doors. Eleazar, to save the plunging team, had now wheeled the vehicle back, and was seeking a place for it lower down the lawn. It was as she stood thus hesitant that there approached her from some point in the bushes a disheveled figure. Turning, she recognized none other than old Sally, her former jailer and sometime friend.

"Sally," she cried; "Sally! What is it? Who has done this? Where are they? What is it all about? Can't anything be done?"

But Sally, terrified beyond reason, could exclaim only one word: "Whah is he? Whah's Mr. Dunwody? Quick!" An instant later, she too was gone.

At the same moment, Dunwody, weapon in hand, dashed around the corner of the house and up on the front gallery. Apparently he was searching for some one whom he did not find. Here he was soon discovered by the old negro woman, who began an excited harangue, with wild gesticulations. To Josephine it seemed that Sally pointed toward the interior of the house, as though she beckoned, explained. She heard his deep-voiced cry.

By this time the names had taken firm hold upon the entire structure. Smoke tinged with red lines poured through the great double doors of the mansion house. Yet even as she met the act with an exclamation of horror, Josephine saw Dunwody fling away his weapons, run to the great doors and crash through them, apparently bent upon reaching some point deep in the interior.

Others saw this, and joined in her cry of terror. The interior of the hall, thus disclosed by the opening of the doors, seemed but a mass of flames. An instant later, Dunwody staggered back, his arm across his face. His hair was smoking, the mustaches half burned from his lips. He gasped for breath, but, revived by air, drew his coat across his mouth and once again dashed back. Josephine, standing with hands clasped, her eyes filled with terror, expected never to see him emerge alive.

He was scarcely more than alive when once more he came back, blinded and staggering. This time arms reached out to him, steadied him, dragged him from the gallery, through the enshrouding smoke, to a place of safety.

He bore something shielded, concealed in his arms—something, which now he carried tenderly and placed down away from the sight of others, behind the shade of a protecting clump of shrubbery. His breath, labored, sobbing, showed his distress. They caught him again when he staggered back, dragged him to a point somewhat removed, upon the lawn. All the time he struggled, as though once more to dash back into the flames, or as though to find his weapons. He was sobbing, half crazed, horribly burned, but seemingly unmindful of his hurts.

The fire went on steadily with its work, the more rapidly now that the opening of the front doors had admitted air to the interior. The construction of the house, with a wide central hall, and stairways leading up almost to the roof, made an admirable arrangement for a conflagration. No living being, even though armed with the best of fire fighting apparatus, could have survived in that blazing interior. All they could do, since even a bucket brigade was out of the question here, was to stand and watch for the end. Some called for ladders, but by accident or design, no ladders were found where they should have been. Men ran about like ants. None knew anything of time's passing. No impression remained on their minds save the fascinating picture of this tall pillar of the fire.

Dunwody ceased to struggle with those who restrained him. He walked apart, near to the little clump of shrubs. He dropped to the ground, his face in his hands.

"What do you reckon that thah was he brung out in his arms, that time?" demanded Mr. William Jones, after a time, of a neighbor who met him a little apart. "Say, you reckon that was *folks*? Anybody *in* there? Anybody over—thah? Was that a bed—folded up like—'bout like a crib, say? I'm skeered to go look, somehow."

"God knows!" was the reply. "This here house has had mighty strange goings on of late times. There was always something strange about it,—something strange about Dunwody too! There ain't no doubt about that. But I'm skeered, too—him a-settin' thah—"

"But *who* was she, or it, whatever it was? How come—in—in there? How long has it been there? What kind of goings on do you think there has been; in this here place, after all?" Mr. Jones was not satisfied. They passed apart, muttering, exclaiming, wondering.

An hour later, Tallwoods mansion house was no more. The last of cornice and pillar and corner post and beam had fallen into a smoldering mass. In front of one long window a part of the heavy brick foundation remained. Some bent and warped iron bars appeared across a window.

Unable to do anything, these who had witnessed such scenes, scarce found it possible to depart. They stood about, whispering, or remaining silent, some regarding the smouldering ruin. Once in a while a head was turned over shoulder toward a bowed form which sat close under a sheltering tree upon the lawn.

"He is taking it mighty hard," said this or that neighbor. "Lost nigh about everything he had in the world." But still his bowed form, stern in its sentinelship, guarded the something concealed behind the shadows. And still they dared not go closer.

So, while Dunwody was taking that which had come to him, as human beings must, the gray of the dawn crawled up, up over the eastern edge of this little Ozark Valley. After a time the day would come again, would look with franker eyes upon this scene of horror. As the light grew stronger, though yet cold and gray, Dunwody, sighing, raised his head from his hands and turned. There was a figure seated close to him—a woman, who reached out a hand to take his scarred and burned ones in her own,—a woman, moreover, who asked him no questions.

"Oh! Oh God!" he began, for the first time breaking silence, his burned lips twitching. "And you,—why don't you go away? What made you come?"

She was silent for a time. "Am I not your friend?" she asked, at length.

Now he could look at her. "My friend!" said he bitterly. "As if all the world had a friend for me! How could there be? But you saw that,—this—?"

She made no answer, but only drew a trifle nearer, seeing him for the first time unnerved and unstrung. "I saw something, I could not tell what—when you came out. I supposed—"

"Well, then," said he, with a supreme effort which demanded all his courage, as he turned toward her; "it all had to come out, somehow. It is the end, now."

She had brought with her a cup of water. Now she handed it to him without comment. His hand trembled as he took it.

"You saw that—?" He nodded toward the ruins. All she did was to nod, in silence. "Yes, I saw you come out—with—that—in your arms."

"Who—what—do you suppose it was?"

"I don't know." Then, suddenly,—"Tell me. Tell me! *Was it she?*"

"Send them away!" he said to her after a time. She turned, and those who stood about seemed to catch the wish upon her face. They fell back for a space, silent, or talking in low tones.

"Come," he said.

He led her a pace or so, about the scanty wall of shrubbery. He pulled back a bit of old and faded silk, a woman's garment of years ago, from the face of that something which lay there, on a tiny cot, scarce larger than a child's bed.

It was the face of a woman grown, yet of a strangely vague and childlike look. The figure, never very large, was thin and shrunken unbelievably. The features, waxy-white, were mercifully spared by the flames which had licked at the shielding hands and arms that had borne her hither. Yet they seemed even more thin, more wax-like, more unreal, than had their pallor come by merciful death. Death? Ah, here was written death through years. Life, full, red-blooded, abounding, luxuriant, riotous, never had animated this pallid form, or else had long years since abandoned it. This was but the husk of a human being, clinging beyond its appointed time to this world, so cruel and so kind.

They stood and gazed, solemnly, for a time. The hands of Josephine St.

Auban were raised in the sign of her religion. Her lips moved in some swift prayer. She could hear the short, hard breathing of the man who stood near her, grimed, blistered, disfigured, in his effort to bring away into the light for a time at least this specter, so long set apart from all the usual ways of life.

"She has been there for years," he said, at last, thickly. "We kept her, I kept her, here for her sake. In this country it would be a sort of disgrace for any—any—feeble—person, you know, to go to an institution. Those are our graves over yonder in the yard. You see them? Well, here was our asylum. We kept our secrets.

"She was this way for more than ten years. She was hurt in an accident—her spine. She withered away. Her mind was gone—she was like a child. She had toys, like a child. She wept, she cried out like a child. Very often I was obliged to play—Ah! my God! My God!"

"This was one of your family. It was that which we heard—which we *felt*—about the place—?" Her voice was very clear, though low.

"My wife! Now you know." He dropped back, his face once more between his hands, and again she fell into silence.

"How long—was this?" at length she asked quietly.

He turned a scorched and half-blinded face toward her. "Ever since I was a boy, you might say," said he. "Even before my father and mother died. We kept our own counsel. We ran away, we two children. They counseled me against it. My people didn't like the match, but I wouldn't listen. It came like some sort of judgment. Not long after we were married it came—the dreadful accident, with a run-away team—and we saw,—we knew—in a little while—that she simply lived like a child—a plant—That was ten years ago, ten centuries!—ten thousand years of torture. But I kept her. I shielded her the best I knew how. That was her place yonder, where the bars were—you see. Nobody knew any more. It's all alone, back in here. Some said there was a funeral, out here. Jamieson didn't deny it, I did not deny it. But she lived—there! Sally took care of her. Sometimes she or the others were careless. You heard once or twice. Well, anyway, I couldn't tell you. It didn't seem right—to her. And you were big enough not to ask. I thank you! Now you know."

Still she was silent. They dropped down, now weary, side by side, on the grass.

"Now you see into one bit of a human heart, don't you?" said he bitterly. The gray dawn showed his distorted and wounded face, scarred, blackened, burned, as at length he tried to look at her.

"I did the best I knew. I knew it wasn't right to feel as I did toward you—to talk as I did—but I couldn't help it, I tell you, I just couldn't help it! I can't help it now. But I don't think it's wrong now, even—here. I was starved. When I saw you,—well, you know the rest. I have got nothing to say. It would be no use for me to explain. I make no excuses for myself. I have got to take my medicine. Anyhow, part of it—part of it is wiped out."

"It is wiped out," she repeated simply. "The walls that stood there—all of them—are gone. It is the act of fate, of God! I had not known how awful a thing is life. It is all—wiped away by fire. Those walls—"

"But not my sins, not my selfishness, not the wrong I have done! Even all that has happened to me, or may happen to me, wouldn't be punishment enough for that. Now you asked me if you were not my friend? Of course you are not. How could you be?"

"It would be easier now than ever before," she said. But he shook his head from side to side, slowly, dully, monotonously.

"No, no," he said, "it would not be right,—I would not allow it."

"I remember now," she said slowly, "how you hesitated. It must have been agony for you. I knew there was something, all the time. Of course, I could not tell what. But it must have been agony for you to offer to tell me—of this."

"Oh, I might have told you then. Perhaps it would have been braver if I had. I tried it a dozen times, but couldn't. I don't pretend to say whether it was selfishness or cowardice, or just kindness to—her. If I ever loved her, it was so faint and far away—but it isn't right to say that, now."

"No. Do not. Do not."

"I don't know. There are a heap of things I don't know. But I knew I loved you. It was for ever. That was what was meant to be. It seemed to me I owed debts on every hand—to the world—to you: I tried—tried to pay—to pay you fair, ache for ache, if I could, for the hurts I'd given you. And you wouldn't let me. You were wonderful. Before the throne of God—here—now, I'll say it: I love you! But now it's over."

"It is easier now," she said again. "You must not give way. You are strong. You must not be beaten. You must keep your courage."

"Give me a moment," he said. "Give me a chance to get on my feet again. I want to be game as I can."

"You have courage—the large courage," she answered quietly. "Haven't you been showing it, by your very silence? You will be brave. You are just beginning. You have changed many things in your life of late. You were

211

silent. You did not boast to me. Sometimes things seem to be changed for us, without our arrangement."

"Isn't it true?" he exclaimed, turning to her quickly; "isn't it the truth? Why, look at me. I met you a year ago. Here I sit now. Two different men, eh? No chance, either time. No chance."

"Maybe two different women," said she.

"No, we are not different," he went on suddenly. "We are something just the same,—for my part, at least, I have never changed very much in some ways."

"You have suffered a great deal," she said simply "You have lost very much. You are no longer a boy. You are a man, now. You've changed because you are a man. And it wasn't—well, it wasn't done for—for any reward."

"No, maybe not. In some ways I don't think just the way I used to. But the savage—the brute—in me is there just the same. I don't want to do what is right. I don't want to know what is right. I only want to do what I want to do. What I covet, I covet. What I love, I love. What I want, I want. That is all. And yet, just a minute ago you were telling me you would be a friend! Not to a man like that! It wouldn't be right."

She made no answer. The faces of both were now turned toward the gray dawn beyond the hills. It was some moments before once more he turned to her.

"But you and I—just you and I, together, thinking the way we both do, seeing what we both see—the splendid sadness and the glory of living and loving— and being what we both are! Oh, it all comes back to me, I tell you; and I say I have not changed. I shall always call your hair 'dark as the night of disunion and separation'—isn't that what the oriental poet called it?—and your face, to me, always, always, always, will be 'fair as the days of union and delight.' No you've not changed. You're still just a tall flower, in the blades of grass—that are cut down. But wasted! What is in my mind now, when maybe it ought not to be here, is just this: What couldn't you and I have done together? Ah! Nothing could have stopped us!"

"What could we not have done?" she repeated slowly. "I've done so little—in the world—alone."

Something in her tone caught his ear, his senses, overstrung, vibrating in exquisite susceptibility, capable almost of hearing thought that dared not be thought. He turned his blackened face, bent toward her, looking into her face with an intensity which almost annihilated the human limitations of flesh and blood. It was as though his soul heard something in hers, and turned to answer it, to demand its repetition.

"Did you say, *could* have done?" he demanded. "Tell me, did you say that?"

She did not answer, and he went on. "Listen!" he said in his old, imperious way. "What couldn't we do together an the world, for the world—even now?"

For a long time there was silence. At last, a light hand fell upon the brown and blistered one which he had thrust out.

"Do you think so?" he heard a gentle voice reply.